Saving
Ian Pope

Saving Ian Pope

CAROL ERICSON

PopWiz Instagram Post

Blind Item #7

This former boybander is nowhere to be found
after rehab stint. Has he gone on another bender
for a career ender?

Part I

LA

Chapter 1

IVY

Fabio wobbled in the slight breeze, and I jumped up from my chair to rescue him. As I grabbed his hunky cardboard shoulders to re-position him, I tripped over the twine connecting him to the stakes of the romance booth. Fabio and I did an awkward dance, and he wound up between my legs in a compromising position. Had been a minute since I had a man between my legs.

"Are you alright? Is this bloke taking advantage of you?"

From my hunched over posture, I glanced over my shoulder into a pair of dark sunglasses obscuring the eyes of the dude with the English accent. I couldn't read the expression in his eyes, but the guy, his face shadowed by a baseball cap, struggled to maintain his composure.

I straightened to my full height, which came to Fabio's armpit, hugging the cardboard cutout to my chest. "I'm fine. Just putting Fabio in his place."

The Englishman cracked a smile and then tipped his head toward the inside of the booth. "I think you have a customer. Go. I'll handle... Fabio."

"Thanks." I relinquished my cardboard boyfriend to the care of the guy with the tattooed arms and headed for my table, stacked with my two latest romance novels. I tripped on the table leg and knocked over a pile of books in front of the woman with a ring in her nose. "Sorry. I'm here."

The woman, her canvas bag from the LA Festival of Books already bulging, picked up one of the books scattered in front of her. "Just the one I want. Can you sign it to Aurora, please? How much?"

I plopped down into my chair, re-ordering the books. "These are free today." Not that I could afford to give anything away.

Aurora clapped her hands together, her long fingernails clicking. "Sweet. I'll take both, then."

As I finished autographing the second book with a flourish, my gaze flicked to the right. The Englishman, the New York Yankees baseball cap pulled low over his forehead, his longish, brown hair sticking from the bottom, had wrestled Fabio into submission and stood beside him, mimicking the studly pose, awaiting my approval. While his body didn't quite match the physique of the iconic romance cover model's, he made up for the lack of beefcake with a boyish sexiness.

I put a finger on my chin and shook my head at him. Hopefully, his guilt for laughing at my predicament would prompt him to storm into the booth and demand the remainder of my stock, so I wouldn't have to lug them home.

At the thought of unloading the rest of my books onto an unsuspecting Brit, a smile stretched my lips as I slid the signed books toward Aurora. "Thanks for stopping by. Hope you enjoy them."

I glanced past the shoulder of my happy customer at baseball cap man, who'd taken a step into the booth, ducking beneath the awning, even though it wasn't necessary. He wasn't particularly tall, more average height, but his aura took up a lot of space. I couldn't see his face, shadowed beneath his hat and obscured by the dark sunglasses, but something about his presence had captured my attention—most likely because a man checking out the romance novel booth was a rarity.

He picked up a book from one of the racks and turned it over carefully to study the back, but I could tell he was as aware of me as I was of him. A little thrill ran down my leg.

I cleared my throat. "Now that you're intimately acquainted with Fabio, you should definitely pick up a romance to read. Have you ever read a romance novel before?"

He glanced up, holding the book over his heart, the tattoos on his hand and arm as colorful as the book cover. "Uh, not that I'm aware of, but I could start."

"Put that one down." I grabbed the two books I'd been hawking all day and waved them in the air. "You should start with these two. I write romantic suspense, so you get a few dead bodies along with the romance. Or you could get them for your mother, sister, aunt, granny..."

He'd been walking toward me, as I blathered on, and parked in front of my table, plucking his sunglasses from his face and hanging them on the neckline of his white T-shirt, some obscure band name printed on the front.

I swallowed and stuttered to a stop while gazing into a pair of warm, brown eyes. Dropping the books, I licked my dry lips and reached for the diet soda on the corner of the table, knocking the empty can over. "Wife, girlfriend?"

He smiled at me, and it reached his crinkling eyes. Some chord of recognition reverberated in my chest, and I gripped the edge of the table to avoid melting into a puddle.

"I don't have a wife, or a girlfriend, for that matter. Are you telling me your books are for women only? You don't believe a man could enjoy a good romance?"

I flicked back my hair and straightened my shoulders. I was supposed to be promoting romance here, not turning away potential readers. "I think you...he could. And it won't cost you a thing to try them out. My books are free today."

His soft lips turned down in an adorable pout. "You shouldn't give away your creativity."

"Oh, I don't, typically." I picked up a book. "It's my publisher. All these books are my promo copies to give away to entice...new readers." *And maybe random hot Englishmen.* "I'm not allowed to sell them. Would you like one? You really should take both because they comprise the beginning of a new series for me and should be read, in order, to understand the whole story."

"What a bargain. I would love both, autographed, please." He traced a finger over my name on the cover, and I shivered, as if he'd trailed that same finger along my cheek. He said, almost in a whisper, "Ivy Chase."

Patting my chest with an open palm, more to settle my heartbeat than anything else, I said, "That's me."

He placed the first book in front of me, and the tips of our fingers brushed as I slid the book closer. The electricity of his touch almost had me dropping my favorite purple pen—the panties were next.

I took a deep breath and flipped open the front cover, placing the tip of the pen on the page. A little blob of purple ink marked the spot. "What's your name?"

"Ian."

Holy shit. Surprisingly, my hand trembled only a fraction as I wrote out his name. I signed with my usual flair, the end of the E in my last name sweeping into a curve. I spun the book around for him and grabbed the second one.

He opened the cover, careful not to crease it, and read the inscription aloud. "For Ian. These words are yours."

I kept my head down, my burning face buried in the second book. What had possessed me to write something so cringe? He must think I'm a total idiot, referencing a song title from his days in one of the most popular boybands in history. Would he dismiss me as an obnoxious fan? A crazed hanger-on? A stalker?

All I could manage for the second book was a shaky signature. I looked up as I handed the book to him and as soon as our eyes met, he threw his head back and laughed, a sound like water bubbling over a pebbly stream bed.

I chewed on my thumbnail as I studied him; then the corner of my mouth twitched into a half-smile. His laugh was pure joy. At least he hadn't dropped the books and made a mad dash for the exit.

He dabbed at the corner of his eye with the pad of his thumb. "Did you really just realize my identity when I said my name?"

"Yeah." I sat forward. "It's not that you're not recognizable or that I don't know who you are. Of course, I know who you are. I was a big fan of Five2Go back in the day. I-I mean now. I'm still a big fan..." I bit my bottom lip. "I should probably just shut up, right?"

He held up his hands. "It's all good...Ivy. I don't need to be recognized everywhere I go." He flicked the brim of his hat. "Small disguises go a long way."

Tilting my head, I said, "It would be a better disguise if you were wearing a Dodger hat. You wouldn't stand out as much...or inspire as much hostility."

"Excuse me, Ivy?" An older woman with a streak of pink in her gray hair plunked her book bag onto the table. "I'm a big fan of your books. I loved that series, Southwest Sheriffs. Nothing like hot sheriff's deputies sweating through their khaki in the desert sun."

As she fanned herself with her hand, she nudged Ian in the arm with her elbow and winked. He winked back before slipping on his sunglasses.

I covered my mouth and coughed. "I'm so glad you enjoyed that series. I'm starting a new miniseries with these two books—four brothers, all US Air Marshals."

Ian muttered, "What are the odds?"

I managed to kick his foot under the table while grabbing a book. "They're free today. Would you like both?"

"Absolutely. Can you sign one to Evelyn, that's me, and one to Alicia? That's my daughter."

I eyed the diminishing stack of books on the table—the fewer the better. "If you have room in your bag, I'll sign two for you and two for Alicia."

The woman's faded blue eyes sparkled to life. "That would be wonderful."

I autographed four books, affixed the autographed by author sticker on each book and stacked them in front of Evelyn. As Evelyn's gnarled hands reached for the books, she knocked them to the ground. My clumsiness was contagious or maybe nobody was immune from boyband charm.

"I've got them." Ian ducked down and gathered them for Evelyn and tucked them into her book bag.

"What a nice English gentleman." Evelyn squinted at Ian. "Are you married? I have a granddaughter about your age, and I could overlook those tattoos."

I smirked as I raised my eyebrows at Ian. What would the nice English gentleman do to get out of this one? He probably had plenty of practice.

He gave Evelyn that crinkly-eyed smile and said, "I'm flattered you'd be willing to overlook the tattoos, but I'm in a relationship." His brown eyes, alight with mischief, shifted to me. *I died.*

Nodding, Eveyln said, "Oh, I see. Very nice."

Heat seared my cheeks, and I placed my hands against them to hide the blush. At least Evelyn had no idea she'd just tried to set up her granddaughter with a global popstar. Thank goodness, her granddaughter would never know, either. She'd probably be mortified.

When Evelyn left the booth, I planted my elbows on the table and buried my chin in my palm. "You see what happens when you venture into the romance novel booth at the book fair? A meet and greet with Fabio and a possible blind date. What *are* you doing here, anyway? Do you live in LA?"

"I haven't for a while." He jerked his thumb over his shoulder. "I came with my manager for the week, and he's here to support a friend of his who's on a panel discussing non-fiction, true crime books. It all got kinda gory for me, so I ducked out."

"Uh oh." I tapped the cover of one of my books. "I'm afraid there's some blood and guts in my books, although nothing too gruesome."

"Hi, Ivy. How's the crowd? Did you give away many books?" Tessa Starr, one of the other romance authors signing today, peered over the top of the box wrapped in her arms.

"Here, I'll take that." Ian took the box from Tessa and lowered it to the ground as Tessa's eyes rounded and her mouth formed an O.

She'd recognized Ian right away.

Tessa stammered, "A-are you...?"

I waved my hand. "Yes, this is Ian Pope. He's helping out in the booth today, assisting with the setup, bringing in readers. He'll even fetch water for you. And this is Tessa Starr, author of the very popular sci-fi robot romance series."

Ian's mouth dropped open. "You write books about people having sex with robots, or is it just the robots having sex with each other?"

"Human on machine. It sounds weirder than it actually is. It's pretty hot once you get past the...mechanics." Tessa grinned. "What's Ian Pope doing in our romance booth, Ivy?"

"It's a long story, but he rescued our Fabio out there, and I was able foist my books onto him. Are you taking my place at this table? The crowd's been good, but I'm giving my books away. Are you selling yours?"

"I am." She dug in the box Ian had set at her feet and popped up with a book clutched in her hand, a robot with a shiny six-pack and a busty woman with her hand on his chiseled, albeit metal pecs. "Twelve bucks—cash, Venmo, PayPal, credit card. You can have the physical book, or I can give you a code for a download."

Ian's mouth opened and closed for a few seconds, and then he dug into the front pocket of his faded jeans and pulled out a crumpled twenty. "I'll take the book."

Tessa twisted her mouth to the side. "I don't have change, yet. Ivy, you have change for a twenty? I'll pay you back."

Ian waved his hand. "That's alright. Keep it."

Tessa squealed and plunked her book down on the table, grabbing my purple pen. She scribbled, what seemed like another chapter on the flyleaf, as I rolled my eyes at Ian, his arms crossed, his fingers drumming against his bulging bicep, his mouth quirked on one side. Ian Pope had a bulging bicep. Since when? I remembered him as a skinny teen with floppy hair in his eyes.

He was going to want to get out of here as soon as possible, before I subjected him to all the other writers signing today.

Tessa handed the book to him. "You don't really have to read it, but maybe some lucky lady in your life would like it. Tell them the robots never get tired...if you know what I mean."

While Tessa gave Ian a broad wink, he added the book to his growing pile of romance novels on the corner of the table.

"I'll be sure to mention that to my...uh...mum."

I giggled, and I hardly ever giggle. This was the most exciting book signing I'd had in...ever. "Okay, the table is all yours. I signed and stickered my leftovers, and I'll put them in the rack with the other freebies."

As Tessa started pulling her table items—stickers, bookmarks, pens—from the box and setting up, I pushed back from my chair and grabbed the empty soda can.

"Thanks for humoring us today." I gestured toward the books now tucked against Ian's side and whispered. "You don't really have to read the books or even keep them."

Hugging the books to his chest, he said, "Are you kidding? Now I have something to read on the flight home."

As I filled the slots of the freebie rack with my books, Ian stayed put. I kept expecting him to wander away. Make someone else's day.

"Well, it was nice meeting you, Ian. You made my final minutes in the booth fly by." I held out my hand to shake his and tried to swallow the little lump in my throat. He must make every girl alive feel this way. I'd definitely succumbed to his charm, his looks, his smile, his eyes...the little freckle on the side of his face near his ear.

He took my hand, and the current that charged through my body at his touch almost brought me to my knees. I managed to stay upright and even smile.

I tried to pull my hand back, but he kept possession of it, squeezing lightly. "My manager, Jack, is still hanging out with his friend, and they're going to another author panel. Do you want to get something to eat with me at one of the food trucks? I-I mean if you don't have a huge, muscular boyfriend or husband picking you up."

Ian Pope stuttered and...blushed?

I held out my left hand and wiggled my ring finger, never happier at my single status. "No and *no*."

"What a relief. So, lunch?"

"Ah, yeah, sure." I grabbed the handles of my bag on the ground and started to hoist it over my shoulder.

Ian stopped me, taking the straps in his hand. "I'll carry that for you."

"Thanks. Evelyn was right." I led the way out of the booth, waving to Tessa, who pointed to me and Ian and made some obscene interlocking gestures with her fingers.

I whipped my head around so Ian wouldn't glance back, and as I stepped into the sunshine, I rubbed Fabio's...abs and silently thanked him.

Chapter 2

IVY

As I caught up to Ian, I cleared my throat. "So, lunch. I think the food trucks are over in front of Dodd Hall, aren't they?"

"What's a Dodd Hall?" Ian tilted his head, as he slung my canvas bag over his shoulder.

"Oh, sorry." I waved my arm in the air. "It's a building across the street. I went to UCLA, and I mostly took classes on this side of campus, so I know all the building names—at least I think I remember them."

"How long ago was that?"

Was he trying to discover my age? I couldn't remember his, but we had to be about the same age, as I'd been in my teen years at the same time as he and his band members had started out, also in their teens.

"I graduated six years ago." I pressed a hand over my trembling heart to suppress the anxiety that consumed me every time I thought about those tumultuous months following my graduation from college.

"And is this where you learned to become a romance writer?" He spread his arms and turned, taking in the leafy quad lined with book booths.

"Not exactly. I was an English lit major, so I did have to do a lot of writing, and it had to be good writing, but it was an entirely different process from writing fictional stories. I read a lot, including romances, and just decided to try one out for myself. I sold the second book I wrote and was recently able to quit my day job to write full time." He didn't have to know that some life insurance money helped me with that move—money I'd sunk into a townhouse in Santa Monica, mostly to protect it from Matt.

He nodded. "That's impressive."

I felt that warmth creeping into my cheeks again. "Ugh, I didn't mean to go on about myself."

Dragging his sunglasses to the tip of his nose, he lowered his head to look at me. "Do you always do that?"

"Do what?" I stopped walking, too distracted to move and worship at the same time. God, I could get lost in those eyes.

"I don't know. Put yourself down or at least diminish your talents." He drew a circle with his finger in the air. "Tapes in your head."

That sounded like one of those pop psychology phrases, and I had no intention of wasting my short time with the very hot Ian Pope delving into my insecurities.

I grabbed his finger. "Tacos or noodles."

"What?"

Pointing to several food trucks lined up on the utility road between campus halls, I said, "So far, I can make out a taco truck and a noodle truck. I'm sure there are more."

Five minutes later, we stood in line at a food truck called Canoodles, appropriately enough because that's what I wanted to do with him... among other things. We both decided on something called Thai Bomb with green curry and tofu.

After we ordered at the window, Ian patted his pockets. "I gave my last cash to Tessa for the robot sex book. They probably take cards or Venmo, yeah?"

"My alma mater, my treat." I plucked my wallet from the bag still hanging over Ian's shoulder and slid out two twenties to pay for the bowls and a couple bottles of water.

As part of the book festival, small plastic tables and chairs dotted the lawn and walkway. I led Ian past the crowds to the shady sculpture garden, where others clearly had the same need for tranquility. We claimed a spot on a bench beside the flowering coral trees, boasting their bright red flowers for the summer.

"This is a great spot." Ian unwrapped his chopsticks and aimed them at my fork. "You're not using chopsticks?

"Never really mastered the art of chopsticks. Way too much work to get food into my mouth." I stabbed a chunk of tofu with my plastic fork. "Why did you come to LA with your manager? Are you making new music? I don't think I've heard anything from you, lately. Okay, I admit I don't follow your career that closely."

With his chopsticks pinched between two fingers, Ian opened his bottle and chugged some water, but not before I caught the shadow that seemed to darken the sparkle in his eyes. Had I said something wrong? Maybe I should've done a surreptitious search on my phone before asking him questions about his career.

While I'd heard and liked some of his solo songs, it seemed as if he'd released them a while ago. But maybe it was because one of the other former Five2Go band members had been all over the news with a big tour and a few acting gigs that had overshadowed the others.

My mouth burning from the spicy food, I twisted the cap off my own water and waited for an answer.

He placed his bottle carefully on the bench between us and wiped his palm on the thigh of his jeans. "You're right. I haven't released anything for a while. I'm working on some songs for a new album and planning a tour, so I took a few meetings here with my manager. And I'm just...uh, relaxing before I get back to work."

I'd been holding my breath and released it slowly between my lips. He didn't exactly sound pumped-up about the prospect of his new music. Now my fingers tingled with the urge to skim through my phone to discover the real story, but an even stronger impulse surged through me to bring the sunshine back to Ian's smile and the warmth back to his brown eyes.

Something tickled the back of my neck, and I twitched and flicked my hair. A split second later a squirrel leapt from the bench over my shoulder and grabbed the fork sticking out of my bowl.

I emitted a terrified yelp while Ian doubled over beside me, his shoulders shaking with laughter. When he popped back up, his grin took up half his face, and his eyes sparkled. He pounded his chest as he choked on his food. "Are you okay?"

More than okay. I'd have to thank that squirrel later for bringing Ian out of that funk.

"Yeah, except that little rodent stole my fork. What's he going to do with it?" I gave a little shiver and rubbed the back of my neck. "I don't like the idea of that squirrel roaming campus armed with a fork."

Ian nodded his head at my bowl. "More importantly, how are you going to finish your noodles?"

I dug through the plastic bag at my feet that had contained our food and triumphantly withdrew a set of chopsticks. "I hope you have all day. That's how long it's going to take me to eat."

"I can run over and get you another fork, or..." he took the chopsticks from me and peeled off the paper "—I can give you a quick lesson in wielding chopsticks."

"I suppose it's time I learned, living in LA, the land of 283 different cuisines. Show me."

Ian put his water bottle on the ground and scooted closer to me on the bench. I liked this lesson already. My eyelids drooped for a moment as I savored his nearness and inhaled his masculine, slightly spicy scent—even if it was the green curry.

"Give me your hand."

Gladly. I held out my hand, steadier than it had a right to be, given the turmoil of my mind and other strategic parts of my body.

He placed one chopstick in my fingers and instructed, "Hold it like you would hold a pencil."

I gripped the smooth wood between my thumb and pointer finger.

"Wait. You hold your pencil way down at the end?"

I whacked his hand with the chopstick. "Good teachers are patient."

"Ow." He rubbed the back of his hand that sported a tattoo with the Roman numeral 52. At least I thought the L was 50, or was that a C? No, 52 for Five2Go, obviously.

"Okay, slide your fingers up toward the top." He tried to tell me where to place the second chopstick, but I got the same result I always did—the pincher chopstick wouldn't pinch.

Shaking his head, he clicked his tongue. "You are seriously uncoordinated, Ivy. Here."

He took the chopsticks from my clumsy fingers and deftly scooped up a mass of noodles. He held the food over the bowl. "Open."

My jaw dropped. Was he going to feed me?

He leaned in, positioned the noodles over my open mouth and lowered them. Like a baby bird, I closed my lips around the chopsticks and sucked the food into my mouth.

His eyes never left mine, so I shielded my lips as I chewed. Instead of feeling gross for eating in his face, this had to be one of the most erotic moments of my life.

He blinked as if coming out of a daze. "See how easy that was?"

"For some. You did the hard part. I'm just chewing here." My tongue darted out of my mouth, and I licked the spicy flavor from my greasy lips.

His eyes darkened to a chocolate brown, and his gaze intensified. He reached out with one finger and dabbed the corner of my mouth. "You missed a spot."

My lips throbbed, and I touched the tip of my tongue to the pad of his finger.

He snatched his hand back as if scorched and then clicked the chopsticks together like a pro. "Another bite?"

I nodded. Could he just feed me noodles forever?

"Oh my God. You're Ian Pope."

Chapter 3

IVY

Ian gave me a twisty smile before turning to face his accuser, a young woman about my age, prime Five2Go fanbase. The blonde clutched the arm of her goggle-eyed friend as they shimmied in front of Ian expectantly.

"I am." Ian flashed a smile. The effect was instantaneous. The women blushed and fluttered and tittered.

"Can we get you to sign something? Can we get a picture with you?"

"Absolutely."

I studied the interaction through narrowed eyes as the women produced a few flyers from their book bags and shoved them toward Ian, along with a pen. It was as if the presence of the women had flicked a switch hidden somewhere on his body—and I wouldn't mind doing a thorough search for the switch's location.

He chatted easily with them, the smile never leaving his face. He accommodated them in every way—signing a few items and even using their phones to take selfies. He hugged them and assured them new music was on the horizon.

My gaze darted among the other people in the sculpture garden, almost expecting a stampede, but after a flurry of interest, everyone had turned their attention back to their own affairs. Even if they did recognize Ian, spotting a celebrity in LA had lost its luster for most residents...except the Five2Go fandom.

When he sat back down on the bench, he shrugged and said, "Sorry."

"No, I mean, whatever. Does it bother you? You were so nice. I'm not so sure I could be that friendly to people interrupting my private time." I snapped the lid onto my half-eaten bowl of noodles, the feeding session lost, and shoved them into the plastic bag at my feet.

Leaning back, Ian folded his hands behind his head. "It doesn't bother me. Not really. It's part of the pact."

"There's a pact?" I tugged on a lock of my hair and wound it around my finger.

"Of course. The fans buy your music, your merch, go to your concerts, and make you rich beyond your wildest dreams. In exchange, you have to give up an expectation of privacy, your..."

"Soul?"

His gaze jumped to my face, and he rubbed the scruff on his chin with his knuckles. "Something like that."

"Ugh." I brushed off my skirt and nudged the bag in his direction for his trash. "Not for me."

"I really don't mind. You never know what someone else is going through. A fan could be having a bad day or a bad week. As a celebrity, you have an opportunity to cheer someone up. I couldn't live with myself if I thought I had contributed to someone's sadness by turning down an autograph." He sat forward on the bench, warming to his topic. "It reminds me of the story I read about a guy who jumped from the Golden Gate Bridge and survived. He had bi-polar disorder and was having an episode. He had gone to the bridge to jump. As he walked along in the fog, he told himself if just one person reached out to him, he wouldn't jump. A couple, German, I think, approached him to ask him to take their picture. With tears streaming down his face, he snapped their photo, but they never asked him why he was crying. He jumped."

My hand covered my mouth and tears pricked my eyes. "That's a true story?"

"It is."

"But he survived to tell it."

"He was one of less than one percent of Golden Gate Bridge jumpers to survive. He said that a sea lion kept him afloat when he surfaced with all his broken bones." Ian shrugged. "So, a sea lion cared more than another human."

"That's an incredible story. You want to be the sea lion."

"I do." He crumpled up a pile of napkins and tossed them into the bag. "I know it's Saturday, and you're probably busy, but if you're not, you wanna hang out for a while? My manager, Jack, is probably going to do something with his friends, and I don't feel like tagging along. I also don't wanna be stuck in the hotel by myself for the rest of the day. I mean...if you're free."

Ian Pope didn't have anything better to do on a Saturday night in LA than spend it with a clumsy romance author? Should I pretend I had a hot date? A fabulous party to attend? A book signing with a thousand fans?

"I'm not busy. I was just going to do a little writing."

He aimed a finger at the books he'd stuffed into my bag earlier. "A continuation of the randy air marshals?"

"Actually, yeah, the fourth and last book of the series. Book three is already done." I pushed up from the bench and eyed the tree behind us, on the lookout for that rogue squirrel. "What did you have in mind?"

He quirked his eyebrows up and down. "Surprise me."

* * *

An hour later, I wheeled my compact SUV up to the curb in front of a small group of one-story, fifties-era bungalows. I loved my little place in Santa Monica, just north of Wilshire Boulevard, a detached house built on a large lot with three other houses. I'd bought it just over a year ago with my share of the life insurance money and still needed a roommate to make my mortgage payments, but it beat renting.

Ian tapped the window with his knuckle. "You brought me back to your place? Bold move, ain't it."

I poked him in the arm. "Just for a minute. I'm going to change out of this skirt and these shoes. I-I thought we'd go down to the pier...if that's okay with you."

"That's a great idea. Never been there."

I did a double take before grasping the door handle. He'd lived in LA and hadn't been to the Santa Monica Pier? "You can wait in the car, if you like. I'll be right back."

"I'd rather come in, unless you don't want me to." He took off his hat, and ran a hand through his wavy hair, longer than I'd remembered from the last pictures I'd seen of him.

When *had* I last seen pictures or video of Ian Pope? I couldn't recall, but his hair had decidedly been shorter and more styled. I liked his messy brown mop that brushed his collarbone and framed his handsome face. Yikes! The cute boy had become a hot man with a hot body.

"Sure, c'mon." I stumbled out of the car, suddenly nervous. Had I cleaned up the kitchen before I left? Put away my vibrator? Made my bed? Not that he'd be in my bed—or anywhere near it—unless some magical transfer of romance power had occurred when we'd both wrestled Fabio.

I practically skipped down the walkway that led to my snug bungalow that had once been part of a small single-story apartment complex of four detached units. I'd snapped up the last unit shortly after the conversion to single-family.

I waved to Janet, my elderly neighbor across from me, watering her potted plants that separated her unit from the shared courtyard. No chance Janet would recognize Ian, even without his hat and sunglasses. Jim Morrison of The Doors, maybe, whom she'd claimed to have seen—

and blown—at the Whiskey-A-Go-Go on Sunset back in the day, but not Ian Pope.

On the way to my place, I led Ian between two rows of plants and flowering bushes that culminated in a riot of pink bougainvillea climbing a trellis next to my door. The jasmine in the pot on the other side of the door provided the sweet fragrance, but the bougainvillea provided the color and Southern California vibe.

It didn't escape Ian's notice, as he closed his eyes and made a show of inhaling the scent. "That's sweet."

Despite my trembling fingers, I unlocked the front door on the first try. "C'mon in. I'll just be a minute."

I dropped my bag on the floor and tossed my keys into the basket on the small table in the entryway.

Shoving his hands in his pockets, Ian strolled into my living room. "Cozy."

"Yeah, I know that's another word for small, but it's big enough for us."

"Us?" He spun around.

"My roommate, Chloe, and I. She rents from me and helps me pay my mortgage." I waved my hands. "Oh, she's not here right now. Her boyfriend lives in San Diego, and she spends a lot of time down there. I don't know why she doesn't just move in with him, but she's also my best friend, and she vowed to stay with me."

He picked up Loki's dog tags from the basket and jingled them. "You have a dog?"

"I did have a dog—a Great Dane named Loki." I rubbed my nose. "He died a few years ago, but I keep his tags."

His face softened, and he dropped the tags. "Aw, I'm sorry. That always hurts."

I took a deep breath, dizzy from all the personal information I was revealing to a stranger—one known the world over, but still a stranger. "I'll be right back. Do you want something to drink? I have some bottles of water in the fridge, no beer, I'm afraid, but Chloe loves her wine, so I'm sure there's an open bottle of white in there."

"Uh, water's good."

"Help yourself." I traipsed down the short hallway and ducked into my bedroom. I shut the door behind me and leaned against it, placing one hand against my chest, measuring my galloping heart.

Was I just imagining this electricity between us? Did he feel it too, or was he just bored? Hard to believe he didn't have celebrity friends in LA he could hang with.

I sat on the edge of my bed and slipped off my high, wedge sandals. Then I unbuttoned my floral skirt and stood up, letting it fall in a heap around my legs. I stepped out of it and grabbed a pair of denim cut-offs from my dresser. I shoved my feet into a pair of flipflops, traded my pink blouse for a green T-shirt and yanked a striped hoodie from a hanger in the closet.

A little out of breath, I emerged from the hallway to find Ian with a framed photo in his hands. My heart skipped a beat when I recognized the picture.

Turning at my approach, he held up the photo. "This is nice. You and your father at your graduation from UCLA?"

"Yeah." I pointed at the two bottles of water on the kitchen table. "I see you found the water."

He nodded. "Did your mum take the picture?"

"She was long gone by then."

Placing the photo back on the bookshelf, he said, "I'm so sorry."

I looked up from transferring items from my tote to the cross-body bag pinned to my side with my elbow. "Oh, she's not dead. She abandoned us years before I went to college."

"Still sorry." He shoved his hands in his pockets. "Does your father live nearby?"

"*He's* the dead one." As I slipped the strap over my head, I saw his confused and slightly stricken face. He must think I'm cold as ice. "I mean, yeah, my father passed away not long after that picture was taken."

"I-I'm..." he thought better of saying sorry again and sputtered, "... th-that's too bad."

I turned my back on him and adjusted my cross-body bag. His words floated over my shoulder, but I had no intention of getting into my past or explaining myself. I'd already revealed too much. I asked, "Are you ready?"

"I could use the loo."

I pointed to the first door on the right-hand side of the hallway. "You can use Chloe's. Hers is the public one. Mine's attached to my bedroom— perks of owning the place. Chloe won't mind, as long as you put down the toilet seat."

He crossed his heart with the tip of his finger. "I promise. I grew up with three sisters, so I've been trained."

As he shut the door behind him, I grabbed the waters and leaned against the wall by the front door, arms folded. Should I text Chloe and tell her what was happening? Chloe would probably just confuse me even more, but maybe my best friend had a better idea about what was going on with him right now.

Didn't Ian have a girlfriend? I knew he had a daughter. Oh, God, yes, he had a daughter with that beautiful English soap actress Sasha. I'd almost forgotten about that. He'd been quite young at the time, and Sasha had about ten years on him. Did he like cougars?

I jumped when he swung open the bathroom door and stepped into the hallway.

He approached me and took the water bottles from where I'd tucked them against my body, his thumb brushing my under-boob. Had he done that on purpose? He said, "I've got those."

The boobs or the water?

He also got the door, opening it for me. As I skirted past him, he patted the top of my head. "Did you shrink?"

Kicking up one of my flipflop-clad feet behind me, I said, "Just swapped out the heels for flats. I know. It's a shock."

Once outside, I leaned my forehead against the door as I locked the deadbolt. Ugh, he probably dated leggy models with a good seven inches on me.

"I'd call it a nice surprise. No matter how high your heels, you'll never be taller than me." He flipped one of the water bottles into the air, catching it and grinning at me.

I doubted I'd ever have the chance to wear heels with him again. He'd already mentioned he was leaving the day after tomorrow. Knowing this would be my first and last time with Ian Pope freed me.

Might as well enjoy it and go out with a bang—with any luck.

Chapter 4

IVY

slid into a parking spot in the public lot next to the pier. I'd timed our visit perfectly—just as families were leaving after a day at the beach and before the teens and young adults descended on the pier for the rides and illicit nighttime activities on the beach.

As we got out of the car, Ian tipped his head back. "I guess I didn't realize the pier had funfair rides."

"The rides have been around for about twenty-five years, and the carousel inside is from the original pier in 1916." I gestured toward the wooden steps leading down the sand. "You wanna take a walk on the beach?"

"Lead the way. It's like being with a tour guide." He adjusted his cap, keeping his sunglasses in place.

I kept mine on, too. The day might be waning, but the sun still hung low in the sky, creating a glassy glare on the water.

As we hit the sand, he grabbed my arm. "Hang on. I wanna feel the sand between my toes. I haven't been to the beach in a while."

I kicked off my flipflops and dangled them from my fingers. Again, I had a burning desire to know more about how he'd spent his year, so far—obviously not at the beach.

After he removed his running shoes and stuffed his socks inside the shoes, he tied the laces together and slung them over one shoulder. He then rolled up his jeans. "I'm ready."

We trudged through the dry sand, and occasionally my shoulder would bump against his arm. Nobody seemed to notice him, or if they did, they'd decided not to make a fuss.

I slid a glance at him from the side of my eye. Did he want them to or not? Fame had to be a double-edged sword. If people noticed you, even if that caused a hassle, it affirmed your relevance. If they gave you your privacy, you'd have to wonder if they'd recognized you, or worse, didn't care.

Of course, I wanted lots and lots of people to buy and read my books, but I would detest the level of fame that Ian had endured. I remembered scenes of frenzied girls chasing the Five2Go boys down the street and mobbing them everywhere they went. I preferred my anonymity.

We made our way to the wet sand, littered with seaweed, shells and other debris from the ocean. Ian jogged a few feet in front of me, leaving his imprint in the sand. I had a sinking feeling he'd leave his imprint on more than just the beach, and I put one hand over my heart, as if that could protect it from what I knew was marching toward me.

I followed him by placing my feet into his bigger prints.

He veered toward the water and danced in the foam from the breaking waves. "Feels good. Dip your toes."

"I'm sure it's freezing. The Pacific is always cold, even at the end of a sunny day."

"Chicken." He splashed into the water as it reached the hem of his rolled-up jeans. "Do you surf?"

"Once in a while—with a wetsuit."

He kicked at a wave, and the arc of water caught the sunlight and glittered like diamonds dropping to the sand. He crooked a finger at me. "Join me."

I inched a little closer to a wave rushing to shore, and the water tickled my toes. "Definitely cold."

Ian swung around and charged toward me. He scooped me up in his arms, as if I weighed no more than a kitten, and carried me back to the water.

I shrieked and kicked my legs, but he held me high above the rolling waves and spun around. I threw my head back and laughed at the sky as the spray from the sea dabbled against my cheek, droplets of saltwater landing on my tongue.

Panting, he lowered me to the ground. "Did you think I was going to toss you in?"

"Crossed my mind, but then you'd have to find a ride back to your hotel." I tucked my fluttering hair behind one ear.

He'd released me but kept possession of my hand, and I let it remain with him. He laced his fingers with mine and tugged me forward.

Hands clasped, we continued our walk on the beach, leaving most of the clutches of beachgoers and their screaming kids behind us as we ventured farther north toward the bluffs.

The fog rolled in quickly, as it often did on a summer night, and I nudged his shoulder. "I don't think we're going to see much of a sunset tonight unless the fog just keeps flowing inland."

He said, "I always found it strange that Malibu could be 20 degrees colder than where I lived, which was about 20 kilometers away."

"You lived in...?"

"Calabasas."

"Ah, yes." I disentangled my hand from his. "The Valley playground of the rich and famous so they don't have to rub shoulders with the people of Van Nuys."

From the corner of my eye, I could see his head jerk toward me. I pursed my lips. I didn't know why that bitchy comment had tumbled out of my mouth. Jealousy, probably.

He chuckled lightly. "Yeah, I guess. I don't think I ever went to Van Nuys, but you would've loved the library in my old house."

"Really?"

"It was a two-story room with a massive number of books and one of them rolling ladders to reach all of them." He took my hand again, more firmly this time. "You said you studied English at uni, and I noticed all the books you had at your place. I suppose you read all the time. You probably know more about English authors than I do—Shakespeare and Chaucer and that lot."

I snorted, despite myself. "Yeah, that lot. Don't you like to read?"

"Honestly, I never had much time for it. Never had much time for a load of stuff."

The sadness in his voice had me squeezing his hand, and I said, "Let's get back to the pier. At the rate this fog is sweeping in, we might not be able to see it."

We retraced our steps in the wet sand, our previous footprints already washed out to sea. We swung hands in companionable silence, broken by the occasional exclamation over something deposited on the beach, which we would scoop up and study before tossing it back into the ocean.

By the time we reached the wooden steps up to the pier, the majority of the beachgoers had left or relocated to the carnival rides.

Ian sat on the bottom step to the side and brushed the sand from his feet. He put on his socks and shoes and rolled down the wet hems of his jeans.

When he finished, I thrust out my hand to him, and he took it as I pulled him up. Face-to-face, he flicked a strand of hair from my cheek. "Your hair...changed."

Smoothing my hand over the back of my hair, I said, "It's the damp air. Makes it frizzy."

He caught another lock of my hair and wound it around his finger. "It's all wavy. Makes you look like a beached mermaid."

Heat rose from my chest to my face, and I pulled away from him. "Better than a beached whale, I suppose."

I tromped up the steps ahead of him, pulling my sweatshirt around my body. I glanced over my shoulder. "Are you cold?"

"I'm English."

We reached the pier, and I said, "I have a surprise for you."

"I like surprises." Ian clapped his hands together.

Although he must've been a few years older than I was, Ian had an adorable childishness about him sometimes. It was part of his devastating charm—at least for me—and probably ever other girl in the Five2 fandom

"Do you like Ferris wheels?"

"Absolutely." He raised his eyes to the big wheel churning around at the end of the pier, its colorful lights flashing, reflecting in his shining eyes. "I even like rollercoasters and those teacup things that spin you around until you're nauseous."

"You're not going to vomit on the Ferris wheel, are you? That could get messy."

"I promise not to, but if I'm feeling a bit queasy, I'll face away from you and hurl over the side."

"Deal." I grabbed his hand, and we threaded our way through the crowds to the ticket booth.

I slid my credit card beneath the window. "Two tickets for the Ferris wheel, please."

"That's thirty dollars."

"Bloody hell." Ian reached for his wallet. "Hang on. If they take plastic, I'll pay for the tickets."

"You're my guest. I got it." I placed a hand on his chest, resisting the urge to run it across his defined muscles beneath the cotton of his T.

I snatched up the tickets and handed him one.

Shaking his head, he said, "Thirty quid? The bloody thing better fly for that price."

We joined the end of the short line. The waiting would come as the wheel stopped for each car to spit out its passengers. I danced from foot to foot. I hadn't been on this Ferris wheel for years.

The sun had officially set, although the fog had obscured its glory. The lights and motion of the pier seemed even more intense against the gray backdrop, and my senses were attuned to every nuance. My nerve endings tingled. I hadn't felt this alive in a very long time.

Ian bumped my shoulder. "Here's our car."

A car swung down to the landing, and the ride operator unhitched the door and let a mom with her two kids out. He held the door open, and I stepped in first, sliding to the end of the red vinyl seat. Ian climbed in after me, and his knee hit my leg as he got comfortable.

As the wheel lifted into the air, I swung my legs. "Ooh, I love that feeling, but especially the whoosh on the way down."

Ian craned his neck, turning his head. "Do you reckon that guy knows what he's doing? Did he shut the door properly? Do you hear that creak?"

I huffed out a breath and patted his shoulder. "Are you scared? Do you want me to hold your hand?"

"Mission accomplished." Ian held out his hand, palm upward. I threaded my fingers through his, and the wheel began to turn, picking up speed. Each time we descended, Ian squeezed my hand, and my stomach dropped. I couldn't figure out if the butterflies were coming from the motion or Ian's nearness and attention.

He slipped off his sunglasses and hung them on the front of his shirt. "I imagine this is loads more scenic during the day or on a clear night. I think you should get your thirty quid back."

I rested my head against his arm. "I know. I'm sorry. There's not much to look at."

"I wouldn't say that." He bumped my knee with his. "It's not bad, though. Up here, cocooned in this fog, barely able to see five feet in front of my own face, I feel like we're in a bubble or rather nestled in a cotton ball. It's like we're floating on our own, hidden from everyone and everything else. Do you feel it?"

I felt all kinds of things. Weirdly, my throat was constricted, and I was having difficulty uttering a sound.

Ian wedged a finger beneath my chin and turned my face to his. I closed my eyes as his lips met mine. He tasted of the ocean—salty, briny, fresh, and unbridled. I moved my mouth against his, parting my lips.

The tip of his tongue slid into my wetness, and I used my own tongue to toy with his. He deepened his kiss and cupped the side of my face with his hand, his thumb stroking my earlobe.

My body tingled in all my regular hot spots and some I didn't even know I had. I smooshed my breast against his arm to get closer, as if I could climb into his kiss and get lost with him in the fog.

When he ended our connection and pulled back, my eyelids flew open. He touched his nose to mine. "Nice."

Nice? Yeah, that word was hardly adequate for the emotions and sensations his kiss had awakened in me. His touch had taken me somewhere else—beyond reason and logic and fear, and the aching loneliness that had engulfed me the past few years.

I managed to whisper, "Nice."

He draped his arm around my shoulders and placed his chin on top of my head. "Magical."

As I turned my head and rested it against his chest, I saw a streak of pink on the horizon. The sun hadn't disappeared, after all. The overcast had lifted just enough to give us a peek of the sun's final show before it dipped into the ocean.

When we got off the ride, my knees shook, and I knew damn well the kiss and not the Ferris wheel had caused my unsteadiness. I hung onto Ian's arm as we walked away from our private bubble and delved into the crowd.

The smell of hot dogs, popcorn, fish, sugar and grease made my stomach rumble. Woman did not live by celebrity crush alone, and that ramen was just a distant memory now. The kiss should've been enough to satisfy me, but it seemed to have set everything on fire, including my appetite.

As if on the same wavelength, Ian stopped and inhaled deeply. "I'm starving, and you must be ravenous since that squirrel stole your fork. Do you want to get something to eat?"

"God, yes." I pointed to the fresh fish stand across from the tourist restaurants. "We can pick out fish there, and they'll cook it however you want. Only downside is that we have to eat it on those picnic tables set in front."

"Sounds good. Please tell me they take plastic. I'm beginning to feel like a kept man."

I'd like to keep him, alright...in my bed for about twenty-four hours. "I'm sure they do. They even have alcohol, if you want to get a beer. I'm driving, anyway."

"I'm good. Do you want something to drink?"

"Just a soda."

We ordered our fish at the counter, grabbed two cans of Diet Coke and sat across from each other at the end of a picnic bench with another couple at the other end.

Ian immediately stretched his hands across the table to take mine. "I hadn't been on a Ferris wheel in years. Thanks for the suggestion."

I disentangled one of my hands from his and took a slug of my drink. Might as well get over my awkwardness right away with a joke. "I only took you up there because I thought it would be a good place to share a first kiss. I'm a romance writer. I'm always thinking about these things."

He tapped his temple. "That's good to know. Do you always...try things out before putting them in your books?"

"Not always." I winked. "I have a very good imagination."

The guy at the fish counter called our number, and Ian jumped up to get our food.

Several minutes later as we were eating, two women approached us. "Hi Ian, can we get a picture with you?"

He dropped his plastic fork and wiped his mouth with a napkin. "Yes, my pleasure."

I continued eating as the women got selfies with him on their phones and had him sign various items. Before he could sit down, another group mobbed him, requesting his picture, his signature, his time. The fandom wasn't limited to females. A young, Latino man held out his tattooed arms to compare his ink to Ian's, and Ian graciously consented to more photos.

As the crowd continued to press on him, they chattered as if they knew him personally. In fact, they seemed to know a lot more about him than I did. They commented on his long hair and how it was different from how he usually wore it. They wondered where he'd been for the past several months and why they hadn't seen him on social media. They asked him about the other boys in the band, and if he'd seen them, talked to them, gone to their concerts. One or two asked him if he was feeling better. Had he not been feeling okay?

As the frenzy around him dissipated, a final fan approached him, a middle-aged woman who wanted a picture for her daughter, who'd plastered her bedroom with Five2Go posters as a teen.

Ian offered to take her phone and do the honors of a selfie and as the woman stepped forward, she noticed me. I'd finished my dinner by this time.

"Oh, are you a couple? Is this your girlfriend, hon? You two look so cute together. Come, come." She gestured toward me. "I'd like a picture of you both."

I plastered a stiff smile on my face, as I swung my leg over the picnic bench, plate in hand. Ian put his hands together in a pleading gesture. He just couldn't disappoint a fan. Had to be the sea lion.

"Sure, let me drop this in the trash first." I tossed my plate into the trashcan and turned back toward Ian. I stood beside him, my jaw aching from the smile on my face.

He curled an arm around my waist and pinched me.

"Thank you, so much." The woman turned away, and I grabbed her arm. "I'm sure your daughter would love a proper picture of her mom with her favorite boybander. I'll take your picture with Ian."

"Thank you, hon. She would like that." The woman handed me her phone and stepped forward to stand beside Ian, who put his arm around her.

With my thumb, I switched to the woman's photos and deleted the two pictures she'd taken of me and Ian. I had no idea what the woman planned to do with the pictures, but I couldn't risk them going out on social media.

Not if I wanted to keep Matt's nose out of my business.

I lifted the phone. "Smile."

Chapter 5

IVY

Ian captured my hand again as we walked back to my car in the lot. "Sorry about that back there. It must be overwhelming for you."

"What about you? I've experienced it with you a few times already, and I'm not even the target. Can't you politely decline?"

"I suppose I could, but then you have people attacking you online for being stand-offish." He shrugged. "You get used to it."

"I know...the pact." I muttered, "sea lion," as I aimed my key fob at my car and pressed it, my car answering with a beep. When we got into the vehicle, I drank some water left over in the bottle in my cup holder and fished around in my purse. "Do you want some gum?"

Not that I was thinking about kissing him again or anything.

He held out his hand. "Thanks."

I dropped a piece in his hand and started the car. "I don't even know where you're staying, but I can drive you there."

"I'm at the Beverly Hills Hotel."

"Of course you are." I wheeled out of my parking space. "No freeway to get there from here, so it's going to be a stop and go drive down Santa Monica Boulevard."

"You're not going to drive me all the way to the hotel and then back to your place."

"I'm not?" My pulse ticked up a few notches. What did he have in mind?

"Just drive home, and I'll get a ride from there."

"Okay." I'd aimed for a bright tone to cover my disappointment and ended up sounding like a deranged Mary Poppins. I clicked through the source button on the steering wheel to get to the music on my phone and turned it up to cover the awkwardness.

Disgraced Phil Spector's wall of sound filled the car, and I sang along with Ronnie as I buzzed down the window. The fog's density diminished the farther I drove away from the coast.

After a few more choruses of oh, oh, oh, oh, I noticed Ian's silence beside me. I jerked my head to the side and stopped singing.

Holding up his hands, he said, "Don't stop. I was enjoying the concert. You're a good singer."

"Ha! Don't be patronizing. I'm karaoke-level decent." I turned my attention back to the road when the light turned green. "Do you like Ronnie Spector and The Ronettes?"

"I like this song—and I like the way you sing it." He scratched his chin. "Do you prefer older music?"

"I suppose I do, but I like all music." I tucked my hair, which had become wild in the damp ocean air, behind my ear. "I like your music."

"Oh-ho, now who's being patronizing?" He rubbed his arms as if suddenly chilled.

I turned down Ronnie and bit my bottom lip. "I'm being honest. Why wouldn't I be? I like your voice—it's strong and versatile, warm and rich."

"Thank you." He turned his head to stare out the window.

He must hear it all the time. I'd heard it from his fans tonight—the gushing, the compliments, the love. And again, the oddity of his life struck me anew. Was it worse to be lonely by yourself or lonely among a group of people who professed to adore you only to turn on you the minute you slipped?

Lonely? I gave myself a mental slap. Why the hell would Ian Pope be lonely? Just because he'd found himself with nothing to do on a Saturday night in LA didn't mean he was lonely. He'd probably been partying all week and decided to tone it down on his last few days. And it couldn't get more toned down than spending his evening on a Ferris wheel, eating fish from a paper plate.

So, I'd drive him to my place, and he'd go back to his world. He could pat himself on the back for being nice to the quirky little romance writer. I'd have an adventure to talk about at parties and at the next meeting of my writers' group.

My fingers strayed to my lips, the imprint of his kiss still vibrant. But I'd always have that kiss on the Ferris wheel.

All too soon, I turned onto my street and rolled to the curb in front of my building. "Should I let you off here, and you can call a car? It shouldn't be long. There are a lot of cars prowling this area on Saturday night."

He snapped his fingers. "I left my books in your book bag."

"I can run and get them for you while you're getting a ride." I threw my car in Park and reached for the ignition.

Ian put his tattooed hand on mine. "I'd rather come in, if that's alright?"

"Sure, yes, of course, absolutely." I put the car in gear and squealed away from the curb before I could string together another series of assents. I pulled into my parking spot, and we exited, walking through the courtyard shared by the four units in the complex.

Classical music floated from Gregory and Stan's place. The scent of jasmine from my own patio permeated the air, and a light breeze stirred the dead blossoms of the bougainvillea scattered on the ground. I moved forward as if in a dream, Ian following so closely behind me, I could feel his breath on the back of my neck.

With my heart pounding, I attacked the deadbolt with my key, and my key chain dropped to the ground. Ian crouched down and swept it up.

"I'll do it."

I stepped to the side to make room for him, and his arm brushed mine as he fitted the key into the lock and turned it with a click. He shoved the key into the door handle and turned it, shoving it open, at the same time.

The door swung wide with a creak, and I hesitated before stepping into the entryway, as if crossing this threshold would alter my life forever. Ian followed me and closed the door behind us. Habit had me reaching back and turning the deadbolt.

Ian dropped the keys on the floor and placed his hands on my shoulders with a caressing touch. He walked me backward and pressed me against the wall, his mouth hungrily seeking mine.

I tasted the spearmint of his gum, but he must've swallowed it or spit it out. I plucked mine out of my mouth quickly and stuck it to the wall behind me. Reaching up, I burrowed my fingers into his thick, wavy hair, stiff with the spray of salt water, and guided his head down to mine. I stood on my tiptoes, and our lips met with a sizzle. The heat snaked through me, and I sagged against him.

He curled one arm around my waist, the fingers of his other hand lightly stroking my neck as he invaded my mouth with his tongue, seeking that connection we'd felt on the Ferris wheel.

I pressed my body against his, craving his touch, his closeness. He broke off our kiss, and his lips roamed my face, pressing against my forehead, my temple, my cheeks, my chin. When he returned to my mouth, I sucked his bottom lip between my teeth.

We'd sort of rolled down the wall, closer to the door to the back rooms. I hooked both arms around his neck and hopped up to wrap my legs around his waist—the signature short girl move. He smoothed his hands along my bare thighs and tucked them beneath my ass to hoist me higher, burying his face in my neck.

Somehow, we still had our clothes on. I wriggled out of his grasp and slid down his body. Feet firmly on the ground, sort of, I peeled off my shirt and dropped it to the floor. I craved the feel of his skin against mine and grabbed a handful of his T-shirt and yanked it up. He raised his arms, and I pulled it over his head.

His bare, chiseled chest looked like a Michelangelo sculpture, and I ran my hands over his smooth skin, tracing along his muscles. He gasped as the flat of my hand reached the waistband of his jeans. With my fingertips, I traced the tail-end of a green tattoo that snaked across his hip bone.

Taking his hand, I tugged him down the hallway to my bedroom. As he stepped inside my room, he glanced at my bed, perfectly made with its floral comforter. He cleared his throat. "Are you sure?"

"No, I just dragged you in here to show you my old CD collection." I walked to the bed and scooped up the skirt I'd worn and discarded today and threw it in the corner. Then I turned around and undid the clasp of my bra, letting it slide from my shoulders onto the floor.

In two strides, he was standing toe-to-toe with me at the side of the bed. He cupped my boobs, running his thumbs across my aching nipples and breathed out, "Beautiful."

He pulled me into his arms and when our skin met, I felt a flash of desire that ignited all my senses. He skimmed his knuckle down my spine and slid his hand into my shorts, caressing my bottom.

I rocked my hips forward just in case he had any more doubts about what I wanted—and I wanted him with every cell in my body.

Taking the hint, Ian unbuttoned my shorts. I didn't even have to worry if I'd worn a good pair of panties because he pulled off everything in one flourish. My shorts pooled at my feet, and I kicked them out of the way.

I moved forward to press my body against his, but he held me off and took a step back. Placing his hands on my waist, he raked my naked body with a glittering gaze from his half-closed eyes.

His unabashed scrutiny made me feel like a virgin on my wedding night, and I crossed one leg over the other.

His hands traced over the outline of my body as if committing it to memory. Then he spoke, his voice rough with passion. "You look like that little fairy...Tinkerbell."

Cranking my head over my shoulder to look behind me, I asked, "Is it the gossamer wings?"

He ran one finger from my throat to my pussy. "Not just the wings, it's your tiny waist paired with your bangin' curves."

The anxiety I'd experienced the past few years, which had caused me to drop the ten pounds I'd gained in college, had a silver lining, after all. I reached out and hooked my fingers in the waistband of his jeans, more to steady myself than to make a move. "Kind of pervy of you to be having impure thoughts about an animated fairy."

He laughed, his eyes crinkling, and instead of breaking the moment, the pure joy of it only enhanced my desire. I fumbled with the button on his fly and then peeled back his jeans. The bulge in his black briefs gave me pause, but only for a second.

Like he did with mine, I yanked down his jeans and underwear at the same time. I smoothed my hand over his hard cock, and he made a sound deep in his throat. I ran my fingernails lightly across his tight flesh from the base to the tip, spreading his pre-cum around his head with my thumb.

Through clenched teeth, he said, "You're going to have to stop that if you want this to last more than a minute."

I batted my eyelashes. "A popstar stud like you? I thought you guys could go all night."

He grabbed my face with his hands and kissed me hard on the mouth, his cock prodding me in the belly. He lowered me to the bed, and I fell back on it. My knees bounced with impatience while he kicked off his jeans and shoes. Then he parted my legs.

Was he going to fuck me like this on the edge of the bed? I liked a man who thought outside the...box. Instead, he dropped to his knees and put his head between my legs, his hair tickling my thighs. When his tongue met my flesh, I squirmed, and words flashed in my mind like a pink neon sign: *I have Ian Pope's head between my legs.*

He breathed out, his warm breath heating me up even more. "You're so fucking wet."

I'd been wet since the minute he fed me those noodles. "Less talking, more...oh, that."

He used his tongue, lips, and even his teeth to cause absolute mayhem in my mind and body—especially my body. If he'd been worried about lasting a minute, I didn't even make it that long. My orgasm clawed through me like a living thing. My hips rose and fell with each spasm of pleasure, and Ian dug his fingers into my ass, riding it out with me, enhancing my high even more with his tongue.

When my ecstasy subsided to a mere tingling of my nerve endings and fluttering eyelashes, Ian laid a path of kisses along my inner thighs. I grabbed a fistful of his hair. "I want you inside me...now."

His head popped up and he rested his scratchy chin on my belly. "Same—or rather I don't want you inside me, but I sure as hell wanna be inside you."

I scooted back on the bed, and he followed. He placed his hands on either side of me and teased me with his cock. I licked my lips. I might be wet everywhere else, but my mouth was dry with anticipation and longing.

He braced himself on one elbow and kissed me with his impossibly soft lips, his hand caressing my boob. "Mm, your tits are so soft."

Had he even felt real ones before? He'd probably been with a lot of plastic fantastic women with perfect, if fake, tits and asses. He'd probably been with a lot of women, period.

Oh damn. Damn. Damn. I had to do the thing. I absolutely had to do the thing, especially with him.

"Um." I stretched my arm to the side, my fingers feeling for the handle of my nightstand drawer. Once located, I yanked open the drawer. Hopefully, he wouldn't look over and see my purple vibrator, which had gotten a lot more use than the item I plucked up with my fingers. "Could you...?"

I held up the stack of condoms, and they unfolded, swinging in the air between us. Wow, it looked like a lot when they were unpacked like this—which could be a good thing. Yeah, I kept condoms next to my bed, but I hadn't used that many.

"Absolutely. Of course." He took the string of foil packets from me, peeled one off and opened it with his teeth.

I raised my eyebrows. Should I...? He answered my silent question by unrolling the condom onto his dick and sweeping the rest of the packets off the bed.

I closed my eyes when he entered me, filling me up inch by delicious inch. When he stopped, I sucked in a breath.

"Open your eyes, Tinkerbell."

I obeyed—of course, I did. I'd do just about anything for him at this point. When I peeled open my eyelids, I met his brown eyes, burning into me. Holding my gaze, he slid out and then plunged back inside me.

Curling my legs around his slim hips, I didn't ever want to let him go. I kissed his neck and his jaw as I ran my nails up and down his back, his muscles hard and tense.

He whispered in my ear, "Baby, you feel so good. So good. I love fucking you."

And then his words turned to gibberish while his pumping picked up in speed and intensity. When I shifted position, he rubbed against my clit, and all the unreleased tension in my body collected in that one, little hot spot. I clenched my muscles, clenched him inside me, until a warm rush that started at my toes flooded my body. I went limp beneath him, my legs falling to the sides, as my orgasm spiraled through me.

His body seemed to go still, and then he emitted a low moan from his throat as he came hard. When he finished thrusting into me, a shiver ran through his frame, and he lowered himself on top of me. He traced my throbbing lips with the tip of his finger and followed it with a kiss.

I rubbed circles on his back, damp with sweat and inhaled the scent of us together, sweet and spicy, our bodies mingling.

He braced his forehead against mine. "I have no words. That was mighty."

"Mighty what?" I pushed his hair back from his face. "Mighty is an adjective not a noun. It has to describe another word."

"Bloody hell. Is this what it's always going to be like with a writer?" He shifted off my body. "I'll just leave it at mighty, and I'll be right back."

He rolled off the bed and headed toward the bathroom connected to my room, presumably to dispose of the condom. At least he hadn't balked at that.

I chewed on my bottom lip. His question had implied that there would be other occasions between us where I'd need to correct his grammar, instead of accepting that this was the very definition of a one-night stand. He was going back to England, an ocean away.

I'd never fallen for anyone this hard and fast, or ever, but my inner therapist told me that's exactly *why* I'd fallen for Ian so hard and fast. The word transient in the dictionary had Ian Pope's face all over it.

And that's just the way I'd wanted it...until now.

Chapter 6

IVY

Tears pricked my eyes, and I dragged the back of my hand across my nose. I scolded myself and my phantom therapist. Of course, he was going back to England. I knew that. I knew the overwhelming sexual tension between the two of us could only have one result. Well, two, actually. I could've said goodnight at the curb and spent an evening with my purple pussy pleaser stashed in my nightstand. Or have one night of wild sex and relive it in my mind once in a while and re-write it in my books over and over.

He came back into the room, his hair damp and sluiced back from his face, the ends curling. He launched himself onto the bed next to me, making the mattress bounce. Then he lay on his back beside me, curling one arm behind his head, the fingers of his other hand idly toying with mine. "Believe it or not, it's been a long time since I had sex, especially sex like that."

"Like what? Mighty?" I draped one leg over his, still needing to soak in his closeness.

"Yeah, like just feeling everything, every sense alive and present. Fully engaging. Haven't had that in so long."

"Me either..." I turned my head and touched the tip of my tongue to his shoulder, which tasted salty and musky "...despite the long trail of condoms in my nightstand. I'm actually hoping they aren't expired. It's been that long."

He threaded his fingers through mine and kissed the back of my hand. "I'm glad you did have them, else I would've packed off to the corner market and bought some, worrying all the way that you'd change your mind."

"I think my mind was made up the minute you rescued me from Fabio."

"I think I rescued Fabio from you, and you didn't know who I was until I told you my name."

"That's right."

"So, you wanted to ravage me before you knew I was Ian Pope?"

"That's right."

The glint in his eye at my answer made me feel a little sad for him. I traced the tattoo on his hipbone, a mermaid, tail up, her head dangerously close to the hair covering his pubic area. "So, you've ensured that you always have a mermaid going down on you."

He snorted. "You have kind of a dirty mouth. I like that about you."

"And I kind of like your mouth, too. It's very versatile. Who knew you could do more than sing with that mouth."

"You have no idea." He lifted his eyebrows up and down. "Do you want some water? I'll get us some water."

"Yes, please. I don't trust the tap water, but we have some filtered water in a pitcher in the fridge, or I think there are a few bottles left."

"I'll get you a glass." Once again, he clambered from the bed, and I watched the muscles of his buttocks clench and release as he walked out of the room. *Sexy.*

I'd left my phone in my bag out there...and some gum on the wall. Otherwise, I'd text Chloe to let her know I had Ian Pope in my bed. I'd have to get some proof, or Chloe would never believe me. Ian didn't seem to mind selfies. Maybe I'd do one with him in bed.

He strode back into the room, carrying a glass of water. "I already drank from this one, but I figured we've already shared so much, we could share a glass, too."

"Great thinking." I tapped my head and took the glass from him.

He settled himself next to me again, and we shared sips of water from the glass. When I put it to the side, he draped his arm around me and pulled me close. Did he have the same feeling as I did? I felt a need to touch him, to keep connected to him. Probably because he was leaving. I dropped my head onto his shoulder.

He asked, "Did you grow up here in Santa Monica?"

"In Hollywood. My parents had a small house in Hollywood—the flats, not the hills."

"Was your father in the business?"

I gave a short, sharp laugh. "Yeah, my father was in the business alright, a lot of businesses, just not show business. My dad was kind of a scammer, a big gambler. In fact, you could say he was an addict—a gambling addict."

Ian's body stiffened beside me. He'd been stroking my collarbone with his thumb, which I'd been finding very erotic, but he suddenly stopped.

"That must've been hard to live with."

Great. If that tidbit about Dad made him uncomfortable, I sure as hell wasn't going to tell him the rest.

"It was. He gambled away every cent my mother earned until she got sick of it all and left." I sighed.

"Your mom raised you by herself?"

"Are you kidding?" My hands curled into fists, bunching up the sheet. How the hell did we get onto this topic? "She's the one who left. She abandoned us. I haven't seen her since."

"I'm sorry." He squeezed me and kissed the top of my head. "And then you lost your father. How did he...pass away?"

I chewed the inside of my cheek before answering. "Hit and run, right on Hollywood Boulevard."

"God, I'm so sorry, Ivy. Do you know where your mum is? Did she ever reach out after your father died?"

"She probably doesn't even know he's dead, and I wouldn't want to see her, anyway." I sniffed, and a tear rolled down my face. I hadn't cried about Mom in years. To anyone.

Before I could dash the tear away, Ian caught it on the tip of his finger. "My poor Tinkerbell."

"It's alright. I mean, it's not alright, but it is what it is." I blew out a breath. "I really didn't imagine this would be our post-coital discourse."

"Post-coital discourse." He said the words as if trying them out in his mouth. "You have a way with words. That would be a great song title. Post-coital Discourse."

He started singing in his smooth baritone. "I gave her post-coital discourse, but it couldn't have gone worse. She didn't like my sass and kicked me out on my ass."

"That's...not bad." I wriggled out from beneath his arm and swung my legs off the bed. "I'm going to brush my teeth. Do you want a toothbrush?"

"Is that an option?" He ran his tongue over his teeth. "I could really use a toothbrush."

"My dentist always gives me extras. I'll leave one on the sink for you." I sprang up from the bed and strolled to the bathroom, feeling his hot gaze following me. I closed the door behind me and faced the mirror.

Running my hands over my face and body, I said, "Same face, same body."

After my day with Ian, I expected to see something different. I puckered my lips, which seemed plumper, and ran my fingers down my jaw, a little red with scruff rash from all the kissing we'd done. Things looked pretty much the same on the outside, but my insides had experienced a massive shift.

I got ready for bed and left a red toothbrush in its package on the sink. When I returned to the bedroom, Ian was sitting up, going through his phone, a slight downturn to his lips.

"Everything okay?" I picked up the glass on the nightstand.

"All good. Do you have that toothbrush?" he held up his phone. "And a charger?"

"Toothbrush is on the counter in the bathroom. I'll get you a charger from the kitchen. Do you want any more water?"

"No, thanks." When he hopped off the bed, he grabbed me around the waist and kissed me before heading to the bathroom.

I scurried out of the bedroom, plucked the gum from the wall, put the glass in the sink, and yanked a charger from the outlet by the kitchen table. When Ian had been out here before getting the water, he'd placed my keys in the basket by the door and hung our shirts over the back of a chair along with my purse.

I tiptoed to my purse and retrieved my phone stuck in the side pocket. I scanned a few text messages—one from Chloe, asking about the bookfair, one from another author, asking the same, and one from Matt, which I deleted without reading.

When I got back to the bedroom, Ian was still in the bathroom with the water running. I slid between the rumpled sheets and plugged my phone into the charger I kept by the bed, leaving it on the edge of the nightstand.

Ian stepped out of the bathroom and flicked off the light. As he approached the bed, I dangled the charger in front of him. "There's a USB port on the lamp you can use."

"Thanks." He plugged in his phone and joined me under the covers. Wrapping his arms around me, he pressed his naked body against mine. "Mm, I was hoping you hadn't put any nightclothes on."

"Little late for modesty, wouldn't you say?"

"I would." He covered a yawn. "It's barely eleven o'clock, and I'm exhausted. You wore me out, Tink."

"Ditto." I pretended a yawn of my own and rolled onto my side.

He cuddled up behind me, slinging a heavy arm over my hip, cupping my body with his. "This feels good, doesn't it?"

"Uh huh." I twisted my head back and kissed his shoulder, burrowing against him. Too good to be true. Too good to last.

Several minutes later, Ian's breathing deepened, and I closed my eyes and waited. I'd felt at a disadvantage all day, not knowing Ian's recent history, especially as I'd practically vomited up my own. When his hold on me slackened, I peeked over my shoulder and lifted his arm from my body.

Scooting away from him, I grabbed my phone from the charger and ducked under the covers with it, using my body to shield the light from Ian, although he seemed completely out of it.

I Googled his name, and his handsome face popped up on my screen. He was more breathtaking in person. I scrolled past a partial discography, a few links to his social media, the requisite Wikipedia entry and then nearly dropped my phone at the first article headline: **Drunk and Disorderly—Ian Pope Tossed Out of Miami Bar**.

Typical popstar behavior, right? I rolled my shoulders, and Ian murmured in his sleep. My finger swiped up the screen.

Ian Pope's Incoherent Red Carpet Rambling
Former Boy Bander Breaks Paparazzi's Camera
Five2Go or One2Gone—Ian Pope's Drunken Antics
Boy Bander Ian Pope Spotted at Ritzy Rehab in London

I put my fingers to my lips as Ian's warm breath stirred the hair at the nape of my neck. Seemed like I'd just fallen hard for someone who had as many problems as I did. Maybe more.

Chapter 7

IAN

Light pressed against my eyelids like a weight. Typically, I didn't even feel like opening my eyes in the morning, preferring the absolution of sleep, but this morning a different feeling pricked my consciousness. I peeled one eye open, and memories and feelings flooded my senses as I pushed the reddish-brownish hair out of my face. *Ivy*.

I'd had just about the best sex of my life last night, fueled by my craving to make this woman all mine. I did a quick check under the covers just to make sure the mermaid on my pelvis hadn't come to life in my arms. Or, wait, I'd called her a fairy, not a mermaid. God, she must think I'm a right git.

All I knew was the minute I saw her grappling with that cardboard hunk with the flowing blond hair, I'd had an overwhelming urge to meet her, talk to her, kiss her. I couldn't explain it, even to myself. I'd examined the feeling yesterday—I'd become an expert in examining my feelings lately—and faced the harsh reality that maybe I just wanted to fuck her.

I hadn't lied to her. It had been a while since I'd had sex and a long while since I'd had sober sex. But as the day wore on, and we talked and spent time together, I knew my desire ran deeper than a quick smash. I hadn't even planned to make any moves on her, but God, those lips cried out to be kissed, those tits begged to be shaped by my hands, that wild hair demanded to be tamed by my fingers.

Now I had a problem. I didn't deserve someone like her, especially after what she'd gone through with her father. My therapist would dub her a co-dependent, someone with a scarred childhood intent on recreating that childhood and fixing it with another addict. Dr. Lyman would warn me away from someone like Ivy. But did Ivy even know about my...issues?

She didn't seem to know that much about me beyond my days with Five2Go. But what was there beyond my boyband days to know? I hadn't seemed able to move past them, myself, except in the most destructive and detrimental ways.

Just one more day with her. I was returning to England tomorrow. I could spend another day with her, and then go back to...what? Back to making an uninspired record with no motivation or vision behind it. Back to threats from my record label. Back to my feelings of shame around my daughter.

One more day. I brushed Ivy's tangle of curls to the side and kissed the back of her neck.

She sighed and wriggled her bum against my cock, making it harder than it already was waking up beside her.

I curled an arm around her and rolled one of her nipples between my thumb and forefinger. She squirmed some more. I wanted to explore every inch of her body, part by part. I wanted to find all her hot spots and tease them just to watch the ecstasy play across her face.

Reaching back, she hit me in the nose before she found the top of my head and ran her fingers through my hair. She murmured something indistinguishable, but it didn't sound like no.

I pulled away from her for a second to grab the condoms I'd thrown onto the nightstand. I didn't need them—clean and sober in rehab meant *clean* and sober, abstinence from everything. Last night had been the first time I'd had sex in about six months, not that I was keeping track. And not that I'd expected her to believe me. Hell, I wouldn't believe me.

When I rolled back toward her placing my hand on her hip, she scooted away from me, almost to the edge of the bed. I bit my lip. Maybe she'd fully awakened and changed her mind. Maybe she regretted last night.

Closing my eyes, I took a shaky breath through my nose. Would be tough to come down from my arousal, but she'd probably thought twice about getting involved with me any further. I couldn't blame her there. I could knock one out in the shower.

Then she put her hand on mine and pulled my arm around her waist. She sighed. "I can't help myself. I want you so badly."

I didn't want any misunderstandings, so I asked, "Is that a green light?"

"All systems ready for takeoff, baby."

I smiled against her back. She said the craziest things sometimes, but she'd called me *baby* and any part of my hard-on I'd lost came roaring back. She also hadn't turned around, but that didn't mean I couldn't make her come.

My hand skimmed down her belly to her smooth pussy, and I slipped my finger inside her foof, already wet and warm. She uttered a perfect little cry and closed around me. With the pad of my thumb, I stroked her clit, and she rocked against my dick with a soft moan.

Replacing my finger with my cock, I entered her from behind, stroking the same rhythm as my thumb. Her legs trembled, and she curled her toes against my shin. In a jerky movement, she pushed back on me, and then she lunged forward and froze, as if suspended. When she crashed, she slammed her bum against my pelvis and came unraveled.

Her orgasm brought me to my own brink, but as I pumped her from behind, I felt a sense of frustration. This feeling had come over me last night, too, the sense that I had to get closer to her, deeper.

I eased her onto her stomach, while she was still writhing from her climax. When I fully entered her, she grabbed the headboard with both hands, her knuckles turning white. I needed to go deeper now, now. "Now."

Every muscle in my body seized, and then I shattered. My release washed over me, and my arms, braced on either side of Ivy, shook. I felt as if I'd transferred every bit of my power into her, and I collapsed on top of her, too weak to move.

My thundering heart pounded against her back, and her delicate frame trembled beneath me, my hot breath stirring her hair. Our sweat mingled, making us one, and I felt our connection with every fiber of my being.

As my cock twitched inside her, and a sucked her earlobe between my lips, Ivy let out a little squeak. "You're squishing me."

I flipped onto my back and patted her nice, round bottom. "Sorry, baby. Good morning."

Still gripping the headboard, she turned her face toward me, her hair covering one eye. "That was the best wake-up call I've ever gotten. Can I turn you into an alarm clock and keep you next to my bed? Instead of hands on a clock, it can have cocks on a clock. Get it?"

Her whole body shook at her ridiculous joke, and she actually snorted into her pillow.

"You are silly." I ran over the knots in her spine with my knuckle. "I just thoroughly fucked you, and you're making dumb jokes."

"C'mon. That was funny."

As she rolled over onto her side, I disposed of the condom on a coaster on the nightstand. Better than tossing it onto the floor.

I lay back beside her, and she pressed her body against me, entwining her leg around mine. She dabbled her fingers on my chest and planted kisses on my shoulder as I buried my hand in her wild hair, massaging her scalp with my fingertips.

"That bit of mighty almost didn't happen. I thought you were going to change your mind. Y-you pulled away from me."

Drawing a circle around my nipple, she said, "I almost did change my mind. I was just thinking about how you're leaving tomorrow, and how this was just a one-night stand—a very nice one, but yeah."

She had a catch in her voice, and I kissed her temple. "Did this feel like a one-night stand to you?"

"Doesn't matter what it felt like, does it?" She screwed up one side of her mouth. "You're a famous popstar, and you're going back to England tomorrow, back to your real life."

"My real life." I didn't even know what real life was, anymore. I'd squandered opportunities and relationships and had fallen so far from my dreams, I had a hard time remembering what they were.

She studied me from beneath her long lashes, her lips parted, as if in anticipation. Did she expect me to tell her how wonderful I had it? Money, fame, adoration. Bitches and watches, as my bandmate, Charlie, once said. I had all that...and nothing at all.

I didn't want to go back to England tomorrow. I didn't want to leave her. I felt a cavernous ache at the thought of walking away from Ivy and never seeing her again. But if I did want to see her again, I'd have to be honest with her.

I met her hazel eyes, still assessing me, and then looked away. I opened my mouth once. Snapped it shut. Closing my eyes, I took a deep breath.

"I'm at a bit of a crossroads right now in my life." I stopped and chewed on my thumbnail. She waited.

"I...umm, I was in rehab for three months. Got out about two months ago. I'm an alcoholic." I held my breath and slid a quick glance at her.

She hadn't moved a muscle. Didn't recoil. Didn't blink. Didn't pull away.

"Made kind of a disaster of things and don't really know where I am right now."

Her chest rose and fell. "I know."

Her words punched me in the gut, and *I* pulled away from *her*. "You know? You knew I was in recovery and offered me your roommate's wine yesterday and suggested I get a beer with dinner? That's fucked up."

I bolted from the bed and searched the floor wildly for my jeans. They lay in a heap at the foot of the bed, and I grabbed them. I was so sick of this shit. So tired of the users and the hangers-on and the exploitative nature of people. Ivy seemed different. They all seemed different. Until they weren't.

Pulling the covers up to her chin, she watched me with wide eyes, her cheeks pink. "I-I didn't know you were in recovery when I offered you the booze."

I tilted my head back and laughed at the ceiling with a harsh, strangled cry from my throat. "So, what? You learned about my situation overnight, whilst you slept, through osmosis or something?"

I practically ripped my jeans apart, trying to turn them right-side out.

Ivy scrambled across the bed on her hands and knees and grabbed me around the waist, pressing her soft breasts against my back. "Stop a minute and let me explain—please."

I stood frozen as she splayed her hands across my chest, placing one over my bruised heart. She pressed her nose between my shoulder blades.

"I didn't know any of that, yesterday. I was a fan of Five2Go when I was a teenager, but I think I mentioned that I hadn't really followed your solo careers, just heard some songs here and there from all of you. I don't read celebrity gossip. My social media, when I remember it, is mostly about my books and other people's books."

She *had* mentioned that. I dropped my tangled jeans on the floor.

"But when I saw you with your fans yesterday on the pier, I felt kinda stupid. They knew more about you than I did." Her voice softened to a whisper. "I remembered you had a daughter, but I didn't know anything about your career or your struggles."

Now she knew about Thea *and* about my issues, and she'd see me for what I was—a terrible father.

"Sit down. If you wanna leave after I speak, then whatever." She pulled me back toward the bed, and I sat on the edge, next to her, elbows on my knees, hands clenched in my hair. "After we...had sex and you fell asleep, I looked you up on my phone. I saw everything then."

Talking to the floor, I said, "That's why you pulled away from me this morning. You'd already made one mistake sleeping with a loser and didn't want to compound the error."

"I don't think you're a loser." She traced a finger over one of the tattoos on my arm. "I think you're incredibly strong. You've been sober for five months. That's a huge accomplishment."

I swallowed the lump in my throat. God, if I cried in front of her, I'd lose my man-card forever. "But your father was an addict—different kind, same mindset. Don't tell me you didn't have those thoughts when you read about my fuckups."

"I did, and you're right. That caused me some hesitation this morning, but you're not my father. He never tried to recover from his addictions. Never tried to be better." She rested her head on my shoulder. "If you don't mind my asking, when did you start drinking to excess?"

Without raising my head, I answered. "Probably about the time we started touring, I mean the big tours. We were still underaged, and management really didn't know what to do with us, so they locked us in the hotel rooms, but they didn't bother to clear out the minibars. I must've tried every kind of booze in the minibar in hotels all around the world. It was also a way to unwind after a concert. We'd be all hyped up on stage, performing for 60,000 fans, and then the lights would go out and the crowd would go home, and we had to go back to the hotel...and silence and loneliness."

"Do any of the other guys have issues with alcohol? Let's see if I can remember. Charlie, Sam, Javeed, and Conor." She tapped my arm as she mentioned each of my Five2Go bandmates.

"Not really. We all dealt in our own ways. Had our own issues." Truth was, I didn't know how the boys were doing these days. I sat up and thrust three fingers in the air. "This is number three for me. I've tried rehab twice before. What do you Yanks say? Three strikes and you're out?"

"We also say, third time's a charm." She grabbed my fingers and kissed the tips. "I'm sorry I offered you that booze. Are you still upset with me?"

"Why didn't you just tell me this morning that you knew?"

"Didn't want it to ruin the moment, honestly." She clambered into my lap, straddling me. "And I wanted you to tell me yourself. Why didn't you mention it yesterday? Would've been the perfect time when I offered you the wine."

"To echo you, I didn't want to ruin the moment. I don't want to put any pressure on you, but for the first time in a really long time, I didn't have any cravings yesterday. The only craving I had was for your body." As I kissed her mouth, I dropped back onto the bed, taking her with me.

She stared into my face, her nose almost touching mine. "All this doesn't change the fact that you're leaving tomorrow, right?"

I placed my hands on her bum and squeezed her soft flesh. "Do you want me to stay?"

Her eyelashes fluttered. "Could you?"

"Would you want me to if I could?"

"If I wanted you to, would you want to? If you could?"

"This is getting confusing." I smiled as I kissed her kissable lips. "I could stay for another few weeks, and I want to. Stay. Here. With you."

"Good." She held my face in her hands and kissed me back.

I felt a surge of excitement that had nothing to do with her naked body lined up on top of mine—well, almost nothing. I just hoped I hadn't made another big mistake in my life...in a long line of big mistakes.

✳ ✳ ✳

When I got out of the shower, I put on my clothes from yesterday. I didn't have a choice, but Ivy planned to drive me to the hotel to pick up my bags. Before agreeing to an extra few weeks in LA, I'd made sure I could stay with Ivy. There's no way I could stay at the Beverly Hills Hotel with Jack gone. I hated staying in hotel rooms, had been in too many of them.

My manager had not been thrilled to learn that I'd decided to spend the next two weeks in LA with a woman I'd just met yesterday. Jack knew my pattern with women all too well—dive in deep, fast only to wake up months later with the realization that I didn't even know these people, didn't have anything in common with them, was bored in their company, and worse, I'd been functioning as their personal piggy bank and prop for clicks and likes on social media.

Meeting Ivy had sparked something different in my soul. Yeah, the sex was out of this world, but maybe it had been so hot because I felt this special connection with her—or maybe because I was sober.

I tied my shoes and looked for my T-shirt, then remembered Ivy had ripped it from my body in the other room. I poked my head out the bedroom door and heard Ivy singing in the kitchen. She really did have a nice voice, even if she wasn't singing one of my songs.

I made a beeline for the chair where I'd draped our shirts last night.

"Oh, looking for this?" Ivy danced forward, holding out the hem of my shirt that fell to her mid-thigh. "You can have it back when I take a shower."

"Looks a lot better on you, anyway." I stepped into the kitchen and took her in my arms, kissing her sweet lips. "You taste like strawberries."

She held up one finger. "There's a reason for that. I made you a smoothie—strawberries, bananas, pineapple, spinach, and some other healthy stuff. Hope that's okay. It's what I usually eat for breakfast. I'm making toast, too, so you don't starve."

"You shouldn't have gone to any trouble." I pivoted in the small kitchen. "I can make my own toast."

"Sit down." She tapped the kitchen table set with placemats, a green concoction in a glass at the corner of one of the placements, and a vase of pink flowers in the center. "This kitchen is too small for multiple cooks. Coffee? Tea? I don't drink coffee, but Chloe has a single-serve Keurig."

I stood behind one chair and picked up the smoothie. "Tea, please."

Ivy flitted around the kitchen and a few minutes later, she set a yellow plate in front of me with toast and handed me a mug of tea. "Sugar or..." she gave a shudder "—milk? Both?"

"Black is good." I dredged the teabag in the hot water a few times before taking a sip and then sat down once I did. "This is all very domestic."

She jerked her head up from her smoothie, a green moustache on her upper lip. "You don't like it? You would've preferred to go out for breakfast. You probably wanted to eat breakfast at the Polo Lounge at the hotel."

"No, no. Stop. This is fine. Thank you." I tapped my lip.

"What? You want a kiss now?" She leaned forward and closed her eyes.

I kissed the smoothie from her mouth and licked my lips. "I was just telling you that you had some green sludge on your upper lip."

Squealing, she grabbed her napkin and swiped it across her mouth. "You must think I'm a total idiot."

"I think you're adorable, and I wanted to kiss you, anyway." I crunched into a piece of toast. "What are we going to do today after I pick up my bags?"

"It's a surprise. I get the feeling you didn't see much of LA when you were living in Calabasas, so I'm going to give you an, I love LA tour for the next few weeks. How does that sound?" She slurped some tea from her mug, her green eyes sparkling above the rim.

I didn't need the tour. I'd decided I already loved LA.

Chapter 8

IAN

I loosened my grip from the edge of my seat as Ivy wheeled into the driveway of the Beverly Hills Hotel, toward its famous sign and beneath its iconic green and white striped awning. She'd driven like a maniac down Sunset Boulevard. Must mean she was in a hurry for me to pick up my stuff and stay with her.

She screeched to a halt several feet past the valet parking attendants. "I'll wait here."

"Are you sure?"

She adjusted her rearview mirror. "As long as these guys with their neat black vests and bowties let me."

"I'll talk to them. I won't be long." I pushed open the car door and stopped the two valets heading towards Ivy's car. "She's waiting for me. Is that okay?"

They backed off. "Of course, sir."

I'd have to get some cash from Jack to tip them on my way out or have them add something to the room charge. *Jack*. Time to face the ogre. Sometimes it seemed as if Jack cared more about my career than I did—of course, that didn't take much these days.

I sailed through the lobby, waved to a few fans some busy bellhop had herded toward the door, and punched the elevator button for my room on the fourth floor, down the hall from Jack's room. I'd texted Jack earlier to let him know what time I'd be here, and the guy must've had his ear pressed against his door because the minute I stepped into my room, Jack called me from a few doors down.

"Hey, Ian." He appeared in my doorway, his face flushed, as if he'd run a half marathon instead of twenty feet. I held the door open for him, and Jack followed me into the room.

I flipped open my suitcase on the floor with my foot. "Did you have a good time with your friends? How'd you like the book festival."

"Yeah, yeah. It was good, mate." Jack sliced his hand through the air to put an end to the trivial conversation. "Who's this Ivy person?"

"Ivy Chase." I slid several shirts from the hangers in the closet and folded them on the bed. "I told you. She's a romance author I met at the book festival—so cheers to you for that great suggestion. We really hit it off, and I'm going to spend a few weeks with her. But don't worry. Ever since yesterday, I've had lyrics running through my head and melodies thumping in my veins. I have some great ideas for some songs, and she has work to do, as well. I can get some serious writing done here."

Jack folded his skinny arms, bunching the sleeves of his polo shirt with his hands. "You already have songs for the album, Ian."

"They're shit. You know it, and I know it. I'm not happy with any of it. They're not reflective of who I am now—after rehab." I stuffed my folded shirts into the suitcase and pivoted to the cavernous bathroom, bigger than Ivy's kitchen.

Jack followed me. "How's that going?"

"My recovery?" I snatched my toiletry bag from the hook on the back of the door and loaded it with products from the sink. "It's good. I feel good. Honestly haven't had a craving since I met Ivy."

"Does she drink? Use?"

"She may drink. I didn't ask her, but she didn't drink anything around me. Drugs? I doubt it." I shrugged. "I don't know, but I'm feeling good."

Jack chewed on his thumbnail, a habit he acquired when he worked for the management team overseeing Five2. "Have you been on social media lately? D-did you see…?

"I saw it, and I don't wanna talk about it." I slammed the bathroom door in Jack's face and changed clothes; the sand still clinging to my jeans dusted the tiles on the floor as I shook them out.

Jack yelled through the door. "You've said good around five times now, even though you've seen what's trending on social media. Don't give me a load of bollocks, Ian."

I swung open the door, and Jack scooted out of the way as I charged past him with my toiletry bag with Jack still yelling at my back. "It's always good, mate, until it's not. Your sobriety is too important right now to risk being around a bad influence."

"Right now? My sobriety has always been important, Jack, and Ivy isn't a bad influence." I snatched a pair of black pants from the back of a chair and packed them down on top of the rest of my clothes. "I don't even blame Jessica for my issues. It's all on me, always has been."

"Where *is* Ivy, anyway." Jack looked around the room for her to materialize.

"She's waiting in her car out front. Do you have some cash on you? I want to tip the valet parking attendants for letting her stay there."

"I'll give you the money as long as I can meet this paragon of virtue." Jack returned to the bathroom to check the shower and then opened the minibar to give it the once over.

I rolled my eyes. "Nothing's missing from the minibar. Let's go. You can check me out later."

I hitched my backpack over one shoulder and dragged my suitcase down the carpeted hallway. I couldn't wait to get out of here. No matter how nice the hotel was it always felt like a prison to me.

As I strode through the lobby, Jack dogged my steps, his six foot plus frame slightly hunched. Jack had been part of my team for about two years, added just after the previous failed attempt at recovery. My therapist had suggested new friends and new experiences, and that had worked—for a while.

I'd met my ex, Jessica at a party, drinking, and I'd jumped right in with her. She was my excuse for falling off the wagon because I wanted an excuse. Unlike Jack, I never blamed Jessica, but our relationship had grown toxic. I broke it off with her before going into rehab for the third time. I figured we'd pick up where we left off when I got out—and so did she—but this go-around I had to try a different approach.

I traveled with a couple of friends to some out-of-the-way places—hiked in Nepal, surfed in Bali, fished in Montana. When the record company pressured me for new music—or else—I thought I was in a good place, but I'd been fooling myself, the craving for booze always on my periphery. That's why I hadn't returned to England right away to see my little girl, Thea, even though I missed her more than anything. I had to be a better person first, and Thea's mother had agreed.

"Money?" I held out my hand to Jack, and he clapped several twenties in my palm.

"Where is she?" Jack cupped his hand over his face, scanning the curb in front of the hotel.

"She parked farther down."

The two attendants who'd been here when we arrived scurried towards me and Jack.

I waved them off. "Just hopping in the blue car up ahead. Thanks for letting her park there." I stuffed some bills into their hands and made a beeline for Ivy's car.

She must've been watching her rearview because she hopped out and popped her trunk. Her cropped white jeans hugged her in all the right places, and her floaty blue blouse hung loosely right above her hips—effortlessly sexy, freshly beautiful. Every time I saw her, I felt like sweeping her in my arms and kissing her—but I didn't want to give Jack any more ammunition. He figured I'd fallen too hard, too fast and would end up in the same predicament as I had with Jessica.

But this was different. Ivy was different. I was different.

"It's about time. Those valets were ready to pounce to get me to move my old junker out of their beautiful driveway." She shoved her sunglasses into her auburn hair, the sun glinting off the red tint. "That's all you have? I was expecting more."

"That's it." I stepped to the side when Jack joined us, fumbling for a cigarette. "Ivy, this is Jack Davies. Jack, Ivy Chase."

Ivy thrust out her hand. "Nice to meet you, Jack. Sorry for stealing your traveling companion."

"I'm leaving tomorrow, anyway. It's all good." Jack shoved the cig behind his ear and shook Ivy's hand, assessing her head to toe.

If she sensed his scrutiny, she didn't seem to mind.

"Did you enjoy your friend's panel at the book festival? Ian told me your friend wrote a true crime book. I've read a lot of true crime, especially from Ann Rule. Have you ever read her stuff?"

I didn't know what Jack expected from Ivy, but clearly not this. Grinning, I hoisted my bag into the back of Ivy's car.

Jack tilted his head to one side and scooped his thinning blond hair back from his forehead. "No, I don't think so."

"You absolutely have to read 'The Stranger Beside Me,' which she wrote about Ted Bundy. She actually knew him and worked with him on a suicide prevention hotline, of all things. Isn't that wild? It's fascinating, and I think it reveals things about Ann that she probably didn't even realize."

I slammed the hatchback. "Anyway..." Ivy took my hand and kissed me on the mouth. She didn't have the same reservations about giving Jack ammunition. "...you should read that book. What's your friend's name and the name of his book? I'll check it out. Always up for supporting my fellow authors."

"Oh, yes, brilliant. I'll text that info to Ian, and he can give it to you."

"Perfect." Ivy aimed a dazzling smile at Jack. "Again, nice meeting you. Hope you have a safe flight home." She pivoted and hopped into her car.

Jack stood, as if stunned, for a few seconds. Then he shook his head. "She's..."

"I know, right? Totally different. You don't have to worry about me. Enjoy your flight." I squeezed Jack's shoulder as I grabbed his hand.

When I joined Ivy in the car, I felt as if I'd turned some kind of corner in my life. I snapped on my seatbelt and twisted toward her. "Where to?"

"I know you like art, so I'm taking you to the Getty Center." She wheeled away from the curb and stuck her hand out the window, waving at the parking attendants. "Ever been there?"

"No."

She clicked her tongue. "Philistine."

"How do you know I like art?"

"When I was scrolling through your past on my phone last night, I didn't see just the bad stuff." She rubbed my arm, giving me chills despite the heat inside the car. "Some of the good stuff snuck in there, too. I read that you're an artist, had done some sketches for charity, and that you often contribute to arts foundations."

"I wouldn't call myself an artist, but I do appreciate art. Can't wait for our first adventure." I snapped my fingers. "Step on it."

* * *

I didn't know what I'd been expecting from the museum, but a tram ride from the parking lot to the top of a hill wasn't it. The views from the grounds were amazing, and Ivy could barely get me inside the museum to look at the actual art.

As I gazed at the city skyline with the mountains in the background, she tugged my sleeve. "We don't have that much time. Let's look at the paintings."

I allowed Ivy to drag me through the Impressionists, which I appreciated, but my interest perked up when we walked into another gallery with several portraits.

We entered one room of 17th Century portraitists and like a homing beacon, I zeroed in on a particular painting of a woman in a dark green, off-the-shoulder dress. Something about her expression arrested me, and I stood before her, my gaze roaming the canvas. I glanced at Ivy, her head tilted to one side as she studied a painting of a man in a ruffled collar holding an old-fashioned instrument.

When I looked back at the woman in the painting, I noticed that the look in her eyes reminded me of Ivy's—something guarded, even secretive. And I had to admit, for all Ivy's openness, she always seemed to hold something back. Her eyes, sometimes green, sometimes hazel, were the keepers of her secrets, just like...I leaned into the painting...the duchess, here.

I aimed my phone at the QR code on the label next to the painting and sank down on a bench in front of it to read about the Dutch master who'd painted the lady and the lady herself. Turns out, the duchess was a spy.

Ivy touched my shoulder. "Are you tired?"

"I'm reading about this painting. I really like it." I slipped a flyer from my museum program guide and turned it over to its blank side. "Do you mind if I sit here for a minute and sketch this and take some notes. Do you have a pen in your bag?"

"I think so." She dipped her hand inside her bag and withdrew a pen. "I'm going out to the gardens. You can meet me there when you're done. Do you want something to eat?"

"Yeah, sure. I'll see you out there." The pen was already moving across the page in light strokes.

Once I'd taken a picture of the painting, done a passable sketch of the duchess, and taken some notes, I stood up and stretched. When I folded the piece of paper and shoved it into my back pocket, I knew I had the beginnings of a song.

I wandered outside, squinted, and clapped my sunglasses back on my face. Ivy had insisted I wear my hat again and I'd obliged her, but I knew the disguise wasn't always adequate to keep my fans at bay.

I found her on the grass near a fountain with two sandwiches and two bottles of water. I sat beside her and kissed her on the side of her head, warmed by the sun.

She repositioned herself on her back and put her head in my lap, looking up at my face. "So, did you have a connection with that painting?"

Running my thumb over the little bump on the bridge of her nose, I said, "I did, yeah. She reminded me of you."

"You mean sexy and irresistible?" She lifted her sunglasses and batted her eyelashes.

"Mysterious."

"*Moi?*" She rolled over and grabbed the packaged sandwiches. "Turkey or ham?"

"I'll take the ham." She was an expert at avoidance. Maybe she was a spy like the duchess.

As Ivy tossed me the sandwich, a woman stepped into the line of fire, and the sandwich hit her on the back of the leg. It didn't even faze her. "Sorry to interrupt, but would you mind signing my Getty Center map?"

"Be happy to." I grabbed my ham sandwich on the ground before the woman crushed it under her heel.

Ivy stood up and dusted grass from the back of her white pants. Unwrapping her own sandwich, she rolled her eyes at me and stepped away. She really didn't like this fame game.

I was about to get to my feet, but another woman crouched beside me, thrusting her map and pen in my face. "Big fan of Five2Go. Do you ever talk to Sam? I'm sorry, but he was my favorite. You were my next favorite, though."

Why did they always have to go there? "Haven't spoken to him in a while, but he's doing well, ain't he?"

"I went to his concert two years ago. Hope he tours again soon." She shoved her sunglasses into her hair, her gaze probing my face. "You haven't been on tour for a while, have you?"

"Planning something for next year." I handed the map back to her.

"That's great. I'll definitely go if you come to LA." She leaned in close, cupping her hand around her mouth as if to tell me a big secret. "Sam may have been my favorite, but you always had the best voice and stage presence."

"Well, thanks for that." I reached for my sandwich. "You have a good rest of your day."

As I prepared to unwrap my sandwich, I noticed two women huddled by the fountain where Ivy had retreated. One of the women pointed at me, and I braced for incoming traffic. This time I stood up. I didn't like being on the ground when my fans approached me. I'd always had nightmares about getting trampled in my Five2 days.

I pasted on a smile as they walked toward me. My expression encouraged their tentative approach. Maybe I should just ignore them, but I couldn't do that to my fans. They'd given me so much.

"Ian! Can we take a picture with you?" They were already fussing with their phones to get to their cameras.

"Sure, sure." The taller of the two women came in for a hug, and I wrapped my arms around her while her friend took our picture. She then got her selfie.

They traded places, and the tall blonde took pics of me and her brunette friend, and then the friend took a selfie. All smiles.

As I handed her phone back to the shorter brunette, she flushed pink. "You know, we don't believe all that stuff that was on social media the past few days."

"Oh, uh, appreciate that." My gaze darted to Ivy, still munching on her sandwich by the fountain, several feet away. "Enjoy the museum."

They walked away, looking at their phones, and I made a beeline for Ivy, my head down. I didn't need any more fan encounters today, especially not in front of Ivy. She didn't seem to be much of a social media fan, which suited me perfectly, right now.

Hopping up on the fountain beside her, I said, "You didn't have to run away."

She studied me as she chewed. "Oh, yeah, I did. I melt into the background when they swarm you...and that's exactly where I want to be."

"I'm sorry."

Waving her sandwich at me, she said, "Don't apologize. You clearly enjoy it, and so do they. I'm not going to rain on anyone's parade, but I don't have to march along in it and get all wet. Do you want to check out the decorative arts or the drawings? We probably have time for just one."

"Definitely drawings, but I need to eat my lunch first." I peeled the tight plastic from my sandwich and took a few bites as Ivy scrolled through her phone. I hoped she hadn't decided to check out the social media sites. I blurted out. "I have a song in my pocket."

"Huh?" She jerked her head up and stashed her phone in her bag. "What's that supposed to mean? Is that some British boyband code for a hard-on?"

I blew out a breath, relaxing my shoulders. "That painting of the duchess back there tweaked something in my imagination. Does it happen like that with your writing? Some image or headline starts you on a path of creativity?"

"Yeah, but usually my inspiration comes from tragic news stories and weird crimes. Must be nice to be inspired by beauty, instead." She sidled closer to me so that our hips met.

We seemed to have complementary magnets installed in our bodies that drew us to each other—unless she was this touchy-feely with everyone. Her touch, her very presence soothed me. Did other things to me, as well, but she seemed to have the same need for physical contact with me as I did with her.

I bumped her hip. "Unfortunately, my motivation for songs doesn't come only from the beautiful. There are enough songs of heartache and loss to tell you that."

"I'd love to hear the song or read it, later, if you're inclined to share." She'd inched closer to me and entwined her pinkie finger around mine.

"You don't have to ask me twice." I balled up the paper from my sandwich and shot it into a trash can. "Let's go check out those drawings."

I was inclined to share a lot with Ivy…just not everything.

* * *

As Ivy navigated the freeway back to her place, she drummed her thumbs on the steering wheel in time to the music on the radio—oldies, of course. "I texted my roommate, Chloe, when we were at the museum to give her a heads-up."

"Okay." My hand tightened on my seatbelt. "Did she have any objections?"

"She hasn't responded, yet, but I'm sure she'll be fine with it. Her boyfriend lives in San Diego, but he travels up here quite often, so there's not much she can say—not that she would. Besides…" she flicked back her hair "—I own the place."

"She helps you pay your mortgage."

"Yeah, and she doesn't have to live with me. She could afford to rent a place on her own or move in with Trent in San Diego. But she's my bestie and has my back."

"Is she a romance writer, too?"

She barked out a laugh. "God, no. She's a social media strategist. She's on contract with some big company right now to update their marketing approach. I don't think she has a romantic bone in her body."

I ran my tongue along my teeth in my dry mouth. Social media savvy Chloe could pose a problem for me. I'd been hoping to skate through this current crisis with Ivy none the wiser.

First real bump in the road since I got out of rehab. It might've been enough to trigger me before, but I felt different this time, stronger. I ran my hand along Ivy's thigh. "Can't wait to meet her."

Ten minutes later, Ivy turned onto her street and glided to a stop in front of her house. She popped her hatchback, and I yanked out my bag and stacked my backpack on top of it. "Thanks, again for doing this. I hate staying in hotels."

"I can imagine." She grabbed my arm and did a little skip.

She probably *couldn't* imagine, but I didn't need to give her any more gory details. I wanted to be open with her, but some things were better left for later in the relationship—if we were going to have a later.

When we got to the entrance of her place, the front door stood open and music poured out the screen door—not mine. I didn't recognize the song, but it had a ska beat that made me want to bop my head.

Ivy pulled open the screen door and muttered, "I told her before to keep this locked."

She held the door open for me as I dragged my bag into the foyer. The music abruptly ended, and I glanced up to see a figure looming at the end of the short hallway. A woman, taller than Ivy—but then who wasn't—had her hands on her hips, a black ponytail swinging behind her as if she'd just stopped dancing or jogging in place.

Ivy tossed her keys into the basket. "Hey, Chloe. Did you get my text?"

"I did." The look she shot me from a pair of icy blue eyes beneath a dark fringe chilled my blood. "I messaged you back. You obviously didn't read it."

"I-I was driving. My phone was in my purse." Ivy stood between me and the avenging woman, who looked as if she was ready to pounce any second. Ivy's head ping-ponged from me to her roommate. "This is Ian."

Chloe wagged her finger in the air. "Yeah, we all know Ian...and his dick. I'm very familiar with Ian's dick. Everyone's seen Ian's dick by now."

Chapter 9

IVY

A fog invaded my brain, and I shook my head to try to clear it. "Would you stop saying *Ian's dick*. What are you even talking about?" I whipped my head toward Ian. "What does she mean? Do you two know each other?"

Chloe sneered. "Apparently, you don't need to know Ian to see his dick."

"Just stop." I covered my ears with my hands. "Ian, what the hell is going on?"

"It's not even my di..." I screamed, and Ian threw his arms out to the side "...todger."

"Todger?" Chloe snorted. "That makes it sound a hundred times worse—like a small, feral animal."

"It can't be any worse. Ian, what's going on?" I folded my arms across my stomach, which had flipped and then flopped. Had I invited a perv into my house? My bed? My life?

Ian took my hand, and I gritted my teeth but didn't snatch it away. "Let's sit down, and I'll explain or at least try to explain."

"This sounds ominous." Something had to be explained. I shuffled my feet as Ian guided me to the loveseat, making a wide berth around

Chloe, still standing there like some kind of hostile Amazon guardian of the home front...forest.

"You, too, Chloe." Ian waved her into a chair like he owned the place, not in the least bit as sheepish as I'd expect someone to be after flashing his privates.

When we were all seated, Chloe crossing her arms, legs and probably her teeth and me holding Ian's hand in a death grip, Ian took a deep breath. "A few accounts on social media have been posting that I've been sending out dick pics to my fans."

I covered my mouth. "That can't be true."

"Thanks, Tinkerbell." He brought my hand to his lips and kissed it. Someone who kissed hands like that couldn't be a perv.

Chloe narrowed her blue eyes and hunched forward. "Why would someone do that? Your dick is currently on everyone's lips."

Ian made a choking sound while I gasped and coughed, pounding my chest with my fist, eyes watering.

Chloe flapped her hands in the air. "Metaphorically speaking."

I recovered enough to ask, "You've seen them?"

"I have them." Chloe folded her hands like a church lady in her Sunday best.

Spreading his hands in front of him, Ian, said, "Well, then it should be obvious that's not me...mine."

Chloe's gaze darted between my face and Ian's...crotch.

"Why would it be obvious?" I crinkled my nose.

Ian ran a hand through his long hair. "I'll tell you later, but those are *not* pictures of me, and I haven't sent anything out to anyone."

"Who would do that to you and why?" Chloe's voice hadn't lost the accusatory edge, but I couldn't blame her. My first instinct was to believe Ian, but he could've sent the pictures earlier when he was—impaired.

Ian shrugged, and he dropped back against the cushions in a defeated posture. I wanted nothing more than to wrap my arms around him and press my warmth into him—even if he was a perv.

"I have an idea who might be behind it, but I don't have any proof. Just hoping people see how absurd it is and drop it. I'm not going to address it. Haven't been on social media in over five months."

"Ugh, that's awful you have to deal with that." I leaned over and planted a kiss on Ian's chin before nestling my head on his shoulder. "Sheesh, Chloe. Do you believe him now? Give a guy a chance. You, of all people, know how this stuff can be manipulated."

"I'm withholding judgment for now." She jabbed a finger at Ian. "But you'd better watch yourself. You may not be guilty of the dick pics, but you're no freakin' angel, are you? And this girly right here is special. She doesn't need a broken heart. She's been through enough."

My intact heart skipped a beat, and I scooted forward to the edge of the loveseat. "Okay. That's enough. Can we just have a truce for right now? And you don't need to worry about me, Chloe. I'm a big girl."

"You don't have to tell me how special she is, and I'm not gonna break her heart." Ian brushed an errant strand of hair from my face and tucked it behind my ear. "Is it safe now? I'd like to unpack a few things, if that's okay."

"Sure, baby. Do you want me to help you?" I captured his hand with both of mine. "I'm sorry this happened to you."

"It's all good, and I don't need help." He pushed up from the love seat. "Maybe you two need to talk."

Chloe cranked her head around to watch him walk toward the entryway to retrieve his bags. As soon as he turned into the hallway toward the bedrooms rolling his suitcase, she spun around.

"What the actual fuck, Ivy. How did you get here?"

"I told you in my text. We met at the book festival. We just hit it off— he's funny and smart and charming, and hot as hell." I clasped my hands together, pinning them between my knees. "I like him."

"Don't forget rich and famous."

"That, too."

"Does he get mobbed everywhere you go?"

"He keeps a pretty low profile. The hat helps. The sunglasses help even more during the daytime. You know LA. People here are more blasé about seeing celebrities than elsewhere and tend to give them their privacy." I twisted my fingers. "Was the dick pic thing bad? Do people actually believe he sent them?"

"I did. Maybe I still do." Chloe lifted and dropped her shoulders quickly. "Of course, I have an ulterior motive for being pissed off about it after you told me he's spending the next few weeks in your bed. People are savage online. You know that, which is why you avoid social media. And Ian Pope has not exactly been a saint the past few years. You do know *that*, right?"

"I looked him up." I curled my leg beneath my thigh, unsure about how much of his life Ian wanted me to share with others. "He was in rehab for three months. Got out two months ago and has been clean and sober since then. He seems fine to me."

"Rehab in some fancy celebrity place." Chloe smacked her forehead with the heel of her hand. "Sounds like a prescription for disaster for a new relationship, or...what is this?"

A smile tugged at my lips. "Not sure, yet, but it's nice."

"It's weird." Chloe kicked her feet up on the coffee table between the chair and the love seat. "You guys have known each other for what? Twenty-four hours? He already has a pet name for you, you're mooning around asking if he needs help unpacking, and it's clear that you can't keep your paws off each other. Sex must be phenomenal."

"It's been closer to thirty hours, and yeah, the sex is great." The smile I'd been battling spread across my face.

"Don't let it blind you to his faults. He's had plenty of fuckups." Chloe threw a pillow at me. I caught it with one hand and buried my warm face in it. She asked, "Does he know about you?"

My head shot up at the same time Ian stepped from the hallway. "Tink, I need to ask you a question. Can you help me with something?"

"Yep, sure." I rose on a pair of unsteady legs. Had Ian heard Chloe's question? As I walked past Chloe, I whacked her on the top of the head with the pillow.

I walked into the bedroom and heard Ian clinking around the bathroom. I grasped the door jamb and leaned into the bathroom. "What do you need?"

He nodded at the counter. "I don't want to crowd you. Where should I put my stuff?"

I squeezed past him and swept up several items that I used infrequently and shoved them into a few drawers. "You can have this space."

Was I really giving a man space in my bathroom? Maybe Chloe was right. I *was* in danger.

Putting away his stuff, he caught my eye in the mirror. "Thanks for believing in me out there. I became aware of the buzz this morning. Jack sent me the pictures and some of the posts. I didn't want to tell you. I reckoned you might find out later, but I didn't want to spoil anything between us. I wasn't trying to hide anything from you. Does that make sense?"

Did it ever.

I slid behind him and wrapped my arms around his waist, resting my head on his back. "It does. I'm just livid that someone is subjecting you to this garbage and that so many people believe it."

He covered my hands with his and moved them up to his chest, so I could feel his heart thumping beneath my palm. "I don't even know if most people believe it. They just get off on the buzz and piling on."

"Who's responsible for it?" I poked my head around his body to watch his face in the mirror.

"I don't know for sure." He dropped my hands and rearranged some items on the counter. *He knew.*

"What do you want to do for dinner? I'd like to take you out to thank you for...today."

"You know what I really want?" I jabbed his side with my elbow. "I wanna see those pictures."

"You naughty girl." He flicked my earlobe with his finger.

Covering my heart with my hand, I said, "For purely educational purposes. You told Chloe it should be obvious why the dick isn't yours.

I'd like to see with my own eyes. Unlike Chloe, I am intimately familiar with your...todger. I'm an expert witness, at this point."

For the first time since we encountered judge, jury, and executioner Chloe, Ian gave me that brilliant smile that could light up a room bigger than this one. "Not sure I like the idea of you ogling someone else's package, but I suppose in the name of judicial fairness, you should have a peek."

We walked into the bedroom, and Ian plumped up a pillow against the headboard and got comfortable, positioning his back against it. He patted the bed beside him. "Get prepared to be blown away."

"Not sure that's the phrase you should be using in connection to dick pics." I hopped on the bed beside him and hovered over his shoulder as he scrolled through his phone.

"Here you go." He held up his phone. "This is supposed to be me."

I gasped. "No fucking way."

Chapter 10

IVY

My eyes almost popped out of my head, and I grabbed Ian's phone to get a better look. "No way. I'm sorry, baby, you are quite well endowed, but this is porno sized. It almost looks CGI-generated."

He jutted out his bottom lip. "You don't have to be that sure that fast."

I snorted and dropped the phone on his lap. "The idea that random people online actually believe that monster belongs to you, and that you'd DM pictures of it to your fans is ridiculous. Emphasis on the dick."

"Told you." He swept the pictures off his display with a disgusted grunt.

"I have an idea." I drummed my fingers on his arm. "Chloe might jump the gun sometimes, but she's very good at her job. She might be able to do a reverse lookup on this picture and find out if it's been used before or maybe even find the real owner."

"And what good would that do me? I'm not going to publicly address this. Oh, hello, Ian Pope here, and I just wanted to let you all know I did a bit of research, and that cock belongs to Harry Dick."

I punched his hard bicep. "*You're* not going to address it at all, but a little army of your fans can. Chloe can start the ball rolling with a few fake accounts reporting that the picture is a phony. Your fans will pick up on it and do the rest of the work. Item debunked and squashed."

"Chloe would do that? She looked like she wanted to punch me in the face fifteen minutes ago."

"She'll do it if I ask her." I slid my hand under his shirt and smoothed it across his washboard abs.

He sucked in a sharp breath. "She's a good friend."

"The best." I hooked my fingers in the waistband of his tan pants and wriggled them close to the dick of the moment.

Closing his eyes, he asked, "What are you doing, Tink?"

"More research. Before I commit Chloe to the task, I have to be absolutely sure this is not the cock in question."

"And how are you going to do that?" He crossed his arms behind his head in a relaxed pose, but his chest rose and fell with each heavy breath.

"Further inspection." I undid his pants and yanked them down his slim hips. I smoothed my hand over the large bulge in his briefs, and he raised his buttocks from the bed. I took the blatant invitation and peeled down his underwear.

Curling my hand around his cock, I breathed out, "Impressive but not porn star quality. I concur. The dick pick is a fake."

"I don't know. You might need to do more to convince Chloe." He gasped as I cupped his sac and circled my fingers around his base, squeezing hard.

"I think you're right." I dipped my head and ran my tongue along the length of him. When I got to the head, I wrapped my lips around it, tasting his slightly salty and tangy pre-cum. As I bobbed my head up and down, sliding his cock in and out of my mouth, he tangled his fingers in my hair and hissed.

When I stopped to reposition myself and adjust my jaw, he stroked my face with his long fingers. "Why do you still have clothes on? I wanna be inside you."

"You were inside me." I pointed to my mouth.

"Don't be cheeky. Get naked."

"When you put it so sweetly and romantically, how can I refuse you?" I pulled off his pants, tangled around his ankles, and then scrambled out of my own clothes, throwing everything over my shoulder, piece by piece. Then I attacked his T-shirt, yanking it over his head.

On my knees, I straddled his legs and drank in the sight of his nude body splayed before me, the hard planes and muscles a work of art to rival his ink. The moment had the shimmering quality of a dream, and I almost pinched myself back to reality, but I didn't want to wake up.

With one hand still behind his head, Ian stroked my thigh with the other, and his eyes glittered below his half-shuttered lids. "I seem to have traded one addiction for another. I can't get enough of you."

We always seemed to be on the same wavelength, and an overpowering need to be one with him again consumed me. I moved forward, positioning myself over his erection.

"Wait." He felt for the handle of the nightstand drawer, and I shook my head. I didn't need the security of a condom anymore. "I believe in your six-month celibacy. I believe you, and you can believe me—I'm on the pill, and I don't sleep around."

Ian didn't need any other explanation, encouragement, or proof. He grabbed his cock and slid it along my pussy, wetting the tip, propelling me into a frenzy of longing. I lowered myself on him, holding my breath as he filled up all my empty spaces.

As I rode him, he reached up and grabbed my tits, pinching my nipples, causing tingles to shoot through my body. I arched my back and moaned. His eyes never left my face, and his gaze scorched me. I couldn't bear the intensity any longer, so I fell onto his chest, still moving against him, forward and back.

He grabbed my ass with both of his hands and pressed my body against his, lifting his hips. I rubbed my clit against his pelvis each time we made contact, as he moved in a circular motion, driving me slightly insane. My orgasm started with a buzz in the pit of my stomach, or maybe it had started in my brain or even my heart the moment I saw his defeated expression over the online smear campaign.

Body, brain, heart—they all contributed to the heat that engulfed me as I came. I cried out and sat up again, throwing my head back, going full cowgirl.

His fingers dug into my flesh, and then he exploded inside me. He thrust upward again and again, the cords of his neck visible, his muscles tight.

I fell forward, flat against his body, my hands on his shoulders, descending from his orgasm with him, my lips on his throat, measuring his pulse as it slowed to a steady tick. I released a long sigh and shivered.

Closing my eyes, I nuzzled his neck, a low growl of contentment gurgling in my throat. I didn't want to move. Didn't think I could move. And Ian didn't seem in any hurry to toss me off, as he zigzagged a finger down my spine.

When he got to my tailbone, he started all over again, dabbling his fingers down my back. "Are you uncomfortable?" His voice sounded hoarse, as if he'd just remembered how to use it.

"No. I could stay here forever. Are you?"

"You're a lightweight, Tink, like a feather that floated down and settled on my body. I'm still inside you."

"Mmm."

He put his hands around my waist and slid me off to his side. I immediately clung to him, resting my head on his chest, my hand covering his heart, and he trailed his fingers through my tangled hair. He said, "You feel it, too."

"I feel a lot of things, baby." I swirled my fingers around his brown nipple.

"It's like no matter how physically close I am to you—we could be pressed against each other along every line of our bodies, your legs tangled with mine, my arm around your waist, I could even be inside you, and it always feels like I can never get close enough." He pulled me tight as if to emphasize his point.

"I do feel it." I reached up and dug my fingers into his scalp. "What's it gonna take? Brain meld?"

With the palm of his hand, he rubbed a circle on my backside. "Maybe something happened that day with Fabio."

"Excuse me?" I dug my chin into his hard pec to look into his face.

"I have a confession." At his words, my heart skipped a beat. "I didn't know who the hell Fabio was. I had to look him up, later."

When my heartbeat returned to normal, I raised one eyebrow. "Maybe you looked up the wrong Fabio because he's not a magician or a spellcaster, throwing around love potions. In fact, he did a commercial for fake butter a while back."

A look of confusion arched across Ian's expressive face, but he decided not to go there. "No, but according to Wikipedia he was the cover model god of romance novels back in the day. Maybe that power put some kind of charm on us. Was it high noon or something when we met? Lightning strike? Venus crossing over the Sun?"

"It was eleven twenty-one and sixteen seconds, not that I took notice or anything. The sky was blue, and I think that transit of Venus is very rare."

"Then I guess it was just very, very good luck that we met each other, after a very, very long string of bad luck for me."

"Me, too." I kissed the scruff on his chin.

"Can we go out for dinner tonight? Someplace nice for everything you did for me."

"Can we not? I didn't do anything special, and besides, we need to strategize with Chloe, you need to keep working on that song, and I need to write a few thousand words on my book tonight."

"Yeah, yeah. Those are all good excuses, but you really don't want to go out with me, do you?" He tugged on my hair.

"I don't like all that..." I waved my hands in the air "—paparazzi stuff. It looks terrifying."

"I think we can find a nice place for dinner, even a trendy place without running into the paps." He ran the pad of his finger along my jaw. "You know how it works? Photographers are not usually hanging around celebrity hotspots all day and night. Someone who needs the press or needs to be seen with a particular person will tell his or her manager or PR team to call the paparazzi with their location and time, looking their best, and getting the desired photo in the tabloids."

"That makes sense, but my excuses are still valid. We have our own PR campaign to launch." I had to make a move, or I'd want to lie all night next to him on this bed, talking silly, falling fast and hard. I sat up and swung my legs over the side of the mattress, planting my feet on the hardwood floor.

"Does this PR campaign mean your further research convinced you that the dick pics aren't me?"

Tilting my head, I tapped my chin. "I don't know, baby. Your package is substantial."

He crawled on the bed behind me, lifted my hair and kissed the back of my neck. "Porn star substantial?"

"Okay, maybe not, but that's what's gonna save your incredibly sexy ass." I hopped off the bed before his kisses could lure me to stay because he might not be as well-hung as Johnny Pornstar, but he had something much more habit-forming...and I was hooked.

★ ★ ★

After we ate our pizza and with the heavy scent of garlic in the air, Chloe and I sat on the loveseat, heads together, while Ian reclined in the chair across from us on his laptop, working on his new song.

It had taken a little more effort to convince Chloe that Ian never took or sent those photos to his fans and after a grudging apology to him, she agreed to help with the rescue effort.

Chloe pulled her own computer onto her lap, sharing the screen with me. "This should be a piece of cake—that's cake, not cock." She snorted at her own joke while Ian caught my eye and winked at me. It warmed me down to my toes, and I smiled back at him.

Chloe saw the exchange and jabbed me in the side with a sharp elbow. "Pay attention. "I'll just download the image to my computer and do a reverse image lookup. I'm surprised nobody's done it, yet."

I hovered over my friend's shoulder, as Chole's fingers flew across the keyboard, clicking, tapping, snipping at lightning speed. "Ah-ha!" Chloe jabbed a finger at the screen. "This particular...member...belongs to one Duke Hammer, two-time AVN award winner for best actor in a feature film."

Ian glanced up from his laptop. "AVN?"

Chloe's mouth dropped open. "You've never watched the AVNs? They're the porn Oscars. And you call yourself a bad boy."

"Must be an American thing." Ian shrugged.

"I've never watched them." I bumped Chloe's knee with mine. "You've never watched them."

"Just fuckin' with you, but it does stand for Adult Video News, and they hand out awards, just like any other self-serving industry."

Rubbing my hands together, I said, "That's perfect. It's the same pose and everything, Ian. Do you want to see it?"

He held up a hand. "I think I've seen enough dicks for today, thanks."

"Is that even possible?" Chloe widened her pale blue eyes, framed with her fake black lashes, and we laughed until tears streamed down our faces.

Ian shook his head. "Now that you've identified the owner, what next?"

"What next, you say." Chloe laced her fingers and cracked her knuckles. "Now we create several fake social media accounts—don't worry; I know how to make them appear legit with posts and friends and followers. A few of these accounts will start posting about how gullible people are. Don't they know this is a famous picture of the incomparable Duke Hammer. How could anyone possibly believe this is Ian Pope's dick. In fact, Ian Pope is rumored to be quite average in that department."

"Whoa, whoa." Ian sat up abruptly, almost upending his laptop. "You don't have to go overboard."

"Ah!" I grabbed a throw pillow and whacked Chloe on the head. "That is *not* true. While Ian won't be winning any AVNs anytime, soon, we hope, he is *anything* but average-sized."

"Thanks, Tink." Ian threw me a kiss.

Chloe stuck her fingers in her mouth. "You two are sickening. I'm just kidding about that last part, but not the first part. This is how we start a reverse PR campaign. Soon enough, Ian's fans will pick up on this narrative and push back."

"You're a genius." I grabbed Chloe's face and kissed the side of her head.

"Joking aside, I really appreciate this, Chloe. It sounds like a lot of work. Send my accountant an invoice like you would any other client."

"I don't need to be paid. I will do this out of the goodness of my heart and because you make my bestie happy." She tapped her chest twice. "I just ask for one thing in return."

"Name it."

"Treat my girlie right and don't fuck up."

Chapter 11

IAN

I returned from my run at the beach and let myself into Ivy's place with the key she'd entrusted to me. She and Chloe had gone out this morning to help a friend move. They'd left behind them the rich aroma of coffee and the sweet scent of flowers from a colorful bunch in a vase in the middle of the kitchen table, set for my breakfast. Ivy had a surprising bent for domesticity, for making me comfortable in her home.

I'd undergone too much therapy to view her compulsion as anything other than a reaction to not having her own mother growing up. Ivy had either been the one to provide the housekeeping or she'd never had that domesticity at all and was trying to create it now. Either way, I wasn't complaining.

I sat down at the table where Ivy had left the breakfast, she'd insisted on making for me every morning. I crunched into the avocado toast as I poured hot water from the electric kettle over the teabag in my cup. I could get used to this, but I couldn't stop time. I had less than a week left in LA. I wanted her to come to England with me, but we'd only danced around the subject.

As I sipped my smoothie, the strawberries sweet on my tongue, I scrolled through my phone, the weight that had been on my shoulders lessening with each new defense of me on social media. Chloe had been spot on. Once her fake accounts started posting about the Duke Hammer connection, everyone jumped on that bandwagon and attacked anyone who dared suggest that I had taken and sent those pictures.

While I was basking in this unaccustomed win, my phone rang, and my manager's name popped up. "Alright, Jack."

Jack got right to the point. "Looks like we avoided fallout from those pictures *and* generated a little buzz. I was brainstorming how to get you out of this, and it looks like your fans took care of it."

"We took care of it, here in LA." I licked a smudge of avocado from my finger.

"What does that mean? Who took care of it?" Jack's voice tended to go up a few octaves when he was nervous, which was most of the time.

"Ivy's roommate, Chloe Dufrain, handles social media for some big companies. She managed it. Did a reverse image search on the picture, found it belonged to Duke Hammer, and started the online push with fake accounts that she created. It worked."

"What did she charge you for that?"

"She didn't." I slurped some more smoothie. "Not everyone is after money. You have a warped sense of the world from being in the business too long, Jack. You should get out more."

"We'll see about that. After she realizes how successful it was, she might come back with her hand out." Jack blew out a long breath as if to relax himself. "Speaking about getting out more, what the hell are you doing out there? I haven't seen anything about you in gossip sites or blind items, which is unusual for being in LA. Aren't you going out?"

"Yeah, yeah, we go out every day. Ivy has been taking me on a tour of LA. Did you know there are mammal bones from the Ice Age at the La Brea Tar Pits?"

Jack coughed. "You went to the La Brea Tar Pits?"

"There, the Long Beach Aquarium, had brunch on 'The Queen Mary,' hiked in Topanga Canyon, took a ferry to Catalina Island and spent the night there, Norton Simon Museum, Descanso Gardens, Watts Towers, went to a Harold Pinter play at UCLA."

"Who? Never mind. That's...great, but you have a record due soon, and your label is not messing around, Ian."

I didn't even feel the tightness in my chest, like I usually did, at the mention of my record label. "I'm on it, Jack. I've been writing songs out here—some of the best stuff I've ever written. Everything around me is an inspiration. I have lyrics coming to me in the shower, on my runs, after..." I was going to say after sex, but Jack didn't need to know everything about my life "—after all these visits. The songs are good, Jack. I reached out to Hugh already, sent him some stuff, and he's really excited about it. He's on board."

"Hugh Smith?"

I knew that would get Jack's attention. Hugh had been part of the song writing team for Five2Go, and I had collaborated with him on several of the band's hit songs.

"Yeah, that Hugh. I can send you a couple of songs today, if that'll make you feel better."

"It would. I'm glad you're getting back to work. You're running?"

"Every day at the beach."

"Are you eating?"

"Uh, yeah." I toyed with the piece of toast on my plate. "Why wouldn't I be eating?"

"Like I said, there haven't been any sightings of you out and about in LA."

"I've run into some fans, but the paparazzi ain't likely to hang out at the La Brea Tar Pits, are they?"

"No, but they hang around Nobu. You can't go out to dinner there one night?"

I scratched the scruff on my chin, debating whether to shave. "Tried that. Ivy doesn't like sushi or sashimi. She's not into those celebrity haunts."

Jack heaved a sigh. "Does she realize she's dating a celebrity?"

"Sometimes I wonder." I smiled to myself.

"Well, people are beginning to wonder about you, Ian. The word is out you were in rehab, but you've been off the grid so long now, people suspect you may have fallen off the wagon or are holing up in your house again."

I squeezed my eyes closed. "That's not happening."

"It's time to capitalize on that dick pic scandal. Got people buzzing in a positive way, for a change. You're going to be releasing a new record soon, only your second solo effort since the band split up. We need a push. You need to be seen—happy, healthy, not punching photographers or stumbling out of clubs at four AM."

"I understand that, Jack." I pinched the bridge of my nose, as pain began to throb behind my eyeballs.

"Just one outing, Ian. I can arrange everything. Just tell me where and when."

For the first time in the conversation, I felt knots in my gut. I knew what Jack meant. It's what I told Ivy last week—celebrities setting up their own pap walks. My management team did it for me before, and sometimes it had backfired spectacularly when I'd been out and about, off my fucking face. I rubbed my chin. "We're going out tonight."

"Perfect. Take her to Nobu. She'll love it."

"I doubt that. We're going to a concert tonight at the Greek Theatre to see Van Morrison."

"Van Morrison."

"Yeah."

"Isn't he about eighty years old?"

"Yeah. What can I say? She loves Van and has seen him loads of times."

"Hmm, I don't know if there would be any other celebrities there, but that won't matter. I'll put in some calls and see if I can get some photographers to the Greek. Pictures of a happy, sober Ian Pope out for an evening with a non-celebrity. Don't worry. I won't give them Ivy's name, if she wants to stay incognito. Even better. Ian Pope out with mysterious auburn-haired beauty. That'll work."

By the time I ended the call with my manager, I had a queasy feeling in my gut. I should probably tell Ivy, so she won't feel ambushed, but if I told her, she might refuse to go, and she really wanted to go. I didn't want to ruin her evening.

Eh, I could protect her. She could put her head down, and I'd tuck her behind me. The hired paps could get their shots, Jack would be happy, and the record company would get off my ass. Ivy didn't have to know a thing about it.

* * *

Later that evening, I leaned into the mirror in the bathroom and ran my fingers through my long hair. I wanted to look half-way decent for the pictures but didn't want to make Ivy suspicious. We'd been dressing down most of the time.

I jumped when she tapped on the door. "Are you almost ready in there? I don't want to leave too late and end up parking miles away."

I swung open the door, and my gaze swept her head to toe. Auburn-haired beauty, indeed. Even though she didn't know it was coming, she looked paparazzi worthy in her light-colored, straight-legged jeans topped with a navy blue, fitted, lacy top with a V-neck, revealing a nice peek at her cleavage. Ivy had great tits, all natural, but she didn't usually flaunt them. She'd complained to me that she got enough unwanted attention to draw any more focus to herself. Ivy didn't like unwanted attention, and the guilt roiling in my chest just got a little more acidic.

"You look fantastic, so sexy." I wedged a finger beneath her chin and kissed her.

"So do you, baby." She ran a hand over my face. "You shaved your scruff, and now you look younger."

"People are going to think you robbed the cradle, you cougar." I growled and made claws.

Smoothing her hands down my short-sleeved, green linen shirt, she said, "I like this. Looks good on you. Just one improvement."

She unbuttoned one more button at the neck and drilled the tip of her finger into my bare chest. "Just don't get any tattoos on your chest. I like it like this."

"Okay, anything else?" I patted the side pockets of my tan cargo pants. "You don't need to do an OOTD check, do you?"

"What the heck is an OOTD?" She scrunched up her nose.

I should've known Ivy would be oblivious to the influencer lingo. "That, my out of touch Tink, stands for outfit of …tedious delusion or something like that, and all the best influencers take selfies of their OOTDs to post on their social media for all the likes and narcissistic pleasure at the fawning compliments."

I realized my tone had turned bitter when she stared at me with her mouth slight ajar.

"Okayyy. No, I'm not going to do that because I don't think anyone gives a fuck what I'm wearing tonight. I only care if you like it, and you do." She ended with a pirouette.

I herded her out of the bedroom because I liked what she was wearing so much, I had an urge to rip it all off her body and worship what was beneath it. I said, "About the parking."

"Yeah, it's a pain at the Greek. I pre-paid, but all I could get was the lot farther away from the venue, and it's a dirt lot with gravel." She extended her leg, a strappy, gold sandal on her foot. "These are okay for walking, though."

"Let me order a Town Car to take us and pick us up. It can drop us right in front of the entrance. You paid for the tickets. Let me do this." She'd never guess my ulterior motive was a quick getaway. Who knows what Jack told the paps. They just might get it in their heads to follow us all the way to Ivy's car, and I'd hate that—even more than I'd hate their flashing cameras.

"Umm, okay. I already paid for the parking, though."

I took her hand and kissed the inside of her wrist. "I'll pay you back for the parking."

Either Ivy didn't realize how much money I had, or she preferred her independence. Before I could even offer, she'd made the plans for the LA trips and always paid for the tickets online. I could barely pay for our dinners or even groceries because she never asked.

Due to the wealth I'd amassed as a member of one of the most popular boybands in history and the investments I'd made with that money, I didn't think twice about it when girlfriends in the past had hit me up to pay for their clothes or trips. I'd been happy to do it, but Ivy's distinct disinterest in my wallet made me feel...special and wanted in a way I hadn't felt in a long time.

"In that case..." she kicked off her sandals "...I'm gonna swap these for a pair of sandals with heels."

Forty-five minutes later, a black limo rolled to a stop at the curb in front of Ivy's place. Ivy covered her mouth with one hand. "It's huge. I thought you said Town Car."

"Yeah, this is all they had on such short notice."

The driver hopped out and opened the door for us. "Greek Theatre, right?"

"That's right." Ivy ducked in first and as I slid along the leather seat, next to her, my knee hit a minibar. The little bottles clinked inside sending me a secret message, one I would've heeded six months ago.

She leaned against me and whispered in my ear, "Did you order a car with a minibar?"

"I think it just automatically comes with the ride. I'm good." I tapped the cover on the bar. "Do you want some champagne? Wine?"

"Absolutely not." She pressed her lips together in imitation of a teetotaling Prohibitionist. She hadn't had one drink since we met. Whether she imbibed when she and Chloe went out with friends without me, I didn't know, but I doubted it. I never smelled booze on her breath or tasted it on her lips.

Chloe drank her fair share of wine in front of me, under an evil eye from Ivy, but I didn't feel any pressure. I hadn't been lying to Jack when I'd told him I'd had no cravings for the first time since I'd been out of rehab. I wasn't going to lie to myself that I didn't feel like taking a drink—many times—since I'd left rehab, but the urge had disappeared since I'd met Ivy. She'd become my new addiction.

On the way to the venue, Ivy asked the driver, Nick, if she could hook up her phone to the Bluetooth. He agreed and Van's voice started belting out songs. I recognized some of them, music my parents played at home, and my Irish bandmate, Conor, was a fan of his fellow Irishman.

Leaning against my arm, she said, "I like to play the music to get into the vibe, but he probably won't be playing any of these songs. He usually plays songs from his current album and more recent releases. Some of his fans from the old days won't go to his concerts because he refuses to play the old stuff, although he'll sneak one in now and then."

"That's a luxury that comes with age. If I tried that, I think my fans would charge the stage and drag me off." I gave a fake shiver.

"Yeah, I don't know if it's age so much as Van just doesn't give a fuck."

I murmured, "Must be nice."

"Nick." Ivy sat forward and tapped on Nick's headrest. "Can I turn this one up?"

"You can do whatever you like, Ivy. In fact, I'll do it for you."

Electronic pinging filled the car and then Van started with a falsetto that I could appreciate and admire.

Ivy whispered, her lips brushing my ear. "Listen to the lyrics. This is us. We're on the same wavelength."

Just in case I didn't heed her direction, Ivy sang along to the song, started dancing in her seat, and had Nick bopping along in the front. By the time we pulled up to the entrance of the Greek, we were in full party mode.

Before exiting the limo, I arranged for Nick to pick us up in the same spot and gave him a big tip just to make sure he didn't forget.

We passed through the security line, and the sultry summer air seemed to press against me. I tipped my head back and sniffed. "It smells like pine, like fruity pine. You have pine trees in LA?"

"There are a lot of pine trees surrounding the venue, but I think they're different from what you'd find up in the Pacific Northwest." She wrinkled her nose. "I'm having a hard time smelling that citrusy pine over that skunky weed."

"Ha, I thought that was just another Southern California plant species."

"It is." She linked arms with me. "Does it bother you?"

"Weed was never one of my vices. Not a fan." I took a deep breath. "I still smell that pine, though."

I veered toward a concession booth. "Do you want something to drink? Margarita?"

"Are you trying to get me drunk, so you can take advantage of me later?" She pinched my side.

"Ivy, I don't need to give you booze to get you going." I draped my arm around her and pulled her close. "In fact, the thought of you drunk and out of control in the bedroom scares the shit out of me."

"Then you can stop suggesting I drink alcohol. I don't need it. I don't want it. And I'm not going to drink it in front of someone who has a mere five months of recovery under his belt. But I will have a Diet Coke."

"Ooh, walking on the wild side."

I looked around at the crowd as I bought Ivy's soda and a bottle of sparkling water for myself. Jack had the right idea to hire the paparazzi. My typical demographic would be swarming me at any other concert, but the aging, mellow potheads here barely gave me a second look. This outing would not have satisfied Jack or the record company without the planned ambush for later.

Once we made it to our seats and the music started, I forgot all about the pap stunt, the online smear campaign against me, and the pressure to produce my album. The bluesy, jazzy songs transported me to another realm, which sparked my imagination with words and phrases crowding my brain for release and the chance to become lyrics.

The performance had captivated Ivy, too, as she shimmied and swayed and nodded her head. She obviously felt the music deep in her soul, and I wanted that reaction from people so much for my own songs. The lyrics I'd written during this idyll in LA had become so much more to me than just words to accompany a melody. I wanted my lyrics to resonate with people, to take them somewhere else, to make them feel and relate and understand.

By the end of the ninety-minute set, I had a fully formed song in my head and couldn't wait to get back to my laptop to get it down. As I stood up and stretched, the real world crashed in on me. I had a pap walk to do, first.

Ivy turned to me, her beautiful face alight with the magic of the night. "Did you like it?"

"Loved it." I engulfed her in a hug, lifting her off her feet and kissing her fully on the mouth. As I led her down our row, I turned my head over my shoulder. "Aren't you glad we have Nick and his embarrassingly huge limo waiting for us out front, now?"

"I absolutely am, especially in these heels." She rubbed a circle on my back. "Thank you."

I'd hold onto that sweet sentiment for now because she'd be cursing me later. On the way to the exit, I got a couple of nods and saw a few people nudge each other when they noticed me. A woman caught up to us and asked me if I'd enjoyed the concert and I replied that I had, very much, but she didn't request my autograph and didn't want a selfie, and I could see Ivy visible relax when the woman moved on and melted into the crowd.

All that changed as soon as we exited the venue.

Chapter 12

IAN

Accustomed to that familiar movement of photographers getting into position, I saw two men approach from the right and another hop off a wall and make a beeline for us.

I took Ivy's hand, lacing my fingers through hers, as I laughed at something she'd said.

The photographers had gotten off several flashes before Ivy even noticed their presence. When the paps stepped in front of us, Ivy reared back, blinking her eyes.

When I felt her body stiffen, I tried to tuck her behind me, but there were too many people around. I murmured in her ear, "It's alright. Just keep walking forward."

The paps kept snapping, but by this time, Ivy had dipped her head, and her long, wavy hair created a curtain around her face.

One of the guys shouted out. "Hey, Ian, are you still sober?"

I flashed a peace sign, but this didn't mollify the aggressive photographer, who'd stopped taking pictures. He continued yelling questions at me. "Are you making music, if that's what you call it? Do you wish you had

Sam's career? How do you feel about your tanking popularity? Has Duke Hammer called to thank you for the publicity?"

I kept walking toward Nick, leaning against his limo. The wanker shouting the questions crowded in too close and bumped Ivy, who stumbled against me and gasped. My free hand curled into a fist at my side, and I elbowed him. "Watch out, mate."

Nick lurched from the side of his limo and charged forward. "Hey, asshole, back the fuck off." With the door already open, Nick herded us into the car and slammed the door. As he got in the front, he cranked his head over his shoulder. "Are you alright, Ivy?"

She managed a weak smile as she sagged against me in the backseat. "I'm fine."

After that assurance, Nick closed the privacy glass between the front and back and started to weave his way out of the parking lot.

Ivy's body trembled against mine, and I hugged her close as I rubbed her thigh. "It's okay. I'm sorry. It's alright. Did you get hurt?"

She swung her leg over mine, almost climbing into my lap, her head dropping to my shoulder. A sob wracked her body, and anger and guilt warred in my chest. "Are you alright, Ivy? I'm sorry that happened."

Turning to look up at me, her green eyes swimming with tears, she smoothed her hand over my heart. "I'm fine. I'm not hurt physically, but I'm devastated over that idiot's questions. Why are people so cruel? You don't deserve that. You're just a human being trying to enjoy a night out. You don't owe anyone anything, especially someone like that with his hateful questions designed to goad you and strike at you. I'm so sorry, baby."

Feeling about two feet tall, I swiped a tear from her cheek with the pad of my thumb. Those paps had just scared the life out of her, and she was sitting here worried about me and a couple of random questions—from a situation that I'd set up.

I let out a long breath. "I'm glad you're okay. Don't worry about that guy. You don't think I've heard those questions before? I have, and worse. Doesn't bother me at all."

Her head shot up. "Just because you adhere to that damned pact, it doesn't mean strangers have the right to attack you."

Her eyes blazed and her cheeks flushed in her defense of me, and something swelled in my chest. Not even my PR team had ever stood up for me with so much passion.

I kissed her trembling lips. "I love...love that you're so vehement on my behalf, but I was more upset that he was invading your space than at his pathetic, juvenile questions. Did it ruin the night for you?"

"Oh, no. The concert was great, and I loved sharing it with you. I could tell you were enjoying yourself and that meant a lot." She shook her head. "I just don't understand why those paparazzi would be stalking a Van concert at the Greek. You saw the crowd—not that interesting."

I toyed with a lock of her hair. Should I tell her? I hated being deceptive, but even more I'd hate the look of contempt and pity in her eyes once I admitted my pathetic need for recognition. "I don't know. It's a concert venue in LA on a Saturday night. Maybe they just figured they'd get lucky."

My answer seemed to placate her, and my kisses had calmed her, reducing her tears to a few sniffles. She still stayed glued to my side, her hand in mine for the rest of the ride home, and I had no complaints about that. The lie had been worth it.

As Nick glided the behemoth to a stop in front of Ivy's place, I rapped on the glass partition and Nick rolled it down. "Somewhere else?"

"No, this is good. Just wanted to thank you, mate, for what you did back there. It helped."

"No problem. I've encountered those guys before, total pricks. They're gonna get someone hurt one of these days." He jerked his thumb to the back seat. "Your girl okay?"

"She's fine. Do you ever do any bodyguard work?" The guy had biceps as big as grapefruits and a chest that could probably repel a bowling ball.

"I haven't done."

"If you're interested, give me your card. I have a lot of friends out here that could use someone trustworthy. I'd give you a good reference."

"Thanks, yeah." Nick reached in his suit jacket pocket and handed me a card. "I'd be interested in that."

As we walked to Ivy's front door, she said, "That was kind of you."

"No, I'm serious. Did you see how that guy was built? And he knows how to handle himself. Charlie lives out here part-time, and he'd be chuffed to find someone like that he could trust."

Chloe had gone to San Diego for the weekend, so we had the place to ourselves, and my mind was still buzzing with ideas, even after the encounter with the paparazzi. I'd meant what I said to Ivy. The photographer's questions had been mild compared to some of the other abuse thrown my way. Did it bother me? I'd stuffed those kinds of feelings down so far, I probably couldn't even identify them if they bit me on the ass. On some level, I almost felt as if I deserved the abuse, but Ivy's defense of me had struck a chord. Why *should* I accept that vilification?

Because you asked for it. You planned it. You invited it.

I pulled my laptop from the charger on the kitchen table and tucked it under my arm. "Would you mind if I stayed up for a while and did some work? I've had this song running through my head for two hours, and I want to nail it down before it escapes me."

"I don't mind." She yawned and then downed a glass of water. "I'm going to bed. Do you want a snack or anything?"

"Do you have anything unhealthy in this house? I don't want fruit. I don't want nuts. I don't want Greek yogurt."

She opened a cupboard, reached in, and dangled a bag of crisps in the air. "These are Chloe's potato chips. I don't think she'd mind if you ate the rest. You've kinda grown on her."

"Thank, God." I snatched the bag out of her hand. "I'll buy her another before I go home."

The words hung between us awkwardly, and Ivy sliced a hand through the air as if swatting them away. "She probably won't even notice." She hooked her arms around my neck, and I put down my laptop and the crisps so I could hug her back. She said, "I'm sorry about those horrible paparazzi. Hope they didn't spoil our night out for you."

"It would take a lot more than a couple of rude questions to spoil any night I spend with you, Tink." I kissed her and said, "Go to bed. Can't wait to see what you have in store for me tomorrow."

She sauntered off to her bedroom, and I planted myself on the sofa, my computer in my lap and the bag of crisps by my side. My fingers flew across the keyboard, as I spewed out all the words and phrases I'd collected during the show.

Once I had the words down, I organized them into coherent thoughts and grouped them into verses. Certain lines jumped out at me that would work as the chorus, and the phrase that ran through my head had already suggested a tune.

By the time I emerged from the cloud of creativity that had enveloped me, over two hours had passed. I saved my work and rubbed the stiffness from the back of my neck.

I tiptoed into the bedroom and slipped into the bathroom to brush my teeth and undress. I turned off the bathroom light before opening the door to the bedroom. Ivy hadn't moved an inch since I'd come into the room, and I didn't want to wake her, although the idea of sleeping right now seemed like something on a distant planet.

As I slid between the cool sheets next to her, she murmured and rolled toward me, turning me on with her naked body. I smoothed her hair back from her face, and along with the lust that tightened my balls, an ache of tenderness throbbed in my throat. Had I almost told her I loved her tonight? That was crazy...wasn't it?

I wanted her to come home with him, but I didn't feel as if I had the right to ask her to uproot her life. She hadn't brought it up, either. Was she waiting for me to make a move? I didn't quite know how I was going to function without her, but I didn't want to saddle her with that burden.

For all her cheeriness, I caught a look in her eyes sometimes—fear, dread, angst—something that didn't match up with her outward sunny disposition. But, while my life was an open, messy book, she kept a tight lid on her background and experiences. A little worm niggled my brain, telling me to run, or at least start demanding some answers, but if she wanted to tell me about her past, I just wanted to give her a clear path to do so without pushing her.

Her fingers found my lips in the dark, and she traced their outline. "I've been waiting for you."

I drew her thumb into my mouth and sucked on it while she slid her other hand across my abs to my cock, already hard for her.

Skin to skin, I moved against her body. She opened up to me like a petal after the rain, and I made love to her. If I couldn't tell her I loved her, if I couldn't tell her I was sorry for tonight, if I couldn't tell her I wanted her to come back to England with me—I'd just have to show her.

* * *

The following morning, I woke up and reached for Ivy, but she'd already gotten up, leaving behind the scent of her floral perfume and the muskiness of our mingled bodies. I rubbed my eyes as the strains of my last hit wafted into the bedroom. Was I dreaming?

I bolted out of bed and grabbed last night's briefs on my way to the living room. I hopped into the kitchen on one leg, pulling on my underwear. "I can't believe it; you're actually listening to my music."

"Why wouldn't I be listening to this banger?" Waving a knife at my crotch, she said, "You need to cover that up in here."

I snapped the waistband of my underwear around my hips and grabbed her from behind. "Be careful with that thing."

She winked. "That's what she said."

"Seriously, are you listening to an oldies station, or what?" I nuzzled her neck and nibbled on her shoulder.

"Don't denigrate yourself." She reached back and tapped my head with the handle of the knife. "Didn't you tell me something like that the first day we met?"

"I'm sure I didn't use the word *denigrate*, but probably." I popped a piece of banana in my mouth.

She asked, "Did you get a lot of work done last night?"

"I did, yeah. So excited about this music."

"So, you'll start recording next week?" Her hands fluttered around the countertop as if she'd forgotten how to make a smoothie.

"Not right away. I'm going to finish the songs with a writing partner, someone I worked with in the days of the band. We might do some of the work in the recording studio. Jack already scheduled time for us." I touched the ends of her ponytail as it swung against her back.

"You'll be busy." She finally found the spinach and stuffed it into the blender. "You'll get to spend some time with your daughter, too."

"Can't wait. I've been in touch with her mum, and she's agreed to let me see her unsupervised. That's a huge leap for her."

"And you." She started piling ingredients into the blender almost at random. "Three more days. I'll take you to the airport."

Was that a catch in her voice? I opened my mouth to speak, but she cranked on the blender, drowning me out. With my smoothie on the way to being liquefied, I reached around her and flicked off the switch. "I'd like you to come with me."

"To England?" Her voice squeaked, and she gripped the edge of the counter.

Stroking her back, I said, "Did you really think I could leave you behind? Is that what you want?"

She turned, wedging her back against the counter and folding her arms. "I can't just give up my life here."

"You'd be able to work. You don't have a nine to five job here. You could use one of the rooms in my house for an office. It's not like you have…"

"Family?" She raised her eyes to my face, and her bottom lip trembled.

"I'm sorry. I didn't mean it like that." I pinched her chin. "I know you have Chloe and your other friends and your writing group and your work at the animal shelter, but you could come back here whenever you want.

You wouldn't have to sell your place. You've been to the UK before. You liked it, right?"

"Of course, yes, but I don't know if I could just uproot my life."

"Sometimes it's seemed to me like that's exactly what you'd like to do, Ivy." I traced the edge of her ear. "But I don't want to pressure you. I know we have something between us, some bond. Am I delusional?"

"If you are, I am, too." She shuffled forward a few steps and buried her nose against my chest. "I've been pushing your departure out of my mind. I don't want you to go. I wish you could stay here with me."

"I know, but it's not just the record. I need to have a relationship with my daughter. I've selfishly squandered the time I could've been with her, and now that I'm...better, I need to restore her trust in me."

"Of course, you do, and I want that for you." She spun around and poured the green sludge from the blender into two glasses. "I could visit."

I squeezed the back of my neck. "Do you want a long-distance relationship where we'd see each other a few times a year? It's not like Chloe and Trent in San Diego. You'd meet someone else, and I'm not tying you down like that."

The thought of Ivy with another man felt like a knife to the gut. She never mentioned ex-boyfriends. I'd glanced at her phone a few times and had seen texts from someone named Matt on a couple of those occasions. Was he an ex? I knew she must have one or two of those. Those condoms in her nightstand were proof enough, and I didn't flatter myself our sex was so hot just because I was Ian Pope. Ivy was a sensual person, loving and demonstrative. She did have the giant purple vibrator in there too, so she could be going it alone, although it's not like we hadn't been able to have some fun with that together.

Handing me a glass, she asked, "What are you thinking about?"

"Uh, sex."

Her eyebrows shot up, and she clinked her glass against mine. "Yeah, I'll miss that, too."

I grinned. "I think I almost have you convinced. It's the sex that'll push you over. Oh, and I even have a dog, if that helps."

"You do?" She crossed her hands over her heart. "A big dog?"

"Just a little thing." I held my hands about two feet apart. "His name is Scruffy."

"Scruffy? Un-ironically Scruffy?"

"Nope, just Scruffy. My daughter named him."

"Then it's a perfect name. I'll think about it. I can't leave with you this week, though." She shoved me out of her way and padded to the kitchen table, set for breakfast in the usual charming manner.

I'd miss more than the sex. In fact, I had the desperate feeling that I wouldn't be able to survive without her.

As she sat down, her phone rang, and she answered it. "What's up, Chloe?"

I carried my breakfast to the table and sat across from her. "Tell Chloe..." I stopped when I got a look at Ivy's pale face.

She stuttered. "A-are you sure?"

"What's wrong?" I hunched forward, elbows on the table.

"It was awful. Yeah, I'll have a look." She paused. "No, I'm sure it's okay. You're right." She leveled a finger at my laptop on the table, and I dragged it toward me.

"Thanks, Chloe. I'll be fine. See you in a bit."

"What was that all about?" I flipped open my laptop. "And what do you want me to do with this?"

She pressed her hands against her pink cheeks. "We're online. Those freakin' paps already sold our pictures."

Chapter 13

IAN

I eased out a slow breath.

"Chloe said there are pictures of us from last night online. Go to those British sites." Ivy stuffed her hands beneath her thighs, and her knees bounced up and down.

Bloody hell. That was fast. I knew exactly which sites to check, and I maneuvered to the first one. I scrolled down the right-hand side, and the thumbnail picture jumped out at me. I clicked on it, holding my breath. This had better have been worth it.

Good picture. I unclenched my jaw. I looked...normal, Ivy a beauty at my side. I skimmed through the shots, and they'd published the ones right after I'd noticed the paps with Ivy still smiling and laughing up at me, even one of us sharing a kiss.

I tilted the laptop toward her, so she could see. "Yeah, that's us."

"Ugh." She covered her face with her hands. "What does it say?"

I cleared my throat. "Ian Pope snapped outside a Van Morrison concert at the Greek Theatre in Los Angeles with stunning auburn-haired mystery woman." My lips twitched. Jack had almost nailed the headline.

"Stunning? Does that really look like me?" She leaned forward, squinting at the display. "I guess it does."

"You look great. What are you worried about?"

Her lips tightened a fraction, and a shadow darkened her eyes. "What else does it say? Did they report on that photographer's nasty questions?"

"Let's see." I tracked my finger along the words on the screen. "Former boybander, blah, blah, blah. Rehab, blah, blah. Troubled singer, blah, blah." I raised my hand. "Ah-ha. Pope looked to be in good spirits, flashing his signature smile." I grinned at Ivy, showing all my teeth. "He and his date seemed to be having a good time as he ushered her to his waiting limo. Well, it wasn't *my* bloody limo, was it?"

"That's not too bad. They must've missed the part when that idiot almost knocked me over. Anything else?"

"It's rumored that a new album is in Pope's future, and there's positive buzz around the songs, written in collaboration with one of the writers who worked with Five2Go." My shoulders relaxed. Jack had done his job.

"How do they know all that?" Tilting her head to one side, she wrapped her ponytail around her hand.

"I do have a manager and PR team behind me, and occasionally they're able to generate *some* beneficial news about me to the press."

She side-eyed the screen once more before taking a sip of her neglected drink. "That's horrible having your face out there."

Tracing the tip of my finger around her head in the picture, I said, "Your beautiful face. They like me again because they like you. They're happy that you're not a celebrity or influencer."

"How do you know all that?"

"I read a few of the comments."

She dropped the toast she'd just picked up. "You're kidding me. There are comments?"

"Don't read them. They can take you down a rabbit hole. Just believe what I say. Very favorable comments about you and your appearance."

She crossed one index finger over the other and held up her hands as if warding off an evil spell. "I don't want to read any comments about my appearance."

"I don't blame you and I don't encourage it, but they are good."

"And you?" Dropping her eyes to her plate, she folded her hands. "Are the comments about you okay, or are they...mean?"

"Like I said earlier, they like you, so they like me." There were still some comments slagging me off but not as many as usual. I ran a hand back from my forehead; was my hairline really receding as fast as my career? Ivy didn't need to know any of that. I snapped my laptop closed. "Enough of that. Let's eat and go to the..."

"Griffith Park. We can take a hike and then go to the observatory later."

"We were in that area last night." I shoved my laptop out of the way and dug into my breakfast. "If we're hiking, I'll skip my run this morning. Got up too late, anyway."

"Okay, you finish breakfast. I'll take a shower first." She carried her dishes to the sink. "Oh, and Chloe called me from her car. She's almost home. Left San Diego early after a big fight with Trent."

"Uh-oh. Does that mean she's going to be in a foul mood." I put my hands over my head. "Should I take cover?"

"I think I was too distracted by those pictures to dwell on her misery or anger—depending on what Trent did this time." On her way to her bedroom, Ivy messed up my hair with one hand and then kissed the top of my head. "Don't worry. I'll protect you, just like you protected me last night."

When I heard the shower start, I jumped back online and scanned through a few more articles with pictures. The stunt had worked out okay. If I'd been drunk, I might've hauled off and punched the annoying photographer instead of poking him with my elbow. But I wasn't, and I didn't.

The front door burst open, and I slammed my laptop shut.

Chloe shouted to no one in particular, "That drive is a bitch, and I don't have to make it, anymore."

She dropped something in the hallway and rounded the corner to the kitchen. Seeing me, she tripped to a stop. "Where's Ivy?"

I tipped my head toward the hallway. "Taking a shower. You alright?"

"Fan-fucking-tastic! I got rid of that jerk, finally." She collapsed in the chair Ivy had vacated. "So, you went to the Greek last night and got papped. Ivy must've loved that."

I licked a bit of strawberry from my lip. "It upset her, but we got through it okay."

"But there are pictures all over the place." Chloe launched herself out of the chair and bent over, opening a cupboard. She studied the contents, intently.

"The photos are good, and she looks great." I felt as if I were mounting a defense of myself, which I was.

"Ivy doesn't care about that shit." Chloe crouched in front of the cupboard. "You see a bag of chips?"

Damn. "I, um, ate them last night. Sorry, I'll replace them."

"No problema." She grabbed a box of sugary cereal instead and crammed her hand inside the box. As she munched, she narrowed her eyes at me. "Good concert?"

"Yeah, it was great."

"Ivy takes all her dates to see Van when he's in town." An orange circle from the cereal was clinging to Chloe's chin, but she chewed on, oblivious, and I didn't feel like helping her right now.

I swallowed. "All her dates?"

"What can I say? She loves Van." She lifted her shoulders to her ears and continued crunching the cereal as if she hadn't just tilted my entire world off its axis.

"Ivy has a lot of boyfriends? Exes?" I hoped they were exes.

"Boyfriends? Who said anything about boyfriends? Ivy doesn't do boyfriends—wait, that came out wrong. She doesn't do the boyfriend thing. Dates a guy for a month or two and then…" Chloe made a fizzing sound with her lips "—gone."

I counted on my fingers under the table. I wouldn't even last a month if she didn't come to England with me. And if she did come with me? Would she leave after a month?

Chloe threw some cereal at me, hitting my face. "Don't get those sad puppy dog eyes. Things seem be a little different with you."

I jerked my head up. "Really? How?"

"She's all over you for one thing." She crinkled her nose. "I mean, you're both all over each other, and it's really annoying." She waved her hand at the table, scattered with colored bits of cereal. "And all this. She wants to make you comfortable, take care of you, please you. It's like she's playing wifey, and I've never seen her like that before. I figured it was because you're a filthy rich popstar."

"That's comforting." I raked a hand through my messy hair.

She leveled a finger at me. "I don't know why she's fallen so fast and hard for you. She can't even get over losing her fucking dog. So, I don't know what kind of popstar, voodoo bullshit you cast over her because she's a goner. All this is not usually her thing, but someone can get starry-eyed when face-to-face with her teen idol."

I opened my mouth to remind Chloe that Ivy had never claimed to be particularly obsessed with me, but Ivy's voice sliced down the hallway. "Chloe?"

Ivy's tone sounded anything but caring and comforting, and Chloe put a finger to her lips. "Yep, I'm back, and I'll tell you everything about that rat bastard once I work off my aggressions at the gym."

"Can you come in here first, please?"

As Chloe walked past me, I said in a sing-song voice, "Someone's in trouble."

Furious whispers skittered into the kitchen before a door slammed. Ivy couldn't blame me for Chloe's big mouth. I hadn't even encouraged her. But she didn't have anything bad to say about Ivy, and the idea that her feelings seemed to be different for me had raised my hopes that she'd come back to England with me.

I'd forgotten to charge my phone last night, so I left it plugged in on the kitchen table, face down, as I got up to clear my dishes and wash everything in the sink.

Several minutes later, Ivy emerged from the back rooms on a cloud of her musky, floral perfume in a pair of cut-off denim shorts, an off-white body suit, and white trainers on her feet.

She dangled a pink hoodie from her fingertips. "It's going to be hot and sunny on the trail, but the observatory might be cold. I'll take a little daypack with water and stuff."

I raised my eyebrows. "Everything okay with Chloe?"

"She and Trent break up every few months." She flicked her fingers. "She's alright."

From the set of Ivy's mouth, I could see she was determined to ignore anything she may have overheard Chloe telling me. She was an expert at dismissing anything related to her personal life while mine had played out on center stage across the media.

"That's...good." I dried my hands on a dish towel and hung it up. "I'm gonna shower and get dressed. I won't be too long."

I nearly bumped into Chloe coming out of the hallway, dressed in workout clothes. She rolled her eyes at me and called out, "I'm off to the gym. Oops, where's my phone?" She went into the kitchen. "Nope that's yours."

Silently, Ivy pointed to Chloe's phone on the coffee table, and she swept it up. "Bye."

Ivy remained silent, so I gave Chloe a wave and headed to the bathroom. I showered, did not bother shaving, and put on some shorts and a tank top. After tying my shoes, I grabbed a hoodie, and the LA Dodgers baseball cap Ivy had bought for me—her thoughtfulness always touched me. Chloe hadn't been wrong about that. Ivy took care of me in a way I didn't deserve.

"I'm ready, and I have my Dodger hat." I veered into the kitchen to grab my phone from the charger, but the end of the chord hung off the edge of the table, empty. Had Chloe taken it by mistake?

"Your Dodger hat?"

I swung around and took a step back when Ivy thrust my phone in my direction, a deluge of negative energy hitting me like a tidal wave. "What?"

"Are you sure you don't want to leave the Dodger cap at home in case the paparazzi happen to be on the trail taking pictures? You wouldn't want them to miss you, would you?"

She knew. Was it too late to join Chloe at the gym?

Chapter 14

IVY

Icy fingers had scrabbled across my skin when I'd picked up Ian's phone and saw the partial text from Jack. Now, facing Ian, the ice had numbed me as his demeanor and posture confirmed the worst. He might be a liar, but he was no good at concealing his emotions.

"I...you..."

I cut him off. "Don't attack me for looking at your phone and texts. It was sitting there, face up, when I was brushing crumbs off the table. It buzzed, and I glanced at it. Kinda hard to miss this text." I brought the phone close to my face and read aloud in my best English accent. "Pap call worked, mate. Good pictures."

He put his hands together as if in prayer and rested the tips of his fingers against his scruffy chin. "Guilty. I approved it, and Jack set it up. I'm sorry. I didn't realize how much it would upset you. I felt like a right prat when you started crying last night."

His words sucked the wind out of my sails, and my shoulders slumped. "You don't even get it. I wasn't crying for myself. I was crying because of how that one guy was treating you, the questions he was shouting. It was vile."

"I appreciate that, Ivy." He placed his hands over his heart. "Your defense of me—it means everything, but I've been dealing with that shit for a very long time. For someone like me, it's the price you pay for the rewards. And Jack's not wrong. It worked. The comments were mostly positive; the pictures generated a vibe and having you by my side only added to the glowing aura. It was a win for me, but I'm sorry it hurt you."

I sniffed. "Why didn't you just tell me? I felt blindsided."

He tossed his hat on the sofa, and then sat down beside it, hunched forward, his elbows on his knees. "I didn't want you to think I was a dick. I don't ever want to seem desperate or weak in your eyes. Does that make sense to you?"

He had no idea how much.

"I don't see you that way. I understand you inhabit a different kind of world, and you thrive on publicity. I think if you had told me, I would've handled it better." I cupped his phone in my hands, and he glanced up, a little closed-lipped smile on his face. I coughed. "Or, maybe not."

"If I'd told you what was planned, you probably would've refused to go out, and I didn't want to ruin your night. That little scuffle at the end of the evening didn't spoil anything, did it? We still had a great time. I got a banger out of it, and as Jack pointed out in his text, the pap call worked."

I opened my hands and walked toward him. "I suppose you'd like to read his text. I'm sorry I looked at it."

He shrugged as he took his phone from me. "I believe that you just happened to see it. Chloe probably turned the phone over when she thought it was hers." He patted the cushion beside him. "Do you want to sit here and read it with me?"

I dropped down beside him, leaving a few inches of space between us. I couldn't let him know I forgave him so readily. I understood better than anyone why he didn't tell me, but it still felt like betrayal.

I leaned over his arm as he began to read Jack's text aloud. "Pap call worked, mate. Good pictures—you know that part." He tapped the message and continued. "Good accompanying article with some positive spin for you. Ivy looked hot—" Ian growled and bit my shoulder "—and fan reaction to her was good. She's a PR dream, and nobody has identified her, yet."

My body stiffened, and I clasped my hands between my knees. *Yet.* Maybe I *should* leave the country with Ian.

"He ends it. Talked to Hugh, and he said you even sent him a song that night. Comeback time, mate." Ian placed a steadying hand on my bouncing knees. "Ain't so bad, huh?"

"Not so bad but a weird way to live your life."

"It's all I've known for a long time, but I like the life you've shown me here. I feel like the moment we went on that Ferris wheel at the pier, we entered a bubble, and it hasn't popped, yet."

"I think that article was the first pinprick."

"I know." He cupped my face with one hand and kissed me. "Let's go on our hike, and I promise there won't be any paparazzi hiding in the bushes."

Maybe not, but with my face splashed across several gossip sites, it might be just a matter of time before someone ID'd me—the real me.

* * *

The following day, Chloe decided to treat me to a pedicure and lunch to apologize for blabbing about me to Ian. I had ripped Chloe a new one, especially for telling Ian I took all my dates to see Van. That wasn't even true. Two guys—one hated the concert and the other used it as leverage to take me to a heavy metal tribute, all-day head-banger that left me with a raging headache.

The night with Ian had been magical...until it wasn't. The stunt worked out for him, so I couldn't blame him too much. I forgave easily—people in glass houses and all that—which was why I was sitting next to Chloe at the nail salon with my feet soaking in bubbling water.

I'd been tuning out Chloe's yapping until I heard the word *England.* Cranking my head to the side, I said, "What arc talking about?"

"I know you have me on ignore." Chloe adjusted her massage chair. "I asked you when Ian was going back to England."

"The day after tomorrow." Saying the words out loud caused a dull ache in my stomach, and I folded my hands across it. "I have one more outing planned for him at the Getty Villa. We started our sight-seeing tour at the Getty Center, so I thought it would be serendipitous to end it with the antiquities at the Getty Villa. Then we can have lunch in Malibu."

"Sounds dull. And?"

"And what?"

"Are you going with him? Are you going to follow him out there? Go for an extended visit? Has he invited you? Wait—" Chloe covered her mouth, her newly painted nails a shimmering blue to match her eyes "—the fuckwad didn't invite you."

I drummed my own nails, short and unpolished, on the armrest of my chair. "He did invite me. He wants me to join him—forever."

"What?" Chloe's jaw dropped. "Girl, no. That's what he said?"

"Sort of. I mean, that was his implication. He said he's not into long-distance romances, and he wants me with him." I giggled and curled my toes as the manicurist scrubbed the bottoms of my feet.

"Oh my, God. You're going, aren't you? Ivy, you have to go with him. He has his issues for sure, but he's so into you, and—" she leveled a long fingernail at me "—he's loaded, mega-rich."

"Yeah, I know he must have some money after his years with the band, but that's not his main attraction, not for me."

"Well, it doesn't hurt, especially given his recent escapades. And *some* money? Are you kidding? He's worth about eighty million dollars."

This time *my* jaw dropped. "No."

"What do you mean? You really don't know? I thought you looked him up."

"I didn't look up his net worth."

"Why the hell not? I did. That's one of the first things I *did* look up when you told me he was at our place sleeping in your bed."

"That can't be right." I scooped up my phone from my lap and did a search for Ian Pope's net worth, praying he'd never accidentally pick up my phone and see my search history. The figure on the screen dazed me. "It says here approximately eighty-five million dollars. What do you do with that much money?"

"Anything you want. *Now* do you see why you have to go with him?"

"I don't lo...like him for his money. He wouldn't be the same person with the same characteristics without his experiences, but money doesn't factor into our relationship. That's gross."

"It will play a role if you have to fly back and forth from the US to the UK. You can't afford to do that. It's just practical. Anyway, like you said, it doesn't matter if he has it or not. You're already in lo...like with him." Chloe gave me a wink.

With our newly painted toes, we hobbled three doors down to a breakfast place and secured a table on the patio in the back. This was just the type of place, the whole block, actually, where paparazzi hung out in their quest for celebrity photos. After realizing how close my place was to Montana Avenue, Ian had suggested several restaurants here for dinner. I'd shot them all down. Maybe if I'd relented, he wouldn't have had to stage his own ambush.

Chloe ordered a cinnamon bun French toast and a mimosa, and I got the açai bowl with a cup of herbal tea. When her drink came, Chloe tapped on the champagne flute with her nail. "Are you ever going to drink again? It's not like you have a problem with it."

"Eventually. I just don't think it's polite or wise to drink in front of someone in recovery."

"Eh. It's not like he's going to get drunk on your kiss." Chloe took a dainty sip of her drink. "He's gonna have to get used to it at some point, especially in the music industry. You remember that guy I dated, Nico, who was a roadie. He said half the concerts he worked were fueled by booze and blow."

I dredged my teabag in the hot water with a trembling hand. I knew you couldn't be responsible for anyone else's sobriety, but you could be helpful and supportive. Ian could navigate his recovery on his own, without me, if he really wanted it.

Chloe asked, "Is Ian going to be touring for this album he's releasing?"

"That's the plan."

"Have you heard any of his new songs?"

"Yeah, he has a songwriting app on his laptop, so he's been working with that, which is what he's doing today. He can compose with it, and he's been putting some of the songs together and sending them to his writing partner. Before you ask—" I held up the swinging teabag over my cup "—they're really good."

"You definitely have to go with him. Just don't sell your place. I'll keep renting it from you. And if he buys you a mansion in the Bu, I'll rent that from you, too."

"Please." I rolled my eyes. "Nobody is buying anyone mansions in Malibu."

"You could always ask." Chloe twirled her finger in the air. "You kinda have him wrapped around your finger."

"What nonsense." But I secretly felt a little glow in my heart even though I didn't completely agree with Chloe. To have someone wrapped around your finger implied you held all the power, but I felt helpless to resist Ian. Every time we made love, he possessed me, body and soul. It terrified me that I'd allowed it to happen.

As the waitress delivered our food, Chloe waved a fork at me. "That smile right there says Malibu mansion."

I thanked the waitress and kicked Chloe under the table, risking my newly painted toenails. "Just shut it. If I do decide to move across the pond, you'll be the first to know, and of course you can stay in my place—in Santa Monica."

We spent the rest of lunch discussing my current book, Chloe's extended contract for work, and gossiping about our friend, Diego, who stumbled across his boyfriend's Grindr account.

Two mimosas in, Chloe got a call from her current client requesting a meeting. After paying for brunch and refusing a ride from me, she hopped into an Uber, furiously crunching mints.

I sent a text to Ian, and he confirmed he was still working, so I decided to give him space and do some work of my own. I'd brought my laptop and when I left the restaurant, I headed across the street to a coffee house to work on my book.

Ian's vast amounts of money hadn't swayed me, but my conversation with Chloe had brought me closer to chucking it all and moving to England. Three weeks ago, I wouldn't have even considered giving up laundry day for a guy. The speed and intensity of my relationship with Ian left me breathless and a little, no a *lot*, scared, but I trusted him. I could trust my heart with him. He made me feel...safe.

Mid-way through a scene where the heroine literally trips over a dead body, my phone buzzed. Without thinking or checking the display, I tapped to answer. "Hello."

"Hey, sis. Finally. I've been texting you for weeks. You have me on ignore, or what?"

My heart stuttered, just like it always did when I heard from my brother. I took my phone off Speaker and held it to my ear. "What do you want, Matt?"

"That's cold. You can start by setting me up with that total smoke show, Chloe. Nothing I like more than a black-haired bitch with fake tits."

I almost choked on my tea. "Yeah, I'll tell her you said that. She'll be swept off her feet at the sheer romanticism. I told you before, she has a boyfriend."

"I know she thinks I'm hot, so you can let her know I'm available."

"Things didn't work out too well for you the last time you dated a woman of that description. I think she got you arrested."

"Nobody's perfect." He hacked. Matt had a smoker's cough already at thirty-two. "How's your *writing career* going?"

I didn't know if he tried for that sneer in his voice every time he mentioned my career, or if it just came naturally to him. "It's going okay. I have two new books out, one ready to go, and I'm working on a fourth." I almost bit off the tip of my tongue. I should know by now, never to brag about success to Matt.

"Any 'New York Times' bestsellers in that bunch? JK Rowling level success? Hell, 'Fifty Shades of Grey' success."

"Sorry, no. Just enough to get by and keep writing."

"That's dull, but you don't have to be coy with me, *Ivy Chase.*"

"Yeah, well you can probably look up the sales yourself. Not that exciting." Matt usually had two reasons for calling—he needed money, or he'd gotten himself into some mess...and he needed money. I didn't have any money to give him, and I'd just about run out of fucks to give about his problems.

He'd gotten the same share of Dad's life insurance money as I did, but he'd squandered his on gambling, booze, weed, and women. The fact that Dad had life insurance had shocked both of us, but Matt pointed out later our old man had probably gotten it as a prelude to some kind of scam or insurance fraud—he just died before he could implement it.

"I'm not talking about your pathetic career, sis. I'm talking about your new boyfriend."

My breath hitched in my throat, and I gripped the edge of the table with one hand as my head spun. "I-I don't have a boyfriend."

"Not only do you have a boyfriend, he's rich as fuck."

Wiping a damp hand on my thigh, I licked my dry lips. "Oh, you mean those stupid pictures at the concert of me and Ian Pope. He's not my boyfriend. I just met him there. Haven't seen him since."

I should've known Matt would see those pictures. He didn't follow celebrity gossip, but he did follow Van. We both got our musical tastes from our father—about the only thing we got from him except for the insurance money. Matt loved Van as much as I did and even had alerts on his phone for any mentions of him online.

I held my breath as Matt mulled over my response.

"You're lying. I saw the pictures. You're holding hands. He kissed you."

I snorted, but my heart was hammering in my chest. "Yeah, 'cuz he's Ian Pope. If Ian Pope wants to hold your hand and kiss you, you're gonnna let him. Nothing else happened. He didn't take my contact info. For all I know, he's back in England. I doubt I'll ever hear from him again."

"He's not back in England, and he's worth eighty-five million bucks." Matt clicked his tongue, which meant he was using his limited brain cells for thinking. "Anything happen in that limo? Did he grab your ass? Force you to give him a blow job?"

"You're disgusting. He had some party to go to, didn't invite me, and had the driver take me home after the driver dropped him off. Nothing happened."

"C'mon, Ivy. Doesn't mean you can't claim something happened. Threaten him. Tell him you'll go to the press and let them know he was drunk and sexually assaulted you in the back of the limo. That shit happens all the time. He won't want his precious comeback to derail, and he'll pay you a couple mil to keep quiet, and you can send a few of those stacks my way."

Matt had done his research, just like Dad had taught us to study every mark. The food I'd eaten earlier churned in my stomach, and I felt as if I was gonna hurl.

"I'm not doing that. I barely know the guy. He wouldn't even remember my name, and besides, he'd probably call an attorney and a private investigator, and once they started looking into my background, we could both be in trouble. Aren't you still on probation?"

"You're not lying to me, are you, Ivy? 'Cuz we both know you're a damned good liar. That's why Dad liked using you so much—that sweet face hiding a whole different kind of animal."

"I'm not lying." I sucked some air into my lungs. My heart was racing so fast, I'd started hyperventilating. "I don't know this guy. Any attempt to get money out of him would be laughably transparent."

"You'd better not be lying to me, sis." Matt had dropped the jovial conman act, and his words held a threat of menace that caused a chill to ripple down my spine. "Because if I find out you're seeing Ian Pope behind my back, I'll fuckin' destroy you."

"Wh-what does that mean? How are you going to destroy me?" My legs twisted into a pretzel beneath the table.

"You know that last con you ran with Dad against the Browne family? The one at the warehouse. The one that cost Dad his life."

I nodded stiffly, even though Matt couldn't see me.

"Remember Dad saw the cameras in the warehouse on his way out and sent me back to get the video." He gave a short laugh that stabbed me in the heart. "I still have that footage, and you're on it, running a con with dear old Dad, as identifiable as you are in those paparazzi photos with Ian Pope."

Chapter 15

IAN

The front door creaked open, and I looked up from stirring the pasta. "Tink?"

Keys landed in the basket in the hallway with a jingle, and Ivy came around the corner of the kitchen. "Wh-what are you doing?"

"Cooking dinner." I spread my arms, water dripping onto the floor from the slotted spoon in my hand. "I'm making some creamy salmon pasta, just to thank you and Chloe for letting me crash here for the past two weeks." Ivy stared at me with rounded eyes, her cheeks pale. "Are you alright? Where's Chloe?"

"She went to a meeting. I thought she'd be home by now." She retreated to the sitting room and placed her bag on top of the coffee table. "You didn't have to do this. Where'd you get the salmon?"

"At that fresh fish shop on Colorado. Road your bike." I tilted my head to the side. "You sure you're okay? You look knackered. Did you get a lot of work done?"

"Not really. You?" She waved a hand at my laptop still set up for my music production, next to her bag.

"I got loads done. Sent stuff over to Hugh." The sauce on the stove started bubbling, and I turned down the heat beneath it. "I'm giving you writing credit on two of the songs."

"What? No." She sank down on the edge of the table, her shoulders rounded. "Why would you do that? I don't deserve it."

"You contributed so many lyrics to 'Muse' and 'Van at the Greek.' Those are my working titles for two of the songs. You helped me so much, and that's the way it works. Those songs wouldn't be what they are without your input. Your way with words and turn of phrase—Hugh agreed. Dead unique, they are."

She shook her head and rubbed her eyes, her chin dropping to her chest. I turned off everything on the stove and ate up the distance between us in a few long strides. Kneeling in front of her, I asked, "What's wrong? Did something happen when you were out? Did you read something?"

God, I hoped Jessica hadn't made good on her threats already. Had Ivy seen something about me? Jack would've warned me if something had popped up. It was like playing a game of whack-a-mole.

Her head jerked up, and her lips stretched into a smile as she placed her hands on my shoulders. "I'm just tired. Bad day writing. Couldn't get anything to work."

Maybe my impending departure was playing havoc with her emotions. I felt it too, but I was just trying to hold onto the thought that I'd be with her after a short while. I began to gather her to my chest, and she flung herself at me so wildly we both wound up on the floor with her on top.

She laughed suddenly, dispelling the shadows on her face, and kissed me hard on the mouth. "How can I help you in the kitchen?"

Before we could roll to our feet, Chloe sailed through the front door and tripped to a stop. "Oh my God. Are you two doing it on the living room floor now?"

I sat up with Ivy straddling me. "We've already done it here. This time we just fell."

"Figures." Chloe sniffed the air. "What is that yummy smell? I know that's not Ivy's cooking."

"Ian is cooking us salmon and pasta for letting him stay here."

"How sweet." Chloe slid her sunglasses to the end of her nose. "I suppose he hasn't seen our bill, yet."

I staggered to my feet, with Ivy clinging to my body. "I'm gonna miss your humor, Chloe."

"Who says I'm joking?" She stopped at the door leading to the hallway. "What time is dinner?"

"About thirty minutes." I carried Ivy to the kitchen and set her down. "Do you want to make the salad?"

"I can make salad, and don't you start on my culinary talents." She smacked me on my backside.

"You have other talents that make up for your lack of expertise in the kitchen." The knots in my gut loosened as Ivy regained her regular sunny disposition. I thought she'd been about to collapse when she came home, and she looked ready to break into tears when I told her about dinner and the song credit. Must've had a bad day.

Later, we shared some laughs with Chloe over dinner, and I played some of the new songs for them. Then Ivy had a surprise request as we were cleaning up the dishes.

"Can we go back to the pier tonight and ride the Ferris wheel again? It closes at ten o'clock, so we have just over an hour."

I parted the curtains over the kitchen sink. "It's foggy again. We won't see the view."

"I know. That's why I want to go." She curled her fingers around mine in the soapy water. "I want to head back into that cocoon with you one more time."

A flicker of fear pinged my brain, but I shook it off. "We'd better bundle up. Baby, it's cold outside."

"Jeans and hoodies, it is."

* * *

I insisted on buying the fifteen-dollar tickets, and we didn't even have to wait in line. The fun fair was almost closed, and apparently the kids were back in school. We climbed into one of the cars. This time we didn't have to pretend or deny our attraction to each other, and we snuggled up in one corner of the red vinyl seat.

Once the operator loaded everyone, the wheel cranked into motion. A solid wall of white obscured our view of the ocean and much of the horizon, except for a thin, dark blue line in the distance.

I pulled her hands into my lap, and she dropped her head on my shoulder. She let out a little gasp each time our car dropped over the peak of the wheel. The fog buffeted us on all sides, the moisture playing havoc with Ivy's hair, curling the ends.

I threaded my fingers through her lush locks and turned her head so I could kiss her mouth. Her lips moved beneath mine, soft and sweet with the vanilla ice cream we'd had for dessert.

I slipped her hand beneath my sweatshirt and pressed it against my chest, over my heart. She whispered against my kiss. "I wanna stay up here forever."

Like a couple of teenagers, we made out on the Ferris wheel, snogging and groping and stroking and sighing, as if we hadn't already gone all the way—several times. All too soon, the ride ended and when our car clunked back to Earth at the starting point, the jarring motion seemed to signal an end to something, a return to reality.

A breath of sadness wafted across my cheek, but I dismissed it. I couldn't wait to start this new reality with Ivy by my side. All things seemed possible.

She must've felt the sorrow, too, as silence prevailed on the ride back to her place. She seemed content to leave her hand in mine or have me stroke her thigh or her arm as she drove. But we had to close this chapter to start the new one.

When we got home, we wasted no time tumbling into bed, but while I would've been happy to fuck her silly, she slowed my hand. With both of us naked, she straddled me as I sat on the edge of the bed. Intimately connected, chest to chest, face to face, I entered her as I stared into her eyes.

She rose and fell against me, and I drove into her slick creaminess. Rubbing her pussy against my pelvis, she grabbed my head, digging her fingers into my scalp. I slid my hand between our bodies, my fingers finding her clit. As I stroked her, she threw her head back and moaned.

Seconds later, she came all over my cock, and I fell back on the bed and flipped positions. She wrapped her legs around me as I pounded into her, abandoning the slow and gentle mood. I came hard and fast, shooting my cum deep inside her, a primeval need to possess her taking over my senses.

She took me in, enveloping me with her arms and legs as we rocked back and forth as one. The rhythm slowed and she loosened her grip on me. I slid from her body and buried my head in the crook her neck. I breathed out the first words that came to my head. "I love you."

Did she move? Did she answer? My body and mind were so satiated, I didn't know or care. As I drifted off, she caressed my face, and her lips brushed against my throat. Did she say it back?

* * *

I woke up on my last full day in LA in high spirits, energized and focused. We'd spend the morning during the foggy hours at the museum, and then when the sun broke through in the afternoon, we'd have lunch in Malibu—not at Nobu—and maybe take a walk on the beach.

Ivy had risen before me and managed to sneak out of bed without making a sound. I grabbed my underwear, in case Chloe was home, and sauntered into the kitchen.

Ivy, her laptop in front of her on the table, snapped it shut, a frown twisting her mouth.

Coming up behind her, I ruffled her hair. "Still having problems with your book?"

"Writer's block. Can't figure out what comes next." She pressed her hands on top of her computer, as if willing words to seep onto on the pages of her book. *I'd been there.*

"Come on my run with me. That always clears my head."

"As long as you don't sprint. I'm not gonna match your pace. I'd collapse."

Cupping my hand under her chin, I tilted her head back to kiss her upside down. "I'll never leave your side, Ivy."

She ducked away from me and jumped up from her chair. "I'm going to take a quick shower first. Do you want to eat anything before we go?"

"I'll grab a banana. I'm gonna skip the shower, so I'll be ready when you are."

When Ivy left the room, I checked my phone and swore when I saw the text from Jack. I tapped it and read the rest with a growing sense of dread creeping through my body like sludge. It always started with something small and innocuous like this—just innuendo. That's how the dick pic scandal began, just gossip until the pictures went online. Maybe Chloe could track the source of these newest rumors and act preemptively.

I didn't need this shit right now. Ivy already had her doubts about coming with me. If she got an inkling of another smear campaign against me on the horizon, it just might push her over the edge.

I texted Jack back that we could look into the issue when I returned to England. I didn't understand my ex, Jessica. The pictures of me with Ivy in the tabloids must've set her off. She couldn't possibly want me back. If she did, she had some odd reconciliation tactics.

I snapped a banana from the bunch and peeled it. I ate it in about four bites on my way to the bedroom. Ivy had finished her shower, and she almost fell over stepping into her running shorts as I surprised her.

"Careful you don't hurt yourself before we even start running." I put on some shorts and a tank and retrieved my trainers from the corner of the bedroom.

"Don't forget your Dodger hat. And sunglasses." She pulled open the blinds and pressed her nose against the window. "Even haze like this can make you squint. Maybe you should wear your running jacket. It looks chilly out there."

Ever since the paparazzi ambush, Ivy suggested I cover up thoroughly every time we went out. She didn't want to take any chances that I'd be recognized.

I gave her a mock salute. "Hat, sunglasses, but I really have to draw the line at the jacket. I'd be ripping it off less than a mile into the run."

She paused adjusting her running bra and bugged her eyes out at me. "Mile? Just how far are we running? I think two miles is my max. I mean, three miles is a 5K race."

"Okay, Miss Roadrunner. Two miles it is, but that's down to the beach and back."

Throwing my hat at me, she said, "We can jog down to the beach, and you can run around for another two miles while I have an ice cream at the pier, waiting for you."

"That would absolutely defeat the purpose."

"*Your* purpose, maybe. *My* purpose is to watch your sexy ass while you run ahead of me."

Shaking my head, I said, "You and your dirty one-track mind."

Ivy's mood had brightened considerably since her jittery appearance in the kitchen this morning, and I planned to bask in it. Definitely not the time to mention this latest assault on my character. I didn't like keeping things from her, but sometimes it was for the greater good, and the greater good was maintaining a light attitude for our last full day together.

Once she joined me in England, I could dump all the bad news on her.

* * *

Despite a bit of fan frenzy at the restaurant for lunch, the day lived up to my expectations. We laughed, joked, kissed, had a table with a view, kissed some more, held hands on the beach. A few times, I'd caught Ivy with a sad or pensive expression, but I put it down to my departure tomorrow.

I'd miss her, but we had an understanding that she'd join me in about a month. She had to finish her book, or close enough, and I had music to record...and another social media fire to extinguish. We'd be busy, and the time would fly. Once we nailed down the date for our reunion, she'd feel better—we both would. Maybe she doubted my commitment to her and this relationship, even though I'd spent the day talking about my home, my family, and my life in England. Maybe she feared I'd leave her like everyone else had left her. I had a lot to prove to her.

We returned to a quiet house. Apparently, Chloe had hightailed it down to San Diego to try to work things out with her boyfriend. I didn't miss that kind of drama, and Ivy didn't play the diva or high-maintenance queen.

I went straight to my laptop on the coffee table and flipped it open. Hugh had promised to review the latest song and send over his suggestions. I called over my shoulder, "Are you sure I can't take you out someplace nice tonight for our last dinner?"

"I'm sure. I relented on your suggestion for lunch today and look what happened."

"Ah, that wasn't so bad." I sank on the sofa in front of my computer and opened Hugh's email while Ivy puttered around the kitchen.

She brought me a glass of sparkling water over ice and sat across from me on the chair. "Do you need to get your boarding pass?"

"My assistant, Penny, already did that for me." I held up my phone. "It came through a few hours ago when we were at the beach."

"Must be nice."

I shot her a glance, but she was staring into her drink. Time to nail things down and reassure her. "Penny's been with me for a while. I went to her wedding and the baptism for her first child. She's the best. Always stood by me. I'm going to send her your contact details, if that's okay. She can book your ticket."

Ivy answered me with a tinkling of ice in her glass.

I continued. "I'm thinking a month. Does that work for you? If you're not done with your book by then, you can finish it at my place. I have a room downstairs that would be perfect for you. It has French doors that open onto the back garden. You can just tell me what furniture you want in there. It's a bit heavy and dark now, but you can decorate the room however you want." I licked my dry lips. She still hadn't raised her eyes from the fascinating water swirling in her glass. "Or you could pick a different room, whatever you want."

The words, which had taken on a desperate quality, hung in the air between us, and a bead of sweat rolled down the middle of my back. "Ivy?"

She finally looked up, pinning me with her green gaze, and a fist formed in my gut. The warning bell that had dinged in my brain yesterday when she'd told me she wanted to go back to the cocoon of the Ferris wheel had turned into a piercing siren, slicing through my head. I could see it all in her face.

"I'm not going to England, Ian."

Chapter 16

IVY

I recoiled from the emotions that played across Ian's beautiful face—disbelief, fear, sadness, anger—they charged across his visage in a matter of seconds, but to me, each feeling lumbered by in slow motion, delivering a powerful, painful punch to my psyche.

I crossed my arms, digging my fingers into my biceps, welcoming the pain of my nails jabbing into my flesh.

"What?" His voice sounded raspy, as if he'd just remembered how to speak.

"I-I thought about it, and I can't go with you. I can't move to England or even try it on for size. Your life..." I flapped my hands in the air "...it's not a normal way to live. I can't exist like that. I'm sorry."

"You're sorry?" He knocked the hat from his head and dragged a hand through his hair. "When did you make this decision? How long have you known?"

"I've been feeling it the past few days but just decided." My tight throat made it difficult to form words. I didn't want to cry.

"You allowed me to carry on like a complete idiot today, talking about our plans, and all the time you were thinking, what a wanker. I'm not going to England with this loser." He swept his computer from his lap and jumped to his feet. "It's because of the pap walk, isn't it? You think I do that sort of thing all the time. I don't."

"No." I pulled a throw pillow from the chair into my lap and hugged it to my chest, while he paced in front of me. "It wasn't the paparazzi stunt. It's the whole lifestyle. I can't do that. It's not normal. Surely, you can see it's not normal for regular people. I'm a regular person." The lie rolled off my tongue. Not that I wasn't a regular person—I was, sort of. I lied about not being able to do it. I could do anything with him. I wanted to do everything with him.

"I don't want it, Ivy. I'm trying to get away from that lifestyle. I thought I could get away from it with you. Have something more lowkey. There are loads of celebrities who manage it. I could. I could manage it with you."

The more he talked, the more my heart shattered and scattered into far-flung pieces. I didn't think I'd ever get those pieces back together in the right order. What I'd have left for a heart would be misshapen and jagged, ripping into my chest with every beat.

"I do think you can have something different from before, but you can do that without me. You're strong and brave and..."

"Don't..." He held up his hands as if to ward off my words "...patronize me."

"M-maybe I could come and visit you, or if your tour takes you to LA we can get together then." Bad idea. Matt would be watching Ian like a hawk for the foreseeable future.

Ian threw his hands in the air. Apparently, he thought it was a bad idea, too. "I'm not doing that. You wanna come to England as a tourist? Oh, here's the London Eye. Let's do the changing of the guard next or maybe high fucking tea at Blenheim Palace." He'd put on a very posh English accent and pranced around the room. "I'm not doing that."

"I'm sorry." I twisted my fingers together.

"Stop saying you're sorry. I'll get my shit and fuck off out of here."

"What?" I tossed the pillow aside and half-rose from the chair. "No. You don't have to leave. Where would you go?"

"Umm, there are these things called hotels. They actually let you stay there overnight if you pay them." He spun around toward the hallway.

Those hotels also had those things called *minibars*. I raised my arms and dropped them. "Please, don't leave. You don't need to leave. It's just one more night. We don't have to talk, if you don't want to. You can work here, and I-I'll give you some space. You stay here, and I'll take off for a while."

Before he could answer, or worse, collect his bags, I launched myself out of the chair, grabbed my purse, my sweatshirt, my keys and slipped out of the house, leaving him with his hands shoved into his pockets and his head bent forward.

By the time I reached my car, I'd already shed enough tears to end the California drought. I couldn't guarantee that Ian would stay at my place, but it would be easier for him to be there without me right now. Did he believe me? I'd raised enough of a fuss about his celebrity and getting recognized that it would make sense to him.

What wouldn't make sense is how I could let the difficulties of his stardom override our deep connection with each other. He'd have to come to his own conclusions about that, but anything would be better than the fallout if I stayed with him and Matt found out.

Matt had already cautioned me about what lay ahead for me if I was really in a relationship with Ian Pope. He had proof of my involvement in Dad's con. I'd seen the tape with my own eyes the afternoon Matt had called me.

He'd also done his research, like any good confidence man. While the crime of fraud might have a five-year statute of limitations, the scam Dad had pulled on the Browne family had also involved bank fraud, and Matt had gleefully informed me that the statute of limitations for that was ten years. I could still be criminally charged for my participation. Did I want to find out?

Of course, I could always tell Ian the whole sordid truth about my life and how my father had used both me and my brother as his accomplices at various times. Matt's tape wouldn't have any power over me then.

I smacked the steering wheel as I pulled into the street. Who was I kidding? If I told Ian, and then told Matt I was staying with Ian, Matt could use that tape against both of us. He could blackmail Ian directly, and if Ian didn't play along, I could go to jail.

Besides, did I really want to tell Ian about my criminal behavior? Ian hadn't wanted to tell me he arranged the pap walk for fear I'd think less of him. The situation with the con was the pap walk on steroids. At least arranging photo ops for yourself wasn't illegal, punishable by twenty years in the slammer.

And then there were the Brownes. Dad thought he could outsmart that criminal family, who had their fingers in auto theft, ID fraud, probably drugs. Figured the Brownes wouldn't go to the cops due to their own illegal activities. The Brownes didn't go to the cops. They'd taken care of Dad the old-fashioned way. They'd killed him. Sure, the hit and run looked like an accident and we couldn't prove a thing, but both Matt and I knew better.

The Brownes hadn't tracked down Dad's accomplice that night. I'd played only a small role and had nothing to do with the money Dad had stolen from them, but it didn't mean they wouldn't be awfully interested in the footage that was stolen from their warehouse that night showing me as the accomplice who ripped them off. Also, Matt and I always doubted the Brownes had retrieved all their money from Dad. Matt had been feverishly looking for it ever since. What if the Brownes believed I had it?

I also had to consider Ian's reputation. He'd been working hard to repair it. News that his girlfriend was a scammer could blow all that to smithereens. No, I didn't have any other choice. Breaking it off with Ian would keep Matt out of Ian's orbit and keep him off my back, too. Matt had already suggested that I could still orchestrate fake claims against Ian to make him pay up.

Dizziness overcame me, and I could feel an anxiety attack gathering. I parked in front of the dog park and buzzed down the window to gulp in the salty sea air. If I could just get through the horrible part of breaking up with Ian, I could protect him and protect myself. He'd get over me soon enough, and I'd be able to limp along, knowing I did the right thing.

I clambered out of the car and let myself through the gate around the big dog side of the park. I dropped onto a bench and watched the pups play, through eyes swimming with tears. The sun hadn't quite set yet, but the lampposts stationed around the park were lit up, spotlighting the dogs as they ran and played and jumped without a care in the world.

An older woman with a gray braid hanging over one shoulder sat beside me, long skirt rustling, bracelets clinking on her arms, the smell of patchouli hovering around her. "Which one is yours?"

I sniffed and wiped the back of my hand across my nose. "None. I used to have a dog, but he passed away a few years ago. I just like coming here sometimes to watch them play. I used to bring him here."

The woman patted my knee. "That's rough. What kind of dog was he?"

"A Great Dane, harlequin. His name was Loki."

"Aww, Loki's over the rainbow bridge now, keeping watch over you."

For some reason, this opened my tear ducts even more, and I covered my face with my hands. I couldn't even get over Loki, how would I ever manage to move on after Ian?

"Do you know what works for me?"

Twisting my head to the side to look at the woman beside me, I asked, "What?"

"When I lost my Ginger, I got another dog a few months later." She tossed her braid over her shoulder. "I know it doesn't help everyone, and some people would see it as traitorous, but it helped me, and I just know Ginger approved. They don't want to see us sad, do they? So, my advice to you, my dear—get yourself another dog."

"I don't want another dog. I want Loki back." My bottom lip trembled. Was I talking about Loki now or Ian?

"Maybe you'll find another Loki to love." The woman jumped to her feet and trotted over to a scrum of dogs. "Who belongs to the German Shepherd. He's trying to hump my Saffron."

My wet sobs sputtered into laughter. I'd have to tell Ian about Saffron and the horny Shepherd. I gasped as a wave of grief tackled me, leaving me breathless.

After another thirty minutes in the dog park, I peeled myself from the bench. Darkness had engulfed the park, and only the pit bulls were cocky enough to stick around.

When I got to the car, I checked my phone. Nothing from Ian. We didn't have any food in the house, and lunch at the beach was a distant, happy memory. Ian needed something to eat—unless he was already at some hotel or out with one of his LA friends. I called my favorite Chinese restaurant and ordered some food.

I arrived before my order was ready and sat in a chair in the corner, drinking hot tea and cracking open fortune cookies looking for hope. When Winnie, the owner of the restaurant set a plastic bag on the table in front of me, she asked, "Are you alright, Ivy? You don't look so good."

"Just a little sad news, Winnie. I'm okay, thanks."

Winnie swept the discarded fortunes from the table. "I'll throw a few more fortune cookies in the bag for you, so you have better chance of getting one you like."

Not even a happy fortune could repair the damage I'd done today.

On the drive home, my foot alternated between heavy and light on the accelerator. I couldn't wait to come back to Ian and make sure he was okay, but I dreaded it at the same time.

With the plastic bag of food banging against my leg and the spicy smells inside making me kind of nauseous, I tiptoed to my front door. I put my ear against the door first, and my fragmented heart rattled in my chest at the silence.

I shoved my key in the lock and bumped the door open with my hip. I almost collapsed with relief when I saw Ian on the sofa, hunching over his laptop on the coffee table, a Diet Coke next to it.

He didn't bother to look up when I walked in. I hauled the bag of food onto the kitchen table. "I picked up some Chinese food for dinner."

"Not hungry...but thanks."

He didn't ask where'd I been for over an hour. Didn't offer up what he'd been doing in my absence. The gulf between us gave me physical pain. "Are you working on your music?"

"Uh huh."

I'm the one who wanted him to stay here. I couldn't complain about how he chose to handle the awkwardness. I scooped some rice onto a plate, spooned the two entrees on top. I couldn't even remember what I'd ordered. I took out a pair of paper-wrapped chopsticks and ran them through my fingers. Maybe that squirrel had brought us bad luck when he stole my fork.

I stabbed a plastic fork into my food. I had enough bad luck to go around. If anything, I'd probably transferred my bad juju onto the squirrel. Some car had probably hit him on his way out of campus that day with my fork still gripped in his tiny, little paw.

Ian had put my glass of sparkling water on the counter, and I grabbed that on my way into my room. I called out to no one, "I'm going to eat in my room. Help yourself."

I perched on the edge of my bed and shoved the food around my plate as I watched some show on the Investigation Discovery Channel about some poor sap who had married a woman who turned out to be a lunatic with a secret life. At least I'd saved Ian from an appearance on this show.

The food turned out to be a bad idea, and now the bedroom smelled like spicy chili and ginger. I shoved open the window and lit a lilac-scented candle and swept my hands in the air as if to usher out the bad smell and invite the good. If only I could do that with my life.

I picked up my mostly full plate of food and my glass and crept to the bedroom door. I peeked into the living room where Ian still sat, glued to his laptop. Did he really find it so fascinating, or did he just want to avoid interacting with me?

In the kitchen, I cleared my throat and dumped my uneaten food into the sink. "Do you want to eat something before I put this away."

"No, thank you."

The perfect English gentleman, even in the midst of this shitshow. "Do you still want to leave for the airport around noon tomorrow?"

"Don't worry about it. You don't need to drive me. I ordered a car already, and I'm leaving earlier. I can wait in the lounge at the airport and do some work."

I gulped back the lump in my throat. He was making this easy on me—too easy. I almost wished he would scream and yell at me, tell me what a horrible, lying, deceitful bitch I was. Tears stung my nose again. I didn't want to sniff, so I let the snot run down my chin. Turning my back on him, not that he was looking at me anyway, I ripped off a piece of paper towel and dabbed my nose.

When he spoke next, I jumped. "If you have an extra blanket, I'll take it and sleep here on the settee."

I gripped the edge of the counter until my knuckles turned white. I hadn't even considered the sleeping arrangements. If I could've lied for another day, I would've been able to spend one more night in his arms before losing him forever.

"You don't have to sleep on the sofa. It's too short. You'll be cramped and uncomfortable. The bed is big enough. I'll take up just a tiny corner."

He didn't respond, so I finished putting the food away and washing the dishes. With everything in order, except my life, I decided to retreat to my bedroom again. On my way, I mumbled, "There are blankets in the hall closet."

Closing my bedroom door behind me, my gaze swept over the room from Ian's suitcase in the corner, mostly packed, to his shoes sitting next to his backpack to the Dodger baseball cap I'd bought him, on top of my dresser, to the bed. I lingered on the bed where we'd spent so many passionate nights, and a few days, exploring each other and being silly and falling in love. A first for me.

My eyes darted to some clothes piled next to his suitcase. He'd mentioned today that he wanted to do some laundry before he left, but with his earlier departure time, he'd probably scrapped those plans. He wanted to get out of here and away from me ASAP.

I crept toward the heap of dirty laundry and pawed through it. I snatched up a white T-shirt and held it to my face, breathing in the unique scent of Ian Pope—some sweat, some saltiness, a hint of his spicy deodorant. I could probably market this masculine smell and make a mint.

Balling it up in my hands, I tossed the shirt into my own laundry basket in the closet. He'd never miss it.

I got ready for bed and for the first time since Ian came into my life and spent that first night with me and many after, I pulled on some pajamas—a pair of blue, cotton PJ bottoms with white, fluffy sheep and a white camisole.

I climbed into my lonely bed and curled up on one side, just in case he decided to join me. The glow from the TV flickered in the bedroom, casting shadows and hues across the walls. I tried to fall asleep, but the activity of my mind kept me alert, prolonging my misery.

After an hour with no progress in the sleep department, I slipped out of bed and padded to my bedroom door. Again, I listened before easing open the door and stepping into the hallway.

The blue light from his laptop illuminated the angles of Ian's face, and turned the tattoos on his arms dull, all the images and words running together into an incomprehensible blur.

He'd slumped back against the cushions, tilting to one side, as his computer teetered dangerously on the edge of his knees. I tiptoed toward the sofa and moved his laptop, securing it on the coffee table and shutting the lid.

He stirred, emitting a soft moan from his lips. He couldn't sleep like this. He'd be stiff and sore for his plane ride tomorrow. Bad enough he hadn't eaten anything all night.

I circled the sofa, coming up behind him and putting my hands on his shoulders, stroking his neck with my thumbs. "Baby, come to bed. Don't sleep out here."

He blinked rapidly and rubbed his eyes, looking around him as if he'd found himself in some alternate universe, less real and more unwelcome than his dreams.

I floated back to my bedroom. He could make his own decision.

Lying back in bed, I closed my eyes; I held my breath as I tracked Ian's footsteps to the hallway. Would he stop, take a blanket and return to the sofa? I'd left my bedroom door ajar, and Ian eased it open.

I eked out the pent-up breath and froze under the covers. I didn't want to scare him off.

He went into the bathroom, brushed his teeth and splashed some water around. When he opened the bathroom door, I raised my eyelids ever so slightly to watch his movements. He stripped down to his briefs, and my heart caught in my throat.

Then he glanced at the bed, turned his attention to his suitcase on the floor, and made a move. Crouching before his bag, he dragged out a pair of gray sweat shorts and a T-shirt. I hoped he wasn't looking for the one stashed in my dirty laundry.

And like me, for the first time since we met, he slid under the covers wearing nightclothes. At least he'd decided to come to bed. He settled on his side, his back to me, his body on the very precipice of the mattress.

I didn't move a muscle, almost forgot to breathe. I'd left the window open, and the misty night air made its way into the bedroom, cooling down the room, spreading goosebumps across my chest.

I inched my foot close to his leg and combed the hair on his calf with my toes. He shifted away from me. A sob rose in my throat, but I clenched my teeth and beat it back. I gave it a few minutes and then stretched my arm toward him and ran my knuckles down his back. He stiffened. But he didn't scoot away this time—of course, he had nowhere to go except the floor.

Heaving a sigh, he rolled onto his back. "What do you want from me, Ivy? Do you want me to fuck you? What would be the point?"

The sharpness of his tone sliced me open, and his crude statement poured acid into the wound.

"I…" What *did* I want? I wanted Ian on top of me, inside me, his hands all over my body, his lips in my hair. I wanted him to love me again. I found my voice, high and breathy. "I know I don't have any right to ask you, but could you just hold me? Just for tonight. Just one last time."

His arm shot out, and he curled it around my waist and dragged me toward him. My body met his, and I molded my form to his muscles and hard planes, soaking in his warmth, a perfect fit. My head dropped naturally to his chest, and my hand covered his heart over the soft cotton of his T-shirt. It pounded beneath my palm.

Tears rolled down my face, soaking his shirt, but I couldn't stop them this time. Couldn't pretend that I didn't want him, need him.

Stroking my hair, he soothed me. "It's alright. It's gonna be okay."

Why was he comforting me when I was the one who'd taken an ice pick to his heart?

"Go to sleep, Tinkerbell. I've got you…for tonight."

In the safety and comfort of Ian's arms, I managed to drift off. The next day, he left.

Chapter 17

IVY

About a month after Ian's departure, actually thirty-two days, seven hours, eighteen minutes, and a smattering of seconds, after his departure, I sat on the sofa in Ian's spot, one leg curled beneath me, and my laptop heating up my thighs.

I stared at the screen and the nonsensical words I'd written. Had I typed those words on the page? My finger hovered over the delete button, but I reconsidered. Better to have bad words on the screen than no words at all. I could always fix bad words. Too bad I couldn't fix my bad life.

Leaving the words, I plunged a spoon into my pralines and cream ice cream, making sure to hit that vein of caramel.

Keys scraped in the lock, and Chloe blew into the house like a Santa Ana wind, hot and fierce. "I cannot believe this client. He didn't like any of my proposals. I wish I could cancel our contract. I'm sick of wasting my time."

Chloe ended her tirade in the middle of the living room, and shoved her sunglasses into her sleek, black hair. She seemed to notice me for the first time. "What are you doing?"

"Writing and eating some ice cream." I waved my spoon in the air.

"That's not just *some* ice cream—that's a pint."

I looked at the carton in my hand, studying the nutrition information printed on the side. "Ooh, that's a lot of fat and calories."

"Exactly." Chloe wedged a hand on her hip.

"Eh, it's Friday night. I deserve it after working so hard all week." I dipped my spoon into the creamy goodness, aiming for a couple of pralines this time.

"You call what you're doing working hard? I read it. It's crap, Ivy. You're writing crap." Chloe leveled a finger at me. "You need to get your head out of your ass."

"It's a work in progress." I side-eyed the ridiculous words on the screen, and my stomach churned. I put down the ice cream.

"You're really staying in again tonight? I'd drag you out myself, except I have a date."

"Another date?" Chloe had been going hard after she'd decided, once again, that she and Trent had hit a wall. "Hinge?"

"That's right, baby. It's wall-to-wall dicks over there, and I mean that in a good way. You should take a look. Although..." She kicked off her heels "...there's another dating app I'm going to try. More exclusive."

"An exclusive dating app?" I sucked some caramel off the end of my finger. "For real?"

"It's called Bluefin. You have to be approved. I think they check your bank statement or something."

"Yours should pass." Chloe excelled at what she did, and she had a solid reputation. The money had started rolling in for her last year.

"It should, right? I heard Austin Butler's on that app."

I said, "Oh, well, then. You'd better get right on that."

"In the meantime, I have a date tonight with Ryan. He's a cryptobro, but in a good way." She picked up her shoes from the floor and hooked the straps around her finger.

"You mean, he actually makes money buying and selling crypto instead of just talking about it?"

"Sounds like it." She dangled her shoes in the air. "I have a favor to ask. Can I borrow those strappy gold sandals of yours? The ones with the three-inch heels, not the flats."

I chewed my bottom lip, sweet with traces of praline. The sandals I'd worn the night of the concert when the paparazzi had surprised us—or at least had surprised me.

"I'll take good care of them. Please." Chloe held her hands together in prayer.

"Yeah, of course. They won't be too small? Aren't you a size eight?"

"They're sandals. I'll make it work."

Shooing her with my hands, I said, "Go ahead. They're in my closet."

When Chloe traipsed into the back, I said goodbye to the awful words and deleted them. I'd never had such debilitating writer's block. The suspense part of the book didn't pose a problem. The romance part had proved to be the sticking point. How could I make my characters happy in love when I couldn't manage it for myself?

"What the hell is this?" Chloe had stormed back into the living room, pinching Ian's face and shaking it in the air.

"It's an Ian Pope pillow."

"What are you doing with a pillow sporting Ian Pope's face? Where did you get this thing?"

I defended my pillow. "It's cute, and I got it on eBay. Quite popular, too. Fourteen sold in the week before I bought mine."

"And what are you doing with it?" She shook him again.

"What does one do with Ian Pope pillows? I put it on my bed and rest my back against it."

Chloe turned Ian's face toward her and narrowed her eyes. "This is a very young Ian Pope, maybe seventeen. I think it's illegal what you're doing."

I hiccupped a laugh. "I'm not doing anything dirty with my Ian Pope pillow."

"Are you sure?" Chloe brought the pillow to her face and started kissing it. "Oh, Ian, give it to me. Harder. Faster."

Shaking my head, I said, "Give me the fuckin' pillow, Chloe."

"You're not putting it between your legs and humping it, are you? Because that would just be wrong." She hugged the pillow to her ample chest. "He's just a baby here."

"Give me the fuckin' pillow, Chloe."

Chloe fired it at me, and I reached up to catch it. I smoothed out Ian's young face. Hugging his pillow and wearing Ian's T-shirt, which I still hadn't washed, eased my pain and loneliness just a little at night.

"Ivy, why don't you just call him? Go over to England and explain everything to him about your past and your dirtbag brother. What's the worst that could happen?"

"Uh…" I put a finger on my chin and raised my eyes to the ceiling "…I could go to prison for thirty years."

"Do you really think the Feds are gonna be all over some seven-year-old case involving a crime family and a conman who's deceased." She crossed herself. "God rest your father's soul."

"I don't know. That's the point, isn't it? I don't want to risk it. And it's not just me, I'm protecting. I'm trying to protect Ian, too. Matt is still pressuring me to reconnect with Ian and accuse him of sexually assaulting me in the limo."

"Matt's a disgusting human being. If you just tell Ian everything, he might end it, anyway, but at least he'd understand your motivation."

"Oh my God, that would be worse. Knowing my past, he might believe our whole relationship was a setup. Do you know what that might do to him?"

"Or he might just forgive you. He's no angel, himself. It would be hard for someone like him to judge you."

"Which brings up another horrible scenario. What if he does forgive me and tells Matt to do his worst—and Matt does his worst. Ian's just getting his reputation back on track. He doesn't need to be linked with a scammer in the press, someone who might land in prison. Social media would rip him to shreds." I hugged the pillow. "I'm not doing that to him. I'm not putting him in that position. He's probably forgotten all about me by now. He hasn't called once."

"You expected him to?" She raised her dark eyebrows. "Girlie, he's a nice guy, but he doesn't strike me as the groveling type. You said the night you broke it off, he barely spoke to you. Didn't plead his case. Didn't try to understand once you'd made it clear you weren't going with him. Didn't even capitulate to your demands to..." Chloe pumped her hips back and forth "...you know."

"I did not demand sex from him." I pushed up from the sofa and stamped the tingles from my sleeping leg. "He just held me."

"Exactly. When a man holds you instead of fucking you, he's done. He's not going to call you—period." Chloe snapped her fingers. "I know what we should do."

"What?" I carried the half-empty ice cream container to the sink and dumped the contents down the garbage disposal.

"We need to neutralize your scumbag brother. We need to get that footage from the warehouse that implicates you. Once we destroy it, Matt has nothing on you."

"I don't even know where he keeps it."

"You said it's on a flash drive, and he showed it to you at his apartment." Chloe tapped a long fingernail on the table. "Does he still live in that crappy bachelor in West Hollywood?"

"Yep. He already had the thumb drive out when I got there, and he plugged it into his laptop to show me the footage." I shivered and gripped my arms. "When he removed it, he shoved it into his pocket. I don't think I'm going to be getting my hands on it."

"The dumbass probably hasn't made any copies. We could break into his place and steal it."

"He's not that dumb. He probably doesn't have it sitting on his kitchen table. All these years, and I never knew he had it. He must've been waiting for the right time to spring it on me." I crushed the ice cream carton in my hand. "And I gave it to him."

"You got Matt out of your life, for now, but you also lost Ian. I don't see how that's a win for either of you."

"It beats the consequences of fessing up." Turning around, I leaned my back against the kitchen counter. "Did you find the shoes while you were snooping around my bedroom?"

"I did. Thank you, babe." Chloe blew me a kiss and scurried off to get ready for her date.

I sat back down with *my* date for the night—my laptop—and did a search for Ian. Holding my breath, I scanned the results, releasing it slowly when I saw that most of the new articles showcased his upcoming music and not any drunken antics. I'd peeked at his social media, which focused on his new album and the first single scheduled from that album, "Muse."

I snarled at the computer. "Ha, surprised he hadn't changed the name of that song yet to 'Betrayed' or 'Sucker Punched.'"

"Talking to yourself now?" Chole twirled around the living room in a pair of black, leather pants, a black corset top, and my gold sandals.

Tilting my head to the side, I said, "You look hot. Does Cryptobro deserve all this effort?"

"I guess I'll find out." Chloe hovered over my shoulder. "Spying on Ian again? I can already tell you he hasn't been up to any shenanigans. Never posts anything personal on his socials. His fans went nuts for his first post after about seven months. He didn't address his rehab at all and just made a series of professional posts about his music."

I cranked my head around to stare at my roommate. "You've been stalking him online?"

"Yeah, I've been keeping an eye on him. The Duke Hammer controversy reversed course and worked to his advantage." Chloe shrugged her bare shoulders. "He's a de facto client *and* my messy bestie's loverboy. I'm gonna follow up on him."

"Thanks, Chloe." I sniffled. "Am I going to have to prepare for an overnight guest?"

"We'll see how things work out." She widened her icy blue eyes, the black eyeliner enhancing their drama. "You're not complaining, are you? Not after you met a guy at a book festival and proceeded to install him in your bed for the next two weeks."

"Just want to make sure you're not inviting any Night Stalkers, Hillside Stranglers, or Golden State Killers into our home."

"Has anyone ever told you that you have an unhealthy fascination with serial killers?"

"It's research." I pinged my laptop with my finger. "Seriously, leave me this guy's name and his socials before you go—just in case I never hear from you again."

"You really are a buzzkill, lately." She patted my head. "Don't worry, Mom. I'll text you all that stuff and let you know whether to expect me... or us, later."

Once Chloe left for her date, the silence in the house overwhelmed me and beat me down, so I scrolled through my phone and blasted some frothy pop music. I usually couldn't write with music playing, but who was I kidding? I hadn't gotten any good writing done for days—maybe weeks, maybe thirty-two days, eight hours—I glanced at the time on my computer—fifty-two minutes, and a smattering of seconds.

By the time I decided to turn in, I'd listened to probably all 40 of today's top 40 hits, with a few Five2Go songs thrown in there just to torture myself. I tucked my laptop under my arm and turned out all the lights. Chloe had already texted me with the news that she was spending the night with Ryan and had even sent a pin to the location of his apartment in downtown LA—suitably trendy for a cryptobro.

I brushed my teeth, undressed, and pulled Ian's dirty T-shirt over my head. I inhaled his scent, still distinguishable but fading fast. If I washed the shirt, I feared I'd lose him forever. If I didn't wash it, I'd probably start growing a bacterial fungus on my skin.

As I passed the squishy barrel chair on my way to the bed, I patted the belly of the stuffed koala bear Ian had bought me during our visit to the LA Zoo. The bear sported Ian's LA Dodger cap—the one I'd bought him. The one he'd left behind. I'd already sniffed the inside of the cap for a trace of Ian, but figured if I started wearing that to bed, Chloe would have me committed.

Slipping between the sheets, I propped up my Ian Pope pillow behind me as a backrest and settled my computer on my lap to watch a podcast on YouTube. I must've dozed off because the ringing of my phone, charging on the nightstand beside me, startled me awake.

I felt for the phone and held it in front of my blurry eyes. The UK number on the display shot a stream of adrenaline to my bloodstream, and I jerked my head up, fully revived. It wasn't Ian's number, and that knowledge caused my heart to pound even more furiously. "Hello?"

"Ivy? It's Jack Davies. We met in LA. Ian's manager."

The blood roared in my ears, and I could barely hear my own frantic response. "Is it Ian? Is he okay? Did something happen to him?"

"Ian's okay." Jack coughed. "He's not fine, but he's okay."

Jack's words had done nothing to calm the thoughts racing around my brain. "What does that mean? Is he hurt? In the hospital?"

"What? No. Nothing like that. He's not injured, but he's not doing great right now. He misses you."

Relief coursed through my body, and my head dropped back and banged against the wall. I closed my eyes and took a deep breath through my nose, but Ian wasn't out of the woods, yet. "What's going on, Jack? How do you know he misses me?"

"He's starting to spiral."

"How? Did he relapse?" I chewed the inside of my mouth until I tasted the metallic tang of blood on my tongue.

"I'm not sure, but if he hasn't, he's close."

I put a hand to my throat. "How's the music going?"

"So far, so good. He's laid down four tracks already, and they're stellar. His vocals are out-of-this-world brilliant, so much depth and emotion. He's wowing everyone in the studio."

"That sounds good." My knees had started shaking so much, my laptop slid off my legs. "What's the problem?"

"Things are not so good in his personal life. His daughter's mother got married last year, and his daughter has really bonded with Sasha's husband. It gutted Ian."

"But he's been able to see Thea on his own?"

"Yeah, yeah. He just feels like he's missed so much, and Thea has this other daddy figure in her life. Just hit him hard."

My hands had gotten so clammy, I couldn't hold the phone anymore. I put it on Speaker and set it down on my lap. "You said you don't know if he fell off the wagon, so how's he spiraling?"

Jack took a sip of something. As it was eight o'clock in the morning in his time zone, I hoped it was coffee or tea. "He started blowing off a couple of the recording sessions. Just not showing up. He had some... uh...friends over at his place the other night. Friends from his party days. Not good people."

I blinked. "His ex, Jessica?"

"No. They're completely over, and she's been waging some kind of hate campaign against him, which doesn't help."

"Is she the one who initiated the dick pic crusade against him?"

"Right. And she's not done with him, yet. So, no, she wasn't at his place, but he's still friends with those other people. They're bad news."

"Then why does he hang out with them?"

"Hell if I know. They're all toadies, yes-men. I think they prop him up and make him feel special when he's not feeling good about himself. And he's not. The record company has gotten wind of the no-shows at the sessions, and they're not happy. This is it for him, Ivy. If he fucks this up, he's done. His label told me he has this one last chance. If he doesn't perform, they're cutting him loose."

I massaged my temple with my fingertips. "I'm sorry to hear this, but why call me? What am I supposed to do about it?"

"You can come to England, Ivy."

I took a painful breath. "I can't do that."

"Look, I don't know why you broke it off with him. He won't talk about it, but I know you could give him the motivation he needs if you came back into his life."

"I have my reasons, Jack, and they're personal. Maybe you can get him some professional help. Doesn't he have a therapist?"

"Refuses to see him. Thinks Sasha is using his issues against him to interfere in his relationship with Thea."

"Well, if he starts drinking again, she could really use that against him. He's just not thinking straight. Doesn't he have any close friends out there? One of the other boys?"

"He's probably closest to Charlie Beck right now, but Charlie's on tour in South America, and when Ian gets like this, he doesn't want to see his old friends or his family."

"I'd like to help him. I really would, but I can't." A roaring headache had a vise-like grip on my head, and I squeezed my eyes closed.

"The record company will pay you."

My lids flew open. "What?"

"Ian's record company, Vivant Records, will pay you to come out here and be with him." Jack spoke very slowly, enunciating every word, as if English weren't my first language.

I still had to shake the fog from my aching head. "What are you talking about?"

"Vivant has invested a lot of money in Ian Pope, a lot of money in this comeback album and the tour to follow. If Ian doesn't come back, his label stands to lose a load of cash. They would have no problem investing a little more by paying you to be by his side to keep him on track. You're also good PR."

"I am?"

"Very positive response to your appearance with him at the concert. Some fans also took some pictures of the two of you out in about in LA and started posting them to their fan accounts. The comments are all favorable. People like you, and they like him better with you."

"This is crazy. I'm assuming you wouldn't tell Ian about this arrangement?"

"Absolutely not. He would be insulted."

"As he should be. I'm not doing anything behind his back like that." *I'll do other things behind his back, but not this.*

"Ian doesn't know what's good for him, right now. I don't see the downside. You want to be with him, he wants to be with you, and the record company is willing to make this happen. It's a win, win, win, for everyone."

My nostrils flared. "You forgot one win—for yourself. If Ian goes down, you're going down with him. No more cushy job, no more perks, no more rubbing elbows with celebrities."

Jack exploded into harsh laugh. "You think it's been a cushy job managing Ian Pope? I'm trying to rescue him from his own bad impulses, and apparently, yours too."

"I can't accept money to date Ian Pope."

"Are you playing hardball with me? Because the record company is in a position to pay you a very generous monthly stipend, and all you have to do is be with the man you love."

"Hardball? You think this is a negotiation tactic?" The pain in my head had migrated to a pain in my gut, and I regretted every spoonful of ice cream.

"Ivy—" Jack's voice had grown cold, and my heart flip-flopped "—do you really think I would allow Ian to meet some woman at a book fair and spend two weeks with her without vetting that woman?"

The coldness of Jack's voice had seeped through the phone and had gripped the back of my neck in its icy fingers. "Wh-what do you mean?"

"The day Ian brought you by the hotel, I hired a private investigator."

I pressed my hands against my fluttering belly. Looked like I might go to prison, anyway. "And?"

"I tried to do a little background investigation on Ivy Chase, but I ran into loads of brick walls. Do you know why?"

He paused, waiting for some kind of response. All I could manage to croak out was, "Why?"

"Because there is no Ivy Chase."

Chapter 18

IVY

I stirred my margarita as I touched my tongue to the salted rim. I'd lost my taste for alcohol when I'd been teetotaling with Ian. I'd been too busy getting drunk off his kisses.

My friend, Diego, snapped his fingers. "If you're just going to play with that, girl, hand it over to me. I need as much booze as I can guzzle down tonight after the day I had."

Pushing her own glass out of the way, Chloe said, "You don't need to suck down her margarita. Our second round is incoming."

"Don't..." Diego held up his hand, the low lights of the bar catching the multiple rings on his fingers and throwing off sparks "...use the word *suck* in my presence. When I think of the effort I put in with that man, I feel like telling him to kiss my gay, Latino ass."

With Diego's words hovering over the table, the waitress, in the middle of delivering our drinks, hit the base of a margarita glass on her tray and the pale-yellow liquid spilled onto the table. "Sorry. I'll get you another."

"That's okay." I blotted the spill with my already soggy cocktail napkin. "I'll take that one." I could barely finish the first one, melting in front of me.

When the waitress finished delivering the other two drinks without a mishap, Chloe lifted her glass. "Don't use the word ass in my presence. When I think of all the uncomfortable things I did with Trent to make him happy, I feel like force feeding him one of these chilies."

Both Diego and I dropped our jaws at the same time and stared at Chloe, obliviously sipping her drink. I shifted my gaze to Diego and said, "Don't you dare ask her."

"What word shouldn't we mention to you, Ivy?" Chloe dabbed her lips with a napkin, leaving a smear of bright red lipstick. "Money?"

I splayed my hands on the table in front of me, touching my thumbs together. "No words are off limits for me. Knock yourselves out."

Diego, fully informed about the situation, hunched forward, stroking his sleek black goatee. "I don't see the downside, Ivy. You get to be with the man, the very hot man, you love..." he cupped his hand around his mouth and leaned toward Chloe "...and stop moping around here, and Ian gets to be with you, which he obviously needs right now, and you can keep your slimy, but also very hot, brother quiet. What's the problem?"

"It's deceitful and disrespectful to Ian. I'd be like a paid girlfriend. I'd hate it. That's why his manager wouldn't tell him about the arrangement. He knows Ian would shoot it down."

"Celebrities have paid girlfriends and boyfriends all the time, and I should know." Diego, a costume designer in the business, patted the breast pocket of his silky green shirt. "Hello, you ever hear of a beard?"

"Except Ian's not gay, sorry to disappoint you, and he doesn't need to pay me to be with him."

Chloe swirled her drink. "Apparently, he does. You have all this shit going on that he doesn't know about; why is this deception any different? This one would actually do him some good. He doesn't have to know. The record company is paying you. It's not like you're suddenly going to be living large off his fat stacks. You're going to be handing it over to Matt. It'll be enough to keep the little weasel quiet, until I can figure out a way to shut him down."

"Ooh, you're going to shut down Matt?" Diego rubbed his hands together. "Do tell."

"I'm working on it. In the meantime, I think Ivy should accept the offer." Chloe took a minute out of giving advice to wrap a strand of hair around her finger and smile at an attractive man sitting by the window. "I wasn't going to tell you, Ivy, but I stumbled across a few hints and rumors about Ian and his inability to finish the album. So, the stuff's out there."

I smacked my hand against my chest. "You're kidding. Who are these vultures roaming around, swooping in on every star's weakness."

"Girl, you have no idea what's going on in the business. It's cutthroat. And Chloe?" Diego tapped her glass with his finger. "I think that guy you're eye-fucking over there is looking at me."

Chloe flopped back in her chair. "It *is* true. All the hot men in LA are gay."

Thirty minutes later and still not through my first margarita, I called it a night.

Diego cajoled. "Come with us to this club. They play a lot of old Motown. You'd love it."

"I'll go with you another time. I promise." I covered an exaggerated yawn with one hand. "That tequila made me tired."

"Girl, you didn't drink enough tequila to lose one inhibition." He wagged a finger at me like a gay granny. "If you're not going back to the popstar, then you need to get a life."

Chloe flicked some bills on the table for a tip, as Diego had put the tab on his card. That's how we usually split the bill, but they wouldn't let me pay anything tonight.

As Chloe pushed back her chair, she said, "Oh, Ivy's going back to the popstar tonight—she has a pillow with his face on it."

Diego arched a plucked eyebrow. "Well, at least you get to sit on Ian Pope's face."

The two of them cackled, as I steered their drunk asses out of the bar and saw them into their Uber. I hopped into my own Uber a few minutes later and headed home. As the driver left the freeway, I scooted forward. "I decided on another destination."

He turned down his classical music, Chopin, if memory served, and said. "Put it in your phone."

I eased back, phone in hand, and entered the new location on the app. Fifteen minutes later, the car pulled in front of the Santa Monica Pier, and I stepped out, pulling my jacket around my skimpy top.

I hadn't even driven past the pier since that last night with Ian—our last real night together when we made sweet love, and he told me he loved me. I ordered a Diet Coke from the same fish stand where we'd eaten our first dinner together and sat at the picnic table where his fans had swarmed him. I didn't believe torturing myself like this did any good, but I couldn't help it.

My phone rang in my pocket, and my heart skipped a beat when I saw my brother's name. Could my life get any worse if I answered it? "Hey, Matt."

"Now, that's a nice greeting. So different from your usual bitchy tone. You must be in love."

My knee started bouncing. "Sure."

"You lied to me, sis. You told me you saw Ian Pope that one night at the concert, but I saw some fan pics of the two of you. Looked all loved up, as the tabloids say."

I sighed. "Okay, I did see him a few times, but nothing happened, and he's back in England. What little we had is over."

"You're trying to tell me you didn't sleep with him?"

"Eww, I'm not answering your questions."

"Whatever, I really don't wanna know, and I heard he's back with his ex-girlfriend, anyway."

I almost dropped my phone. "I didn't hear that. Where did you read that?"

"It doesn't matter, but since you did spend some time with him, it puts you in a better position."

"Better position to what?" My hand was gripping the wooden picnic table so hard, I'd leave with slivers.

"Suggest to him that he sexually molested you, and you're ready to go public unless he pays up."

My stomach lurched. "I already told you. I'm not doing that, and I'm sure his team would go after me so hard to discredit me and ruin me, the whole scheme would collapse...and then I'd have no chance of getting him back."

Matt sucked in a quick breath, and I could almost hear the wheels turning in his head. "Are you saying there's a chance?"

"There might be." How long could I hold Matt off by dangling this prospect in front of him? At least it would make him drop the blackmail plan. "You know what Dad used to say. Every good con takes time to set up. Every mark has to be cultivated."

"You're all in now?" His voice had grown high with suspicion.

"I didn't say I was all in, but what you said about his ex, kinda pissed me off. Sparked my competitive nature." I licked my lips, tasting the salty air.

"Good, good. Dad always said you had all the elements of a successful shark. What's the plan?"

"I'll take it under consideration. Just don't do anything stupid in the meantime. If I go down or you try to go at Ian Pope on your own, you'll risk any chance, already slim, we might have."

"Deal, but I'm not giving you much time. You could be conning me as we speak."

"I could be." The edges of my phone cut into my hand as I squeezed it. "If I can swing this, will you give me that flash drive?"

"I just might." He coughed his raggedy smoker's cough. "I don't like holding anything over your head, sis. I almost forgot I had that old flash drive, but when I saw you with Ian Pope, I suddenly remembered. I wouldn't do it if I wasn't desperate. One more con for old time's sake. It'll be fun."

When I ended the call, I sat on the bench, cupping my phone in my hands. Then I lumbered to my feet, feeling about ninety-years-old, and bought a ticket for the Ferris wheel. What did Matt say? For old time's sake.

I returned home at about eleven o'clock to an empty house. Chloe and Diego must be having a good time. I left the light on for my roomie and got ready for bed. I dragged my laptop with me and searched the internet from one end to the other for any news about Ian with his ex. Had Matt just been messing with me?

I smoothed my hand over young Ian's face on the pillow and glanced at the time on my laptop again. Still too early. Maybe I should've gone to that club to eat through the hours. I switched over to YouTube to watch videos and downed more Diet Coke, although I was already so wired, I didn't need the caffeine to stay awake.

Finally, the clock hit one AM, and I reached for my phone. Jack Davies picked up on the first ring. "Ivy?"

"I'll do it."

PopWiz Instagram Post

Blind Item #12

The 1/5th singer is all set for a raging solo
comeback, but his main squeeze may be in for a
fright as the singer pours on the sleaze at this
fishy site.

Part II

London

Chapter 19

IVY

By the time the wheels of my British Airways flight hit the tarmac at Heathrow Airport, I'd convinced myself I was Mother Teresa on a mission to save a lost soul. It had taken almost the entire ten-and-a-half-hour flight to get there, though. Even after my second glass of champagne in the first-class pod, courtesy of Penny Barrett, Ian's assistant, I could still taste the betrayal on the back of my tongue.

I'd felt dirty working out the details of the arrangement with Jack, but when I'd asked Ian if he still wanted me and he told me to get on the next flight possible, I'd sloughed off all the filth and donned a halo.

I hadn't just popped up out of the blue to call him. That might've seemed a little suspicious. Seeing info about "Muse," the first single from the album, which listed my name on the writing credits, had offered me a good excuse to call him.

When he didn't answer my call, I'd died inside a little, but then I sent him a text asking him to phone me back. He called late afternoon, which translated into late night for him. Had he drunk-dialed me?

He seemed sober as we danced around with small talk, asking about each other's work, and he'd assured me his was cracking along. I thanked him for the song-writing credit, and then one thing led to another. I cried, totally from the heart, no faking needed and told him I missed him. He responded in a rough voice that he missed me, too.

That's when I asked him, and here I was.

I'd never flown first class before and thought I might be able to sleep with all the space and amenities, but that hadn't happened. Now, I rubbed sandpaper eyes and tried to smooth out my wrinkled shirt. I'd be making a pit stop in the airport bathroom to brush my teeth and hair and change from the shirt to a sweater. The sky looked dreary flying into the airport, but my mood was anything but.

I took my phone off airplane mode and texted Ian that I'd landed. I stared at the phone's display until the response bubbles popped up.

Waiting for you out front

Butterflies swarmed in my belly, and I squeezed my eyes closed. I could do this. The most important thing right now was being with him and supporting him. I could compartmentalize the other stuff just like these pods in first class separated me from the other passengers. I could do a TED Talk on compartmentalization.

Once off the plane, I hit the bathroom and fluffed myself up—teeth, hair, a little makeup, a spritz of perfume. I didn't want Ian to take one look at me and regret his decision.

I sailed through customs, and a burly guy the size of a brick wall met me in the baggage claim area. He introduced himself as Jovan, Ian's bodyguard and driver.

All I had to do was point out my bags on the carousel, and Jovan, with the serious black beard, grabbed them and hoisted them to safety, as if they were Barbie suitcases.

He reached for my carry-on, and I clamped it to my side. "I'll keep it, thanks."

"The car's just out front."

Ian probably hadn't wanted to come inside to meet me and cause a stir. Of course, now that I didn't have to hide from Matt anymore, I didn't care if the paps caught us.

Matt hadn't asked many questions about how I was finagling a monthly payment from Ian, and I wouldn't have told him the truth, anyway. It was always best to play your cards close to the vest when it came to Matt.

The sliding doors parted, and we stepped outside into the cool air, me following the brick wall. He pointed up ahead to a black sedan with tinted windows. "Car's right there."

I swallowed and kept putting one foot in front of the other. The car door swung open, and Ian stepped outside with a bouquet of yellow roses in one hand. All sense and reason evaporated, and I ran full tilt toward him.

He braced himself for my assault and didn't even stagger when I threw myself against his chest and wrapped my legs around his waist. He hugged me tightly and spun around with me in his arms, saying my name over and over. When he set me down, he cupped my jaw with one hand and rained kisses down on my wet face. What could I say? I was a sap for happy reunions.

When Jovan slammed the trunk of the car, Ian and I jumped, and then laughed. It felt good to laugh with him. We got into the sedan, which was much more reasonable than the one he'd hired in LA for the concert. No minibar.

He handed the roses to me, and I buried my face in their petals, inhaling the soft, powdery scent. But I'd rather smell him. I put the bouquet on the seat beside me, and leaned against him, my nose planted in his neck. Yep, still smelled the same—masculine, fresh, and a little spicy.

Running my hand through his short hair, I said, "You cut it."

"Do you like it? I can grow it out again."

I shook my head. "Suits you. Sets off your jaw line, even with the beard grown out."

"You're wearing your hair straight today." He wound a lock of my blown-out hair around his finger.

"Easier to keep neat on the plane. Do you want me to go wavy?" Wavy hair was nothing. I'd probably tattoo his name across my...chest, if he asked me to.

"I like it both ways." He glanced at Jovan in the front seat, tugged on my hair to pull me close, and whispered. "I like it wavy and wild when we're in bed though."

I didn't need further invitation. I snuggled next to him, hooking my leg over his, and we snogged our way out of Heathrow Airport, our hands wandering here, there, and everywhere.

By the time I came up for air, Jovan had driven us to the outskirts of the city. Peering out the window, I peppered both Ian and Jovan with questions about the area for about an hour straight until Ian tapped on the glass and said, "And that's an English cow."

I punched him in the arm. "Very funny." A sign at the side of the road caught my attention, and I bounced in my seat. "Look, Milton's cottage. You never told me you lived near Milton's cottage."

"Not sure I knew I did." He scratched his beard. "Who's Milton? Jovan?"

Jovan adjusted the rearview mirror. "That's John Milton, the writer, from I don't know...two hundred years ago. His cottage is open to tourists."

Ian sank is head in his hand. "Oh, God. Not John Milton of 'Paradise Lost.'"

"Is there another?" I put my hand to my chest and quoted, "This paradise I give thee, count it thine."

"Jovan, help me. You're going to make me take you there, aren't you?"

"That would be nice, but I can go by myself. It's close? Are we almost to your place?"

"About three kilometers."

I tilted my head. "After a ten-hour plane ride, you're gonna make me do math? What's that in miles?"

"About two. We're almost there. Are you tired? Hungry?"

Horny. "I'm a little tired. I could probably go to bed." I winked at Ian, and he gave me that crinkly-eyed smile, so I knew I'd *really* made him happy.

A short time later, Jovan drove up to a tall gate with trees on either side. He left the car idling and hopped out to enter a code set on a stone pillar on the outside of the gate. By the time he got back into the sedan, the gate had slid open to reveal a long driveway.

I sat forward in my seat and oohed and ahhed at the beautiful, Georgian-style, brick-façade house that sat at the end of the driveway. Long windows lined up symmetrically on either side of the dark green, paneled front door with fanlights at the top. I breathed out, "It's gorgeous."

"The house is great, but I bought it for the grounds. It sits on about five acres. There's a pond, stables, but I don't have any horses, and a swimming pool."

"A swimming pool in England? That's...optimistic."

Jovan parked the car and as he handled my suitcases, Ian ushered me into his home. I crept inside on my tiptoes. The modern interior was at odds with the exterior, but the furnishings were light, airy, and tasteful.

With my head tipped back, admiring the vaulted ceilings, I remarked, "You're like a real adult, living in a real adult house, and it's so sparkling clean."

"Your house is an adult house...and I have a housekeeper, Sharon, who manages everything." He took my hand and pulled me down two steps into, what I'd call a family room. As he nuzzled my neck, he said, "I want to fuck you in every room in this house. Let's start right here."

I wriggled out of his grasp. "Ugh! I'm not having sex with you in my condition. I feel gross. I've just been on a plane forever in the same clothes, breathing stale air, wrapped up in a blanket. I'd like to take a shower first."

"Then onto the master suite, m'lady." He swept me up in his arms and charged toward the stairs. He took them two at a time without breaking a sweat or breathing heavily.

He nudged open the door to a large room, masculine but not heavy or dark. The scent of the room mirrored Ian's own—woodsy, spicy, and fresh. He set me down on the patterned rug that covered the gleaming hard wood floor.

"This is our room, baby. Bathroom's that way—don't be long."

The look in his smoldering brown eyes almost had me abandoning the idea of a shower and getting down and dirty right there and then, but he gave me a little push and turned and walked out of the bedroom.

* * *

Twenty minutes later, I stepped from the bathroom into the bedroom on a rush of steam and lilac and tripped to a stop at the sight of a naked Ian splayed out on his bed, one arm behind his head, propping it up, his legs open, one leg bent, his hand stroking his massive erection, and a huge smile on his face.

My toes curled against the floor. "Is that smile for me, cowboy? Or is it for that hand between your legs?"

"Why shucks, lil' lady. It's for both." His Texas accent wasn't half bad. "So, why don't you mosey over here, saddle up, and ride ur cowboy."

That was the best invitation I'd had in a long time. I let my towel drop to the floor with a swish, and sprinted toward the bed, jumping on the foot of it, landing at his feet.

"Whoa, there, missy. I admire your enthusiasm, but you don't wanna crush the...*cojones*."

"Your Spanish is as impressive as your..." I nudged his hand aside and trailed my fingers along his stiff, smooth cock "...Western accent. You're quite multi-lingual."

"I'd like to show you how multi-lingual I can be." He stuck out his tongue and wiggled it. "And your hand feels loads better than mine."

I leaned forward to kiss his dirty mouth and gasped as I spotted the ink on his chest. He hid the tattoo quickly with his hand.

"You rat." I smacked his hand. "Remember that time I told you to keep this beautiful expanse of flesh ink-free?" I ran my hands over his pecs, which were even more chiseled since the last time I'd felt him up. Hopefully, he'd been exorcising his sorrows with exercise instead of drowning them with drink.

"Do you wanna see it?" A smile played across his pouty lips.

"I'm gonna see it, eventually, unless you plan to keep a T-shirt on in my presence."

"Definitely not doing that." He slowly inched down his hand to reveal curling green vines of ivy.

I covered my mouth as tears pricked the back of my eyeballs. "That's... beautiful and sweet. When did you get that done?"

"I designed and sketched it myself. I got it done before I knew you were coming back to me. Before that was even a glimmer of hope." As he traced the tattoo with his finger, he said, "You know how you always sleep next to me, with your head on my shoulder and your hand over my heart." He tapped the ivy tattoo. "Right here. I missed that so much, I had to put some ink on the spot."

I slid off his body and cuddled next to him, covering the tattoo with my hand, his heart beating beneath it. He was right. That's exactly where I'd placed it. "You know what I did to keep you with me?"

"Huh."

I had no intention of telling him about the Ian Pope pillow. "I stole one of your dirty T-shirts before you left."

"What?" He drew back to look in my face. "I thought one was missing. You thief."

"I wore it to bed most nights and never washed it."

He crinkled his nose. "That's disgusting, Tink, and you were worried about taking a shower after a plane ride. You didn't pack that dirty thing and bring it along, did you?" He spread his arms. "Because you've got the real thing, now."

"Ooh, and I'm glad I do." I rolled on top of him again, straddling him. Enough talk. Time to get down to business.

Stroking my thighs, he asked, "Did you change anything about yourself since I saw you?" His half-lidded eyes flicked over my body, causing a rash of tingles everywhere they lit.

"I may have done a little damage with those thirty pints of ice cream I downed when you were gone." Ugh. Too early in the relationship for those kinds of confessions. Not too early to get a stipend for deceiving him, but definitely too early for the ice cream revelation. I sucked in my gut.

His hands traced the outline of my body, and I sat still, afraid to breathe. "Mmm. Any extra calories from the ice cream must've wound up in all the right places." He squeezed my ass.

Had my ass gotten bigger? Then the squeeze turned into a caress, and thoughts of ice cream and calories and fat asses flew out of my brain. I rocked against him with encouragement.

"You gonna go cowgirl on me or should I do you like a proper missionary."

"I don't think a proper missionary would be doing the things your gonna do to me."

He grabbed my waist and flipped me onto my back. My legs flew up in the air, and he took the opportunity to slide into my wet pussy. I didn't need much physical foreplay with Ian, although we'd enjoyed plenty of that in the past. Our banter got me hot, and I could tell from his hard cock that it worked for him, too.

I sort of expected soft, sweet lovemaking from him after our time apart, but walking out of the bathroom to him fondling himself with that big... grin on his face firebombed that expectation. To show how much he missed me, he did me every which way and twice from behind.

I came—a lot. He came once—hard and wild.

All the activity after sitting for eleven hours wore me out. Spent, I released the hold my legs had around his hips, and my head lolled to the side. He kissed my neck. "I missed having you in bed."

My eyelids fluttered. So tired, but I had something important to tell him.

Sitting up next to me, he said, "Get some sleep, Tink. I'll make some dinner for later, or whenever you wake up."

As he made a move, I reached out and grabbed his wrist. "Wait. Can you stay with me until I fall asleep?"

"Absolutely." He smoothed my hair back from my face. "I'm not going anywhere, Ivy."

"Baby?" I murmured.

"Yeah?"

"I love you."

"I love you, too." He pressed his soft lips against my forehead.

Yeah, he loved me now, but he'd change his tune if he ever found out about my deal with the devil. I'd just have to make sure he never, ever found out.

Chapter 20

IAN

I couldn't wipe the smile off my face. Ivy hadn't changed a bit, still cheeky and sexy and a little bit needy. I didn't mind that last part. We clicked because we had corresponding pieces that meshed seamlessly... and I didn't mean sex, this time.

Ivy had come to me partially broken, a crack somewhere in her psyche. I saw it in her hazel eyes sometimes. In the way she clung to me. The way she tried to anticipate my needs and support me, as if I'd leave if she didn't. That just wouldn't happen. Outside of my family, I never felt so accepted and understood by someone, especially a partner.

I didn't know exactly why she changed her mind about being with me. I was afraid to dig too deeply. That characterized a big chunk of my relationship with her. She pushed back every time I tried to delve into her past.

Her mum's abandonment must've really done a number on her. Ivy hadn't even told me how old she was when her mum left, but I had the impression she was young. And the woman had never reached out to Ivy since then. Never bothered to contact her own daughter. That had to leave scars.

Her father seemed a poor substitute—unstable, gambler, probably a drinker. I yanked open the fridge door, almost pulling it off its hinges. I didn't want to be that kind of father to Thea. Ivy could barely keep the disgust from her voice when she talked about her dad.

As I grabbed the steaks out of the fridge and tossed them onto the counter, my phone rang. I checked the display before answering. "Hiya, Jack."

"Ivy get there okay?"

"She's upstairs napping. I'm going to cook dinner, and we're just gonna relax."

"Good, good."

The oven beeped for the pre-heat, and I put my phone on Speaker while I put the potatoes on the rack inside. "You sure seem interested in Ivy all of a sudden, when you were so suspicious about her before."

Jack cleared his throat. "I just realized that this might be the real thing. C'mon, mate. You do tend to jump into relationships feet first, only to get burned later. Things moved fast with Ivy, like they usually do with you. I thought it was the same old, same old. But I can see it's different with her. She seems to be a good influence on you."

I slammed the oven door. "It's mutual. I ain't the only one benefitting from our relationship. She needs me, too. That's why it works."

"Yeah, I can see that." Jack paused, which meant he was ready to change the subject. "I...uh...there's something brewing about you out there, I mean, outside of your new record, which is getting phenomenal buzz."

"You mean rumors?" The idea of new gossip swirling around me didn't have the same impact on my peace of mind as it usually did. With Ivy here, by my side, the online barbs couldn't pierce my armor. "Not interested. I haven't been on my socials in months. Whatever you're doing with official posts about my music seems to be working, so keep at it."

"That part is going great. You know about some fish website or something like that?"

"Fish? Like fishing? What are you on about?"

"Nothing. Never mind. I'll take care of it. Has Jessica tried to contact you? Made any more threats?"

I plopped the two steaks onto a cutting board. "I have her blocked every way to Sunday, so no. Is this rumor coming from her?"

"Probably. Like I said, I'll handle it. You're taking a few days off from recording?"

"Just till Ivy gets settled here. Ronnie is doing some re-mixing right now with a couple of the songs, so it's a good time to break. I've never completed an album this fast. Reminds me of the days with the boys when we done this shit on the road between concerts."

"Haven't seen you this passionate about your music since then, either. So, it's all good, mate. Vivant is thrilled."

"Well, if the record company is thrilled, I guess that's all that matters." I jabbed a fork into one of the steaks to flip it over to season the other side, pretending it was everyone at Vivant Records.

"They do pay the bills. I'll let you go. Say hello and welcome to Ivy for me."

Jack had been expressing doubts about Ivy just last month when I told him she'd broken things off with me. Seemed chuffed at the time. Now he was all Team Ivy. Better for my manager and my girlfriend to get along, anyway.

Scruffy's nails tapped on the tile floor, as he trotted into the kitchen, nose in the air. "This ain't for you, Scruffy. Maybe later."

A piercing squeal had both me and Scruffy jumping.

Ivy, another one of my T-shirts floating around her body, clapped her hands together. "Oh my, God. Is this Un-ironically Scruffy?"

"The same." I nudged the dog with my toe. "Go say hi, Scruffy." I didn't have to tell him twice.

As Ivy crouched down and snapped her fingers, his little paws scrabbled against the floor in his haste to reach her. He tried to nuzzle her between the legs.

I know exactly how you feel, mate.

Unfazed, Ivy picked him up and put him in her lap, scratching behind his ear as he looked at her adoringly.

"He's so cute and friendly." She sniffed. Either she had an allergy to Scruffy, or she was remembering her own dog.

"Oh, I see how it is." I raised a fork in the air. "I'm here, too. I'm cute and friendly."

She continued her baby talk with Scruffy. "Look at you. Such a cutie-patootie. Little loverboy. You're a good boy. Who's a good boy?"

"Uh, I'm a good boy, too." I thrust out my lower lip.

She finally looked up from cuddling the dog. "Oh, I know. You're a *very* good boy." She chucked Scruffy under the chin and then hopped up on the counter next to the raw steak and crossed her legs, the T-shirt riding up her bare thigh.

As if I could resist her. I dropped the pepper and moved in front of her. I parted her legs and slid between them. "Did you have a good nap?"

She entwined her arms around my neck and touched her nose to mine. "Quite nice, thank you."

"Is this a thing, now?" I plucked the material of my T-shirt away from her body. "You're going to steal all my T-shirts?" I sniffed the neckline. "All my *dirty* T-shirts. This from a woman who had to shower after a plane ride where she literally just sat in a seat for ten hours."

"I told you. I like the dirty ones because they smell like you." She grabbed a handful of the shirt, brought it to her nose, and inhaled.

"I'm right here. You can smell me anytime you like." When she'd pulled up the T-shirt, the hem of it rode up over her hips, exposing her bare... everything. My hands burrowed beneath the material and encircled her small waist. "You saunter in here, wearing my dirty T-shirt and no knickers. Does this mean we're starting in this room?"

"Starting? We already christened the bedroom." She jumped off the counter and tugged down the shirt. "And not in front of Scruffy."

* * *

I was excited to give Ivy a tour of the house and grounds and to show her around the village. She loved the office I set up for her on the ground floor with the French doors that opened onto the garden. The village charmed her, and she swooned at every old, decrepit building, insisting that we have lunch one day down the pub, minus the alcohol.

I still hadn't given her the bad news about that, but I was working up to it.

She'd befriended the pub owner, the flower seller, and the rector at the parish church, who talked her ear off about the history of the village and the church and the graveyard. She officially knew more people here than I did.

Just like in LA, we lived in our own little bubble with me playing tour guide, this time. I even took her to Milton's cottage, which was closed at this time of year, but I was able to arrange a private tour for her of the house and gardens. We cooked at home, went out for a few meals, watched movies in the home theater, played with Scruffy in the yard, and shagged every night.

After a few days of this idyll, we had to move into the real world, and the prospect had scared the shit out of me. We'd never functioned as a couple with work and responsibilities. Would it change anything between us?

As I went back to work in the London studio, I left her at the house alone, and she finished unpacking, set up her office, and puttered around the village, doing God knows what. She was also able to work on her book and finished it her first month here. That fact put me at ease. We seemed to fall into a comfortable pattern, and I treated recording like a nine-to-five job, making it back home for dinner every night.

As I was making good progress on the album, I decided to ask her to join me at the studio one day.

Her eyes sparkled at the invitation. "I'd love to go. Will you be able to sing a song for me? Aren't you done recording the vocals for all the songs?"

"I am, but I can record another version of 'My Duchess.' That's the song I wrote about the painting at the Getty. That's the first ballad I'm going to release as a single from the album, unless we go with 'Lost and Found.'" I raised my hand and ticked off my fingers. "'Muse' is going to be the first single, followed by 'Van at the Greek,' both mid-tempo, and then 'My Duchess.' Like I said, unless the record company lets me go with 'Lost and Found.'"

She tilted her head as she scooped some mashed avocado onto a piece of toast. "I haven't heard 'Lost and Found.' That's the one you wrote right when you came back to England, isn't it? Why wouldn't the record company want you to release that as a single?"

"I actually started writing it on the flight home from LA." Right after she dumped me. I pulled at my beard. "The lyrics are really personal. I mean I think all my lyrics this time around are personal but 'Lost and Found'...I don't know. I get into some things that my label would rather not have me put out there."

"I hope you can do what you want. I can't wait to hear them all put together. It's kind of like having a baby with you and watching it grow." She waved her hands in front of her pink cheeks. "I mean, not with you and not that I'd know."

Was that a Freudian slip? Although our connection had deep roots, Ivy always wielded a shield to keep me from getting too close. She'd kept her feelings about kids to herself. She hadn't met Thea, yet. My daughter had been at Jasper's house in Italy with Shana and Jasper, and I didn't want to rush anything, yet. I did want to introduce Ivy to my family up north, and they were anxious to meet her, but she'd hedged around the idea without committing to it. The notion seemed to terrify her for some reason, as if my family wouldn't like her.

I sat down across from her, delivering a cup of tea. "I imagine it's like writing a book. It starts with one idea or one character, and then you have a finished product that you share with other people."

"I guess, but this time I'm on the outside of the creative process looking in. I know the songs from their infancy, from a few words and phrases and hummed melodies. I'm excited to hear the end result. And I haven't been to the city, yet."

"We can spend the night. Sharon will look after Scruffy. Would you rather sightsee than sit in the studio all day?" Ivy had some kind of innate drive to explore everything, like if she didn't know the history of a place she couldn't sit back and fully enjoy it. I was just waiting for her request to check out every display in the British Museum.

"Oh, no. I'd much rather see…and listen to how you work, if I'm not going to be a distraction."

"Not at all, but you might be bored."

"I don't think so." She crunched into her toast. "I don't know anything about the process, so it'll be fun to learn."

I suddenly had a frightening vision of Ivy questioning Ronnie, the producer, and Hamza, the sound engineer, about the whole procedure. I put a finger to my lips. "As long as you're very, very quiet."

"Are there going to be any of the musicians there, or are they all done with their parts?"

"There might be a few there if Ronnie needs them to re-record anything. Dennis Foster might be by to do some guitar bits." Another scary thought slammed me in the chest. If Denny showed up today and started talking, I could be in a world of hurt. I had to get ahead of this.

"Ivy…"

She dropped her toast. "I know. If I'm going, I'd better get out of your T-shirt and into the shower. Won't be long, baby."

Before I could stop her, and let's face it, I didn't try all that hard, she'd pushed back her chair, kissed me on the ear, and dashed upstairs, with Scruffy at her heels. That mutt was obsessed with her. I knew the feeling.

I'd lost my appetite, so I cleaned up the kitchen and followed Ivy upstairs on lead feet. She was singing in the shower, not one of my songs, so I sat on the edge of the bed, pulling Scruffy into my lap. This would go better if I had the cute dog with me.

She burst into the room, tucking a towel around her body. As she glanced up, she yelped and dropped the towel. I couldn't do this with her naked.

"You scared me." She grabbed the towel, replacing it around her body, as if I hadn't seen and worshipped every inch of it, already. "Are you trying to rush me? I'll be just a few minutes. I'll put on my makeup in the car. Are you driving us in one of your fast machines, or is Jovan taking us?"

"Jovan is taking us. I thought we could spend the night at my flat there, maybe go out to dinner, or do whatever you want once I'm done." No shame in trying to butter her up before I dropped the bomb.

"Wait, wait." She tugged the towel tighter. "Flat? You have a flat in London?"

"I thought I told you about that. It's on the South Bank, just a small place in a building, an apartment. I keep it if I'm working late or there's some event that runs late in the city."

"You never told me that." She turned toward the dresser and pulled open the top drawer that contained her knickers.

She acted like it mattered. If she thought I'd kept that bit of information a secret for some reason, I'd better come clean right now about that other secret. "Uh, there are a couple of things I haven't told you, Ivy."

She froze, and her back stiffened. "That sounds ominous." She spun around, clutching a pair of silky knickers to her chest and keeping the towel wound around her body.

"It's..." I scooted Scruffy from the bed and patted the mattress beside him "...sit here."

"I'm scared."

"You don't have to be scared. It's not great news, but it shouldn't change anything between us. At least, I hope it won't."

She practically dragged her feet across the rug to the bed and sat next to me, leaving about six inches between us. Her knee bounced. "Wh-what is it? Did you discover something?"

"What? No." I shook my head and rubbed my knuckles against my beard. "I'm no longer six months sober."

Chapter 21

IVY

Relief surged through me like a warm wave. Then I crossed my hands over my galloping heart. I'd been afraid his news involved my deceit, and I'd allowed my selfishness to make me feel some kind of way. Now, I felt another kind of way.

I scooched closer to him and took his hand. "So, whaddya got right now?"

"Thirty-seven days—two days before I found out you were coming back to me, so even before I knew you'd changed your mind about being with me, I stopped. I mean, I stopped pretty quickly. It happened on two different nights, but I totally fucked my sobriety, and I'm back at the starting gate."

"Congratulations on thirty-seven days of sobriety." I brought his hand to my lips and kissed the LII tattoo on the back of it. "I know you've probably been beating yourself up, but don't. You know how this goes. W-was it bad?"

"Like black-out drunk bad?" He laced his fingers with mine. "The first time wasn't pretty, but I didn't go out in public. Didn't go out the second time, either, which involved about four and a half glasses of whiskey, impaired but not totally off my face."

"Four glasses of whiskey would have me on my ass."

"One glass of whiskey would have you on your ass." He flicked a piece of hair from my cheek. "And that's a good thing, but I could tell my tolerance was off, so that's a good thing, too."

I put my arm around his shoulders, broad enough for me to lean on, but now he needed to lean on me. I squeezed him close. "Did you call your sponsor?"

"I did all that." He took my hand dangling over his chest and pressed his lips against my palm. "I don't want you to think it was because you broke up with me. I don't want to put that pressure on you. And I'm not making excuses for myself. It's always up to me. That decision is always on me."

"Was it Thea?"

He jerked his head up. "Why do you ask that? Who told you that?"

Oh shit. Jack had told me, but I didn't want Ian to know I was talking to Jack about him behind his back. That might lead to other discoveries. "You sort of told me. I mean, you didn't say you'd fallen off the wagon over it, but I could tell you were bummed about her connection with Shana's husband, Jasper."

"Yeah, fuck me." He sank his head in his hands. "I was over there, and Thea called Jasper *Daddy* right in front of me. Wrecked me."

My heart ached for him, and I rubbed a circle on his back. "I can't pretend to know what it's like to have kids or even a family, for that matter, but I'm sure that's not uncommon with stepparents. And it's better that Thea have a stepdad like Jasper than some total asshole, right? You want her surrounded by loving people."

"Of course, yeah. I'm just being selfish."

"That's not selfishness. That's human. And you are one of those, despite all your many talents. Just think, we can now celebrate your two-month sobriety together, and we can celebrate your however many days sobriety right now." I crawled into his lap, discarding my towel and straddling his hips because, well, sex made everything better, right?

* * *

On the eighty-minute drive into the city, Ian talked about his music and the album. His infectious enthusiasm practically bubbled out of him, and I prayed so hard that the record would exceed all his expectations. He needed this so badly—more than he needed me. He just didn't know it.

When we got to the recording studio, the charged atmosphere settled my fears about the fate of the album. The guys in the studio had the swagger of pros who knew they had something special.

While Ian talked to Ronnie about a few issues and the plan for the afternoon, I picked Hamza's brain about what he did as a sound engineer. Ian kept sliding glances at Hamza until he said, "Just blink twice, Hamza, if you need to be rescued."

I stuck my tongue out at Ian, and Hamza answered, "No, mate, really. Never had no one so interested in my job before. Ivy makes me feel like a right legend."

"Thing is, she really wants to know." Ian winked at me.

I smiled back, but I had a nauseous feeling in the pit of my stomach. Ian treated me so well, better than anyone had ever treated me before. I felt so safe in that man's arms, and he took his care of me very seriously. He couldn't even lie to me about his relapse, and I know it had pained him to tell me about it. And what was I doing to him? How could I keep this deception going any longer?

But the lie was keeping me safe, too. Keeping both of us safe.

Ronnie pulled out a chair next to his, facing a board of lights and controls that looked as if it belonged to a spacecraft. "Sit here, Ivy. You can ask me as many questions as you like. My job is much more important than Hamza's."

"Bro." Hamza threw a balled-up, greasy paper napkin at Ronnie. "We'll ask her at the end of the session."

"Do not put me on the spot." I wrapped my arms around Ian from the back, poking my chin between his shoulder blades. "What are you going to sing, baby?"

"I'm going to record 'Lost and Found' again. I'll play the piano, and we're just waiting for Dennis and his guitar."

On cue, a tall guy with scraggly blond hair and a wispy goatee, tats clawing their way up his neck, burst into the room. "Sorry I'm late, lads. Bit of a sesh last night."

Ian's back grew rigid beneath my touch, and I figured Dennis's sesh included copious amounts of booze. Must be difficult for any addict to navigate the perilous temptations of the music world.

But when Ian turned around, a smile stretched across his face. "No problem, mate. We're gonna record 'Lost and Found' again. I'll be on piano, since Giles isn't here, and I'm not calling him. This is just a one-off I'm doing for my girl. This is Ivy. Ivy, Dennis."

Dennis's long fingers wrapped around my hand. "Oh, nice to meet the missus. We been hearing nothing but Ivy this, Ivy that."

"I hope followed by good things." I disentangled my hand from Dennis's.

"Nothing but good. It's quite sickening, actually." Dennis nudged Ian in a way I didn't like. I hoped the guy could at least play guitar.

"Are we ready?" Ian smacked Dennis on the back. "Let me just get some water."

As Ian went to the back of the room to get a bottle of water, I settled beside Ronnie, excitement fizzing in my veins. Ian placed some water in front of me on his way to the recording booth where Dennis had already taken a chair with his guitar. Ian sat in front of the piano and ran his fingers across the keys.

Ronnie gave them some directions, and then Ian started to play the opening chords of the song, which I hadn't heard before. When he began singing, his rich baritone voice gave me chills, and the personal lyrics cut me like a razorblade on the wrist. By the second verse of the song, his usually smooth, liquid tone roughened around the edges, and the emotion in his voice carved a hollow in my heart.

His feelings kaleidoscoped across his face, and he squeezed his eyes closed as if to reach deeper into his soul. When he hit the achingly beautiful high notes in the chorus, it was like he peeled open his chest to expose his heart, and the pulse in my throat throbbed in response.

The air in the studio had stilled, the performance hypnotizing all of us. Without realizing it, I had pushed back my chair, my body inclining toward the recording booth where Ian sang not only his life, but mine, too. His words evoked feelings in me that I'd successfully buried for years.

I stepped off the dais and floated toward the glass separating the booth from the studio, as if in a dream. I flattened my hands against the window, whether in an attempt to make him stop or to drown myself in the sensations, I didn't know. Tears rolled down my face, unabated, and dripped off my chin.

The song ended on a whisper, and I couldn't move, couldn't breathe. Someone sniffled behind me.

When Ian opened his eyes, his gaze met mine through the glass. He covered his face with his hands, and his shoulders shook. I had to go to him. Running my arm across my nose, I clawed at the door handle to the booth and yanked it open.

Ian's head jerked up, and he rushed to me and wrapped his arms around me. We clung to each other, while Dennis sat in the corner, his hand pressed against the strings of his guitar, his head bowed.

Ronnie's voice over the speaker in the booth finally cut through the tension. "That's our version, and if the record company doesn't release it as the lead single, they can fuck right off."

✷ ✷ ✷

After the session, we'd walked to an Indian restaurant a few blocks from the studio and sat across from each other, sipping mango lassi. I ripped off a piece of naan. "I take it the original version of 'Lost and Found' didn't sound like the one you just recorded."

"Not even close." He reached across the table and stroked my cheek with the back of his hand. "You should've been in the studio with me for every song."

I threw up my hands. "It wasn't me. That was all you, baby."

"Inspired by you—like everything I do."

I didn't deserve him. I didn't deserve any of it. "You know what I think it was?"

"Huh."

"I think telling me about your relapse sort of brought it all home to you again. You ushered those feelings to the surface and tapped into them when you sang the song."

"Very interesting, Fraulein." He raised his hands and drummed his fingers together. He'd become a student of my deflection methods.

"Are you channeling Sigmund Freud? You know, there's a Freud Museum in Hampstead where he lived the last year of his life after he left Vienna."

"Spare me." He jabbed his fork into a piece of lamb and pointed it at me. "You know what my therapist says about you?"

I pressed a napkin to my face. "You told your therapist about me?"

"Of course. Tell me you've never been in therapy without telling me you've never been in therapy."

I had my reasons for avoiding therapy, but now I wanted in on my second-hand analysis. Hunching forward, I asked, "What did he say about me?"

"I don't think you're gonna like it."

"Now you really have to tell me. Don't say he ordered you to leave me." I took a gulp of water. If the therapist had any common sense at all, that's exactly what he'd tell Ian.

"If he had, I'd fire him." Ian fussed around his plate, obviously regretting he'd ever mentioned his therapist, but when he glanced at my face, he realized I'd become a dog with a bone. He sighed. "He said you use sex as a way to form a deep bond with me without actually letting me in, emotionally."

Damn, that therapist was good. "That's just ridiculous. He can't remote analyze me." I peered at Ian's face in the flickering light from the candle on the table. "Do you think he's right? You don't think we're emotionally close."

He stretched out his hand and toyed with my fingers. "I feel like you're a piece of me. That without you, I'm not whole. Does that sound like a clichéd song lyric?" He shrugged. "It's true, and I would call that emotionally close. Do I think you use sex sometimes to avoid topics you don't want to discuss? Yeah, but, um, I'm not complaining about the sex."

"Well, that's a relief. At least he didn't tell you to dump me."

"Never gonna happen."

Turned out, Ian's flat was not within walking distance of the restaurant, so we took a taxi to a high-rise building on the south side of the Thames, west of the Tower Bridge. We stepped into a swanky lobby after Ian entered a code at the front door. When we got into the elevator, he entered another code as he pushed the button for the 32nd floor.

Although the elevator ride offered a smooth ascent, I braced my hand against the mirrored wall of the car. "How often do you stay here?"

"Not too often. When I work late or if there are events to attend in the city."

The elevator doors whisked open onto a floor that I could already tell just housed Ian's flat. Hadn't he told me this place wasn't very big? He lied. He opened the door for me, and when I stepped across the threshold, a chill dripped down my spine. The amazing view of the river drew me to the window, and I zigzagged around modern furniture pieces to get there. "Nice view. Horrible décor. I'm pretty sure the designer who furnished your house didn't do this place."

"I bought it furnished." He raised his eyebrows. "You don't like it?"

"The setting is lovely, but it's so cold in here."

"I haven't been here for a month. I'll turn on the heat." He grabbed our overnight bags and veered down a dark hallway.

"I didn't mean the temperature, although it is freezing." I hugged myself and rubbed my arms. "I mean the atmosphere. No warmth or humanity."

He returned to the room, and his arms replaced mine. "It's just for one night, Tink. I have a few things to finish in the studio tomorrow morning. You can sleep in or go sightseeing. I hear there's a good exhibit on the Silk Roads at the British Museum. Then we can have lunch and do something else before Jovan takes us back."

"I can manage one night here. Can I have some water?"

He pointed at the kitchen. "I think there are bottles in the fridge. I need to make a few calls."

I wandered into the kitchen, which sported every modern appliance known to mankind. It all sparkled with newness. I pulled open the fridge door and drew back sharply when I saw an unopened bottle of champagne cooling its heels inside. Did Ian know this existed?

I wanted to grab it and toss it out the window, but I might kill someone from this height, and then the police would have another reason to arrest me. Instead, I snatched some water and slammed the door shut.

Ian's voice from the other room stopped, and I called out. "Baby?"

"Did you find the water?" He poked his head into the kitchen, his phone clutched in his hand, his gaze shifting to the bottle I held up. "What do you need? I have one more call to make. Also, your phone buzzed in your bag out there."

I jerked my thumb over my shoulder. "There's a bottle of champagne in the refrigerator."

"Oh, yeah. Right." He squeezed the back of his neck. "It's leftover, not new. You can have some, if you like."

Digging one hand into my hip, I said, "I won't drink in front of you. Should I open it and pour it down the drain?"

He whistled through his teeth. "That's a very expensive bottle of bubbly. Take it home and give it to someone. Don't worry. I'm not going to creep in here in the dead of night and pop a bottle."

"Ian, is this where you fell off the wagon? This...place?"

"It is. Don't worry. It's not gonna happen again." He held up his hands, crossing one finger over another. "I'm not even tempted by that champagne in there. Had forgotten its very existence."

No wonder this flat gave off bad vibes. "Yeah, I know. I'm not worried about that. You said my phone rang?"

"Yeah." I followed him into the other room and slipped my phone from my purse, as he started another call. I glanced at Chloe's name on the display and then checked for a text message. Nothing. Must not be that important, and I was too tired for Chloe's drama right now.

With Ian still on the phone, I crept down the hallway to the rooms in the back. I found the master suite with our bags in the corner. The plush, white carpet cushioned my steps as I walked to the window. Who had white carpet?

I pushed aside the drapes and pressed my hands against the cool glass. Lights blinked on the bridge below, and the gray mist clinging to the banks of the river seemed to have seeped into this building and swirled its way up to the 32nd floor.

As I turned, a glint of light at the end of the window ledge caught my attention. A short, squat whiskey glass glared back, the amber liquid in the bottom daring me. I clenched my hands, hot anger coursing through my body. An urge to do violence thumped in my veins again, just as it had when I saw the champagne bottle. My hands itched to pick up the glass and smash it against the blank, white wall. What had he been drinking? Whiskey or champagne? Both? He'd mentioned whiskey for the one occasion, but hadn't said anything about the other relapse, the worse one.

"Ivy?" Ian sailed into the room, still high from the studio session and whatever conversations he just had with Ronnie and his business manager.

I pinched the rim of the heavy glass between my fingers and turned around. "You left this here."

He blinked. "That you can toss down the drain."

"Is there a half-full bottle of this around here somewhere?" I cranked my head back and forth as if looking for it in this room.

"I dumped that." Cocking his head to the side, he asked, "Are you alright?"

I wrapped my hand around the glass and squeezed. "I just hate seeing evidence of your...downfall."

His eyebrows shot up to his hairline. "Downfall, is it? That's a bit harsh. What happened to you're only human, Ian, and now we can celebrate your two-month sobriety together?" A smile twisted his lips as he took a light tone, but it didn't reach his eyes.

"It just makes me angry—not with you. It's like I'm hating on inanimate objects." My hand sliced through the air. "And I don't like this place."

He strode toward me, snapping the wire of tension that vibrated between us. He took me by the shoulders and skimmed his fingers along the sides of my neck. "You're right. It's rubbish. I'll get rid of it."

"No." I shook my head. "I'm being...I'm just tired."

He cuddled me close and stroked my hair. "Who tried to call you? Was it Chloe?"

"Yeah, but she didn't leave a message."

"Maybe you'll feel better talking to her."

"I'll call her later." I waved at the bed, which at least looked comfortable. "I'm going to watch TV. Is that alright with you?"

"Do what you want, baby. I have a few things to finish, and then I'll join you. Find a movie." He took the glass from my hand and turned to leave. "Oh, there's a Jacuzzi tub in the bathroom if you wanna relax."

I muttered to his back, "Of course, there is."

Chapter 22

IVY

'd been half hoping that Ian would join me in the Jacuzzi. Maybe all I needed to exorcise the bad juju of this place was a good fuck. This flat had done a number on me, plucking all my strings. Why wouldn't Ian have a bachelor pad in London? The past month, he'd made the ninety-minute trip back and forth only because I was at the house. Of course, he wouldn't do that all the time.

The news of his relapse earlier today had affected me more than I'd admitted to him...or myself.

I studied the skin on my hands, wrinkled like a prune. I couldn't wait for Ian any longer. I shut off the jets and flicked the drain open with my big toe. I shivered as I stood up to grab my towel from the cold rack. I'd have to speak to management about installing towel warmers in this dump.

As I stepped from the tub, Ian entered the bathroom, naked, because of course. "Damn, I was just going to climb in with you."

I wiggled my puckered fingers in his face. "I couldn't stay in another minute."

He moved toward me and took the edges of the towel. "Let me help you." He trailed the towel down my chest and rubbed my tits, cupping them from beneath and massaging them.

I arched my back in encouragement and whispered, "Twice in one day. You think you can handle it?"

He blew a puff of air from his lips. "That was hours ago." He swiped the towel between my legs and then dropped it, replacing the terrycloth with his fingers. He teased my clit, bringing me to the brink of my climax. My knees weakened, and I dug my fingers into his shoulders.

I took me by the waist and pulled me toward the vanity, facing the mirror. He bent me over the counter and growled, "Spread your legs."

The command in his voice made me wetter than the water in the tub. I obeyed, and he moved behind me, stroking my ass with his hard cock. With his voice rough with desire, he said, "Look at me in the mirror."

I raised my gaze to the glass, and his brown eyes smoldered as they sought mine. As we locked onto each other, he spread me open, easing his cock into my pussy. I lunged forward with his first thrust, and he reached around and shaped my breast with his hand. He pebbled my nipple with his thumb and forefinger, withdrawing and then plunging into me again, lifting me off my feet.

He slowed down. "Argh, I can't last when you're looking at me like that." He slid his hand from my boob to my pussy and found my clit still throbbing from his previous attentions.

Talk about not lasting. Two flicks later, I was coming all over his hand and grinding my ass against him. He exploded inside me, and squeezed his eyes closed for a few seconds, the only time we broke our visual contact.

When he finished, he stepped back, creating a separation between our bodies, and ran a finger down my spine to my tailbone. "I like watching us fuck. We need to get a mirror for our bedroom."

"Bow-chicka-wow-wow. Maybe a round bed and red velvet hangings while we're at it, Duke Hammer." I laugh-snorted at my own joke, and he laughed with me, picking me up from behind as I kicked my legs in the air.

For the first time since entering this bachelor pad hellhole, the stiff tension between us dissolved. Ian's therapist obviously didn't understand the therapeutic value of a solid shag.

* * *

I survived the night, safe in Ian's arms, and the following morning, he got up early to work out in the gym downstairs. He returned to me still lounging in bed like a lady of leisure.

As he finished dressing, he said, "I'm going to pick up something to eat on the way to the studio. Do you want me to come back here first and drop off something for you."

"I can figure it out. I'm not that hungry."

"You can use the gym, if you like."

"Pass." I plucked my phone from the charger and scrolled through my email. "I might just check out that exhibit at the British Museum you mentioned."

He gave me a thumbs-up. "That's a great idea. Explore on your own."

"I see what you're doing." I narrowed my eyes. "It's a big museum. I'm sure there are many visits in our future."

"Great." He grabbed his shoes. "Did you call Chloe?"

"Not yet. It's about one in the morning for her. I'll give it another nine or ten hours."

He sat on the edge of the bed to tie his shoes and cranked his head over his shoulder. "You know, I selfishly never thought about it, but you must be a little homesick."

Flicking back the covers, I crawled toward him and balanced my chin on his shoulder. "Wherever you are is home to me—even in this God-awful townhouse."

"I mean, if you want to invite Chloe out here for a visit and your friend Diego, that's cool. I'll pay for their airfare, and they can even stay in this…" He waved his arm around the luxuriously appointed bedroom with views of the Thames "…God-awful place."

"That's sweet." I kissed him on the side of his neck. "I'll ask them."

"No, you won't. I'd have better luck calling Chloe myself and inviting her."

"What does that mean?" I asked.

"You never take anything from me, not even a coat, which you definitely need for our weather, and you wouldn't be in our weather if it weren't for me."

His words hit like darts to the chest, and I fell back against the pillows. I didn't know how much longer I could continue taking money from him...or his record company. Maybe he wouldn't care if I told him. He didn't seem all that thrilled with his label, Vivant, anyway. I tickled his back with my toes. "My coat's fine, and I'll ask Chloe and Diego if they want to visit. Maybe *they'll* come to the British Museum with me."

"Brilliant idea."

He kissed me goodbye, making a fuss over how I'd get to and from the museum and where, how, and when I'd get breakfast. He left me his credit card on the dresser with instructions to use it for everything. As if I needed to buy anything at the British Museum.

After he left in a flurry, I stood frozen in the middle of the cavernous sitting room, wearing his T-shirt, staring out the window at the gray expanse of sky. I had to tell him the truth. He deserved that.

The payments had shut Matt down. He wasn't threatening me or Ian anymore, but if I admitted everything to Ian, Matt would have nothing to hold over me. Ian would tell me to hit the road, and Matt could do his worst.

How hard would it be to spend fifteen years in federal prison for bank fraud? I'd get a lot of writing done there. Pretty sure they had a gym, library, maybe even a frozen yogurt machine.

Any scandal Ian faced from his association with me would fade away after a month or two. Hell, it might even increase sales for him. And all it would cost me was...everything.

I spun around and stomped to the bedroom, pulling Ian's T-shirt from my head. Maybe I could wait until the first single dropped. Everyone would be so hyped about Ian's new music, they wouldn't notice that his girlfriend...ex-girlfriend was a felon. Of course, it might leak that his record company was paying that girlfriend to...sleep with him. *Oh, that would be bad.*

I showered and changed into the clothes I brought with me. Ian had left his credit card next to my jewelry on the dresser. I ignored it as I put on a couple of rings, including my mom's engagement ring she'd left behind when she bailed on us. When I reached for my gold hoop earring, I knocked it from the dresser, and it flew into the air.

After scouring the floor with no luck, I dropped to my hands and knees to get a closer look. I peeked under the dresser and then crawled to the bed. The duvet had slipped down on this side, and I flipped it up to peer beneath the bed.

The earring had landed next to a bit of clothing, and I snagged it with my finger. I dragged the item from under the bed and held it up in the air. Screaming, I dropped the pair of silky black women's underwear.

* * *

Silk road, silk panties. I stared at the decorative sheath and dagger from ancient Korea inside the glass, and violent thoughts gamboled across my brain. I'd never asked him about the champagne in the fridge. He told me he drank whiskey. Who had drunk the champagne? The owner of the thong?

"No way."

"Excuse me, luv?" The old woman standing next to me eyed me up and down from behind her giant glasses.

I gestured at the dagger. "Just hard to believe somebody would use something as beautiful as this to slit someone's throat. That would have to be a really special murder."

The woman's eyes widened, almost bug-like behind her glasses, as she sidled away from the crazy Yank.

Ian was not the cheatin' kind. Despite his overall gorgeousness and the nearly naked underwear ad I discovered he'd done a few years back, I had never felt one ounce of jealousy or suspicion about him with other women. We had phenomenal sex. Nobody cheated on that.

I tried to brush aside the little voice that whispered in my ear that I hadn't been around for about a month. I hadn't been around when he fell off the wagon. Hadn't I read that he'd had sex in the bathroom of a club with some random woman during his drinking days?

My phone buzzed in my pocket, and I pulled it out in front of the bronze Buddha. My heart skipped a beat when I saw the text from Ian asking if I was having a good time and telling me the session was running over, and he'd be later than expected. My finger hovered over the display and then I shoved the phone back into my jacket. Was he going to be late because he was fucking someone else in London?

I shook my head. I was just spiraling now. There had to be an innocent explanation for the panties. He had two sisters living in England; maybe one had borrowed the flat. I'd ask him when I came back. Just clear the air.

Unlike me, he didn't lie.

My stomach growled as I wandered through the display of the spice route, which detailed all the different foods that were introduced around the world thanks to the Silk Road. So, when I reached the end of the display room, I headed downstairs to the café.

I'd been too numb this morning to stop for breakfast and too distracted to think about lunch. I entered the half-empty café and stood in a short line to order. I decided on some soup and a cup of tea, and smacked down Ian's credit card to pay for the eight-pound tab. Let him pay for my lunch for putting me through this agony.

When I picked up my soup, I headed for a corner and settled on the plastic chair. I pulled my phone from my pocket and saw that Ian had texted me a question mark. I pressed my finger on his previous text and gave him a thumbs up.

I slurped a few spoonfuls of soup and checked the time on my phone. I counted backward on my fingers and figured it was late enough to call Chloe. I needed a sounding board.

Holding my breath, I tapped her number. *Please answer.*

Three rings later. "Ivy, what the fuck? It's the middle of the night here. Wait, are you alright?"

"I'm fine." I almost sobbed at the sound of Chloe's irritated voice. "And it should be about six AM there, not the middle of the night."

"It feels like the middle of the night."

I held the phone away from my ear as rustling, smacking noises came over the line. "Chloe?"

Chloe whispered, "Be right back, babe."

I asked, "Where are you going?"

Chloe, her voice louder now, snapped back. "Not you. Someone's in my bed."

"Not Trent."

"God, no. It's Cryptobro."

"I thought you…" I closed my eyes and took a sip of my tea "…never mind." I couldn't keep up with Chloe's revolving door of men since she and Trent broke up.

"Are you calling me because I called you earlier? I didn't want to text or leave a message, but you didn't have to call me back so early in the morning."

"Yes and no." I chewed the corner of my lip. "I mean, you go first. Why'd you call? And why didn't you send me a text message?"

Chloe gasped. "You saw it, didn't you?"

"Saw what?" Chloe couldn't possibly know about the black undies.

"That blind item on PopWiz."

I poured more hot water over my teabag. "The who on what?"

"PopWiz. You know that account on Instagram that posts blind items about celebrities."

"I have no idea what you're talking about, Chloe. That's why you called?"

Chloe cleared her throat. "I have something to tell you, and I didn't think it was appropriate for a text message—or a voicemail."

I pressed a hand to my chest. "You're getting married."

"No!"

"You're pregnant."

"No!" Chloe clicked her tongue like a schoolmarm. "This isn't about me. It's about you."

"Me?" My voice squeaked.

"Okay, I'm just gonna say it." Chloe took a deep breath, apparently marshaling her nerves. "Remember, I told you I was joining that exclusive dating site—BlueFin."

"I remember. Better class of guys, yada, yada." I stirred my soup, wondering when Chloe was going to get to the point and what it all had to do with me and PopWiz. Had that site posted something about me?

Chloe continued. "I got accepted."

"Congratulations. Did you match with Austin Butler? Why is this about me?"

"I'm getting to that. I created my profile, and there's a chat you can join with other female members—and boy was there chatter."

"About what?" Chloe's words began to permeate my brain and take shape. Celebrity gossip. Celebrity dating site. My palms got sweaty, and my hand shook when I picked up my teacup.

"About Ian Pope. He's on BlueFin."

Chapter 23

IVY

I plunked my cup back in the saucer, and hot tea sloshed over the sides, burning my fingers. "Th-that's not possible."

"It is possible, babe. I saw the profile. Has his picture and everything."

"Could it be old?" Had he met black panties on BlueFin?

"No. I mean, the account *could've* been created at an earlier date, but the messages are current."

"What messages?" I pushed my soup bowl away, dug my elbow into the table, and sank my forehead to my palm.

"This is where it gets bad."

"*Gets* bad?" My knees were bouncing up and down so hard, I was shaking the whole table.

"He's been sending private messages to members about...stuff."

"Stuff? You mean sex?" I laughed, but it came out more like a croak from my dry throat. "I don't believe it, Chloe. That's not Ian. Have you already forgotten about the dick pics? It's a setup."

"Oh my God. Has he been peeing on you?"

"What? No! What are you talking about?"

"Sex in public?"

"No, I mean, does doing it in the backyard count?" I dragged a hand through my hair. "Why are you asking me these questions?"

"Those are the kinds of things he's suggesting in his messages...kinky shit."

"You mean kinky pee." I smacked my hand on the table and laughed. "This is as fake as Duke Hammer's dick."

A couple two tables over, studying their phones, jerked their heads up in unison. They must understand English.

Chloe huffed. "Duke's dick isn't fake. I read all about him after that fiasco. Quite the esteemed career."

"I don't believe any of it, Chloe. His ex has some kind of vendetta against him. This stinks."

"He's never given you any reason to doubt him? Hiding his phone, working late."

"N-no." I sealed my lips and proceeded to shred a napkin to bits in my lap.

"You don't sound so confident anymore." Chloe whistled. "Hang on. Why'd you call me at five o'clock in the morning?"

"Six."

"Spill."

"Ian confessed to me that he relapsed when we were apart—but just twice. He's back on track." Now it was my turn to beat around the bush.

"Okay, well that's not unusual, and that's why you went out there. You suspected he might be spiraling without you. He's good now?"

"Doing great." I gathered the mangled pieces of napkin and dumped them on the table. "We went to the recording studio yesterday, which is why I'm at the British Museum."

"You're at the British Museum right now? Did you see the mummies?"

"No, I'm here for some exhibition." I drew in a long breath. "Anyway, after the session yesterday, we went to his bachelor pad in London."

"He has a bachelor pad? Uh-oh. Fuck-buddy central."

"Stop. But, yeah, it's stark and modern and sterile. Anyway, I found a puddle of whiskey in a glass in the bedroom and a bottle of champagne in the fridge, so I put two and two together, and he confirmed that's where he relapsed."

"Alright. Where is this going, Ivy? Is that where he asked to pee on you?"

"Enough with the pee." I rubbed my chin. Did I want to open the floodgates here? "After I left this morning, I also found a pair of women's black panties under the bed."

Silence echoed over the line. "Chloe?"

"That cheating SOB. He boozed it up, banged some chick, and now he's on BlueFin making perverted requests."

"I don't think so, Chloe. I *know* he's not on BlueFin. That's not his real profile."

"And the panties? That's the oldest tell in the book of cheating."

"There has to be a good explanation for it, Chloe. Everything between us is so wonderful. He turned over the office in his home to me, he cooks dinner sometimes, he sang me the most beautiful, heart-breaking song yesterday, we screw like bunnies. It's perfect, except..."

Chloe coughed. "Except for the cold bachelor pad, the panties under the bed, and the account on BlueFin."

"That's not what I was going to say." I clutched the phone to my ear. "Except for my deception. How can I even give him the third degree about the underwear when I'm keeping such a terrible secret from him?"

"Just because you're taking a little money on the side—to benefit both of you—doesn't give him license to cheat."

"I just don't think he is."

"Is that why you called me? So you could defend Ian and convince yourself."

"Maybe. I'm going to give him a chance to explain everything, and maybe I should explain everything to him, too."

"That's a bad idea."

"Weren't you the one telling me before I left that I should confess all?" I took a small sip of my lukewarm tea.

"That was before I found out he was a cheating rat bastard."

"You always believe the worst of him. You even thought the dick pics were his." I put my hand to my throat, as the rest of Chloe's words surfaced in my brain. "What were you talking about earlier when you mentioned that PopWiz account?"

"That's what I'm saying, Ivy. You may be in La-La Land, but the word is already on the street that Ian has a profile on BlueFin. PopWiz reported it in a blind item."

The half bowl of soup I drank sloshed in my stomach. Not again. The online attacks against Ian had revved up, and the timing couldn't be worse. "If it's in PopWiz, it must be true. Do you hear yourself right now? It's just garbage."

"It might be, but if you think outing yourself to Ian right now with your past is a good idea, you're still in La-La Land. You'll both be prime fodder for online attacks."

"I'm going to get to the truth today. If it turns out this is another scheme against him, do you think you could help again?"

"If it turns out he's not a cheating rat bastard, I'll see what I can do. I just want to make sure you're okay, Ivy. You're in love for the first time, and I want it to work out for you." Chloe sputtered. "Oh, wait. I have more news."

"Oh, God." I patted my chest. "I don't think I can take any more. What next? Ian Pope wanked off in front of Princess Kate?"

Chloe laughed. "This one doesn't have anything to do with Ian, at least not directly. Wait for it." She paused dramatically. "I got a camera into Matt's apartment."

"What?" I shot up straight in my seat. "What were you doing in Matt's apartment? Did you break in?"

Chloe snorted. "I didn't have to break in. You know Matt's always had a thing for me."

"Oh, God, no. You didn't sleep with him, did you?" I covered my eyes as if to block the image from my mind.

"No, although your brother is seriously hot. You know, his eyes are greener than yours, much prettier, and what he lacks in work ethic, he makes up for in the gym. Built like a…"

"Okay, okay. What excuse did you give him for dropping by, and what are we going to do with a camera? Wait, are you watching my brother in his apartment?"

"I do check in once in a while, and you don't wanna know what he's up to in there. Anyway, I went to his place to give him your dad's watch. You meant to do that, right? Told him I was cleaning house and found it."

"Then, what? He went to the bathroom, and you installed CCTV in his apartment?"

Chloe scoffed. "It's just one of those little stick-on cameras. He'll never find it."

"You're trying to see if he takes out the flash drive that contains my guilt and what, strokes it, licks it? I appreciate the effort, but what's the plan?"

"You're going to call him all in a panic one day—let me know the day and time—and ask him to make sure the flash drive is safe and secure."

"He'll just tell me it is and hang up."

"Give him a reason to worry. He checks on the flash drive, I catch its hiding place on camera, and then we go in for the kill. *Then* I break into his place and steal it, or I make the big sacrifice and sleep with him, before I roofie him and nab the drive."

Drumming my fingers on the table, I asked, "Wouldn't you roofie him first and *then* steal the drive? Why would you need to sleep with him?"

"Just to make sure he's good and drowsy."

"You wouldn't roofie someone. That's illegal, and it's giving me the ick."

"Alright, alright. I'll just wear him out in bed."

"Now you're really giving me the ick." I tugged on my earring. I must be losing it because this plan of hers sounded like it might work. "If we're gonna do this, you're not doing the hard part on your own. I'll fly out there and help you get the flash drive. I can find another way to distract him, or you can break in while I take him outside."

The adrenaline pumping through my system fueled an optimism about my predicament I hadn't felt since I accepted Jack's offer. We could do this. I could save myself, save Ian, and we could really be together with no secrets between us. Not that he'd ever kept any secrets from me. He'd been painfully open with me from the start. And I'd done nothing but lie.

"You like the plan?" Chloe couldn't keep the I-told-you-so out of her voice.

"I do like it, Chloe. I think it could work. Then I could be with Ian without any fears or reservations."

"Just cool your tits. Before I go to any effort to clear your path to happily ever after with the popstar, you need to make sure he's not a cheating rat bastard."

Chapter 24

IAN

I checked my phone for about the hundredth time on the ride from the studio to my place. Anxiety nibbled at the ends of my nerves. Why had Ivy been silent today? She could've been so wrapped up in the exhibition she hadn't had time to respond to my texts properly. I'd expected her to bombard me with pictures of...silk, or whatever she was seeing at the museum.

I tapped my fingers on the stack of boxes next to me. I'd gotten so worried about Ivy wandering around London in her thin jacket, I'd called Sarah to bring some coats to the studio for her. Of course, I didn't have a clue what size Ivy wore, but Sarah was able to figure it out from pictures and my description.

When the car dropped me off at my building, I balanced the three boxes in my arms and rode up the elevator, jabbing the button for the 32nd floor over and over, as if the repeated motion would make it go faster. I burst through the door and dropped the boxes straight to the floor.

Ivy, standing at the window in the dark, twisted her head over her shoulder. In the muted light, her face was a pale oval, and her eyes huge.

"Thank God, you're home." I ate up the distance between us in two long strides and gathered her in my arms, squeezing, just to make sure she was real.

She squeaked, and I loosened my hold. "That's some greeting."

"Why are the lights out? Where have you been all day?" I ran my hands down her arms. "I was worried."

"Worried? I was at the museum." She scooted out of my embrace and flicked on the recessed lighting over the sofa, keeping her hand on the light switch in case she changed her mind and decided to cast us into darkness again.

"I expected some texts and pictures of the exhibit. I kept looking at my phone and—nothing." I crossed my arms over my chest. "You took The Tube, didn't you?"

"I did. I enjoyed it." She tipped her chin toward the boxes. "What's in there?"

"Coats. That's another thing. You were running around London all day in that ridiculous jacket, and it's freezing outside. I had my stylist bring some coats to the studio."

"Are you nuts? Who does that?" She gave the boxes a side-eye. "I can shop for my own coat."

I cocked my head and studied her closed-off face. Looked like she'd had a bad day. "Well, you weren't doing it, and Sarah had some stuff to show me for the upcoming tour, anyway. From what I described, she was able to figure out a size for you. I picked out three coats, so you can return what doesn't fit. Do you want to try them on?"

"Um, sure." She finally gave up her dominion over the light switch and moved toward the back rooms. "Bring the coats and follow me to the bedroom. I-I have something to show you in there, anyway."

I quirked my eyebrows up and down. "Tinkerbell, I've seen it all before." I couldn't raise a smile from her, so I gathered the boxes in my arms and staggered into the bedroom. The coats seemed to get heavier each time I carried them. I placed them on the floor, in a row.

She perched on the edge of the bed, her hands clasped between her knees, her head down. Her long hair created a shield around her face, hiding it from me.

I sat next to her, and her shoulder bumped mine as the mattress dipped. She inched away from me. It felt like miles. Hooking a finger around her thick hair, I pulled back the curtain. "Did something happen today? You said you had something to show me."

"Yeah. I-I found something this morning."

The blood drained from my head so fast, I felt dizzy. "Online? You found something online?"

Her head jerked to the side, and her nostrils flared. "No, right here in this bedroom."

My gaze darted around the room wildly, desperately searching for the thing that had caused my warm sunshine to be replaced by this ice princess. "What?"

She bounced a little and said, "I found it underneath the bed, and I left it there."

Took me a half second to drop to my knees and peer beneath the bed. I reached for the black knickers and dragged them out. Holding them with my fingertips, I asked, "Are they yours?"

"They're not mine. I hate thongs." She gathered her hair into a ponytail with one hand. "I mean, yeah, sometimes the outfit requires a thong, but usually I don't wear them. So, no. Not mine."

I dropped the knickers, understanding punching me in the gut. "They're not mine."

She lifted her feet up, away from the offensive thong on the floor, pulled her knees to her chest, and wrapped her arms around her legs. "I didn't think they were *yours*."

Still crouching beside the bed, I fell back on my bum. "You know what I mean. They don't belong to anyone I know, at least, not well."

Ivy's mouth dropped open, and she hugged her legs tighter.

"Wait. That's not what I meant, either." I dragged a hand through my hair. She didn't really believe I'd had another woman up here. "Can I explain?"

"I'm waiting, but you're doing a shit job of it so far."

I stayed on the floor. "Both times I relapsed I told you they happened here. The first time was with some old...friends. The second time was when we had a late session in the studio, and I invited a couple of the guys, a couple of the musicians, back to my place—Denny, who you met, and Giles, who plays keyboards. They picked up some booze on the way—the whiskey, the champagne, and some beer."

"Do they know you're in recovery?" Her jaw hardened, and she had a murderous gleam in her eyes.

"They do, but c'mon, Ivy. They're not my keepers. They can do what they want. It's up to me. Always up to me."

Her little hand formed a fist. "I knew that Denny was trouble the minute he walked into the studio with that scraggly beard and the smirk."

I rolled my eyes. I'd better keep Denny away from her from here on out. "They came up here to party, and that's when I drank the whiskey."

"Drugs?" She pulled her bottom lip between her teeth, and I thought she was going to draw blood.

"No drugs, which I never used anyway, just the booze."

"And women."

I held up my hands. "Not for me. I left before that portion of the party started."

"You left Denny and...the keyboardist here by themselves?"

"After a few rounds, Denny got the brilliant idea to call a woman he's been casually dating."

"Fucking." She practically growled.

"Whatever. He's an adult, and so is she. You've suddenly become a pearl-clutcher over sex?"

"Go on." She flipped her hand through the air, as if giving me leave to continue.

"Once Denny mentioned the women, I bounced. Told them they could stay at my place, but that I was out of there. I had Jovan drive me back home, fell asleep in the car." I jabbed a finger at the knickers on the floor. "Denny obviously shagged his...friend, and she left those behind."

"Eww, they had sex in your bed? Aren't there like three other bedrooms in this place?"

"Exactly. Eww." I rose to my knees and hobbled before her. "Do you believe me?"

"Sounds sort of plausible, except for the part where you'd leave a party raging in your own place, and one of the guests decides to fuck in the host's bed, and the *friend* leaves her panties behind."

I snapped my fingers. "I'll prove it to you. I'll call Denny. I haven't spoken to him about the knickers, right? Didn't even know they were there. I'll put him on speaker phone."

"You don't have to do that. I believe you." Her lashes swept her cheeks, and she wouldn't look me in the eyes.

"I don't want you to have any doubts, Tink. I need to prove it to you, so this is settled between us. I don't want any misunderstandings or deception between us." I jumped to my feet to retrieve my phone from the other room.

When I returned, she'd un-pretzeled her body, her legs swinging from the side of the bed.

I scrolled through and found Denny's contact info. I tapped to call him and enabled the speaker.

He picked up after two rings. "Hey, bro. That was some good work today. So proud to play on this record with you."

"Thanks. You guys are brilliant. Hey, Denny, that night you and Giles were here..."

"Yeah, epic night, lad. Too bad you missed all the fun, but when I met your missus yesterday, I could understand why you skipped out. Ivy's a stunner, proper fit, she is." Ian held his breath, willing Denny not to say anything else about Ivy.

"Emma brought two friends with her, and since you didn't stay, guess who had a threesome." Denny made a crowing sound. "This bloke."

I glanced over at Ivy, and she stuck a finger in her open mouth like she was vomiting. Yeah, definitely better to keep these two apart. "Congratulations. Did someone have sex in my bed because I found something underneath it."

"Bro, not a used condom."

Ivy made a gagging noise, and I pressed my finger to my lips. "Not that bad. It were a pair of black knickers. Belong to Emma?"

"Not sure. She never said. Might belong to one of them other birds, but I'm pretty sure you can toss 'em."

"So, you *did* have sex in my bed? Bro, that ain't right."

"Yeah, sorry about that. Emma got caught up looking out your window, and I got caught up in her. I did leave the bed messed up, so housekeeping would change the sheets. They did change the sheets, right?"

Ivy scrambled off the bed with a squeal, and I gave her a grin, relieved to have her back and relieved Denny proved my innocence—even though he was a wanker. "Sheets changed."

"Okay, then. All good?"

"Cheers, Denny." I ended the call and held up the phone. "Does that work?"

Ivy skipped toward me and threw her arms around my neck. "I knew you didn't do anything. I was scared, but I knew there had to be a reason those ugly things were under your bed."

I kissed her, like I'd wanted to since I walked through the door, her sweet lips a cure for everything bad. "Okay, settled. Do you want to try on the coats now? I need to keep you safe and warm. Oh, and would you mind if we did the find my phone thing on each other's phone—especially if you're going to be traipsing around London on your own. I mean, you don't have to if you think it's creepy or stalkerish. I would've been less worried about your silence today if I could've seen you were still at the British Museum."

"Yeah, that's cool. That's fine." She shook her finger. "Of course, that doesn't work if someone attacks me, steals my phone, murders me, and stashes my body in the Underground."

Frowning, I shook my head. "And then goes to the British Museum with your phone? That's devious."

She covered her mouth. "Oh. Speaking of devious. There's something else I found out today."

Just when my pulse had settled to a normal rate, her words made it race.

"Before I tell you..." She put her hand over her heart "...I just want to let you know, I don't believe it, especially after the panty explanation."

"Must be bad. Should I sit down?" I backed up to the edge of the bed.

"You probably should, but only if you're absolutely sure those sheets are clean."

I sank to the mattress. "What did you find out?"

"I talked to Chloe today." She paced in front of me, twisting her fingers—never a good sign. "She joined a dating app, called BlueFin."

Ivy looked up at me expectantly, and I shrugged. She continued. "It's an exclusive app. You have to apply and be accepted based on things like net worth and..." she flapped her hands in the air "...probably what kind of car you drive." She stole another look at me as if this was supposed to make any sense at all. It didn't.

"Anyway, BlueFin accepted her, and she created a profile on the site."

"Good for Chloe...I guess, but I'm not getting the connection."

Ivy squeezed her eyes shut and wrinkled her nose. "She told me you also have a profile on BlueFin."

"Huh? Me?" I poked myself in the chest just to make sure.

"Yes, but I told her it was a fake." She chewed her bottom lip. "Right?"

"You think I have a profile on a dating app? Like, I'm actually trying to get dates out here while I'm living with you?" Ivy had said she didn't believe it, but that's not what this looked like. How many times did I have to defend myself?

"No, no. I don't think that." She folded her arms across her mid-section. "And this Ian Pope doesn't seem to be actively trying to get dates, but he is proposing some kinky activities. You don't want to pee on me, do you?"

"What!" I sprang from the bed and waved my arms in the air. "Is that what this fake Ian Pope is suggesting? That's what people think *I'm* into?"

"It's just like Duke Hammer, so obviously fake." Ivy stroked my back as I followed the pacing route she'd already worn into the carpet.

"But it's not apparent to some people, is it? Chloe thought it was me, or she wouldn't have called you." I shrugged away from her. "You must've had your doubts, especially after you found those knickers. Wait a minute. BlueFin? Fish site."

"Yeah, I think it's kinda fishy, too. What kind of dating app doesn't vet its users?"

"I'm thinking about something Jack asked me a few days ago, something about a fish website."

"Jack knows?" Ivy kicked the pair of knickers across the room. "Why didn't he do something about it if he knew?"

"I don't know. Jack knows more than he lets on. He doesn't tell me everything, and then only when it reaches critical proportions." I clasped my hands behind my neck. Could Jessica be responsible for this, too?

Ivy had crossed the room to the window and stared out, her forehead pressed against the glass. "Isn't this critical? You're releasing your single shortly. The focus should be on that, not your kinky tastes."

I lifted one eyebrow. "What else am I demanding over there on BlueFin?"

Raising her shoulders to her ears, Ivy said, "I'm not sure what else. Sex in public places."

"Does sex in the back garden count?" I gave her a wink, and she turned a pretty shade of pink and poked me in the back.

"So, it *is* you."

"That *other* Ian Pope sounds like an alright bloke, after all." I put my hands on either side of her, bracing them against the window. "You know what I've been fantasizing about ever since I brought you here last night?"

Her eyes got glassy as she ran the pink tip of her tongue across her lower lip, making me instantly hard. "What?"

I tapped the glass with my fingernail. "Taking you right here against this window in full view of...well, nothing because it's a straight, unobstructed view of the river. So, I'm not quite as pervy as that other Ian Pope."

Tilting her head, her hair fell over one of her beautiful hazel eyes. "Boats?"

"Pretty sure someone on a boat wouldn't be able to see in a window this high."

She licked her finger and drew a line on the glass. "We'd have to clean the window after. Couldn't leave that mess for housekeeping."

I had a mess alright. My mind snapped like an elastic band, jolting me back to reality. "Do you think Chloe could help?"

Ivy had been on her tiptoes, her teeth against my neck, and she nipped me.

"Ow." I rubbed the spot.

"Did Denny and his threesome give you some ideas, or are you just trying to compete with the other Ian Pope, now?" She punched my bicep with all the force of a butterfly, a violent butterfly. "Chloe *cannot* help us."

"Oof. I wasn't thinking about that, Tink." With my fist, I erased the smudge on the glass she'd made with her spit. "I was talking about the BlueFin profile. Can she do damage control on that app? I'd insist on paying her this time."

She slumped against the window, her hands behind her. "Maybe."

I kissed her plump, pouty mouth. "I'm sorry, baby. We can play out the window fantasy later. I'm gonna call Jack about this recent assault."

"Can I listen in? Then I'll call Chloe to see what she can do on BlueFin to shut down the scam."

"Let's go in the other room." I nudged a box on the floor with my toe. "Can you start trying on these coats, so I can return the ones you don't want to Sarah."

"I'll do it while you're talking to Jack." She picked up one of the boxes and did an exaggerated stagger. "What's in here, a rug?"

I took the box from her and carried it into the sitting room, while I located Jack's number on my phone. I placed the box on the coffee table and called Jack. He didn't answer, so I texted him.

Ivy jerked her thumb over her shoulder. "Do you want something to eat?"

"Not hungry. You go ahead. I'm gonna change clothes."

As she wandered into the kitchen, I walked into the bedroom. I took off my socks and unbuttoned my shirt, letting it hang open on my chest. Sitting on the edge of the bed, I ruffled my hair. Had Ivy really gone through the entire day thinking I fucked some other bird, and then gone through half the day thinking I'd created a profile on a dating app and sent pervy messages? At least she'd given me a chance to explain before jumping down my throat the minute I walked into the flat.

My gaze wandered around the bedroom. I hadn't put much thought into this place. I'd never considered it a home away from my primary home in the country. It had always been a crash pad—a very expensive crash pad, but not much more. It also held loads of...uncomfortable memories for me. I'd partied here more times than I could remember. I'd woken up hung over, unable to recall shit from the previous night, reading about my fuckups the next day along with everyone else. Maybe I could start changing all those memories. Create new ones. It would be cheaper than selling.

I could hear Ivy clinking around the kitchen, so I called out her name.

"Yeah, did you change your mind? Do you want something to eat."

"I do want something to eat. Come in here." When she showed up at the bedroom door, I wiped the grin off my face and tried for bad boy moody.

"Yes?" Her eyes widened. "Ooh, you look sexy sitting there with your shirt open."

"Then take off your clothes."

She smiled and wriggled in place. "Thought you weren't in the mood." Grabbing the hem of her jumper, she pulled it over her head and tossed it into the corner. She had another shirt beneath the jumper, and she peeled this off, too and dangled it from her fingers before letting it drop to the floor.

Waving her hand at me, she said, "Your turn."

I leaned back on my elbows and spread my legs open, my bulge on full display. "We're not doing that."

"N-no?" She sucked in her bottom lip, which made me even harder than I already was. She undid her pants and tugged them over her hips. She kicked them away and crossed her legs, putting one foot on top of the other. "Now, is it your turn?"

I lodged my tongue in the corner of my mouth and shook my head.

"Okay." She flipped her bra straps from her shoulders and dragged the backstrap to the front to unhook it. Then she threw it behind her. I didn't make a move, and she crossed her arms over her chest to cover her tits. "Now?"

I rubbed my cock through my pants—didn't mean to but couldn't help it. "You're not fully naked, yet."

"I see what you're doing." Turning her back to me, she hooked her thumbs in the elastic of her knickers and slipped them over her round ass. She glanced over her shoulder and gave me a wink. "Come and get it, big boy."

"Not so fast." She spun around, her mouth forming an O, and I said, "You know those high heels you were wearing at the studio yesterday?"

"Yessss."

"Put them on."

"Really? I..."

"Do it."

She narrowed her eyes, and they glittered in the low light like a cat's. "Are you going all Fifty Shades on me?"

I flattened the smile from my lips and repeated, "Do it."

She flounced to the closet and ducked inside while I readjusted my cock. My nuts were aching already. How did that Fifty Shades bloke hold out for so long?

She strutted out of the closet, the stiletto heels on her feet causing her tits and ass to jut out at a sexy angle. Licking my lips, I sat forward and shrugged off my shirt.

"Ooh, now we're getting somewhere." As she took a step toward me, I held out my hand. "Stop, turn around, and go to the window."

She jerked her head toward the window and the twinkling lights on the shore across the river. "W-won't someone see me?"

"I told you, there's..." I stopped myself and roughened my voice "—maybe they will."

"Oh, I know. You're trying to be like that *other* Ian Pope from BlueFin. The kinky one."

I put a finger to my lips and then pointed to the window. She walked toward it, her hips swaying seductively, and my balls tightened.

When she reached the window, she turned around, placing her palms against the glass behind her. "Are you going to do me against the window in view of...whatever's out there?"

"Maybe—if you're a good girl."

Her lips parted, and she put a hand to her throat. "What do you want me to do?"

"Touch yourself."

Her fingers went to her pussy so fast, I knew she was already turned on, and a bead of sweat rolled down my back. As she started playing with herself, I asked, "Are you wet?"

She gasped and whispered, "Yes."

"Keep going. Make yourself come. I wanna watch."

At this point, Ivy didn't need any encouragement from me. Her head fell back, hitting the window, but she didn't seem to notice. She let out a groan, and my racing pulse had me almost panting.

A flush of heat rose through my body, and I undid my pants, peeling them open. The tip of my cock stuck out the top of my briefs, and I rubbed the bead of pre-cum around the head as I watched Ivy fall apart at the window.

She squeezed her eyes closed, and her legs trembled. "I can't...I can't..." she slid down the glass into a squat, her knees spread apart, her fingers still buried in her pussy. She cried out when she came, rocking forward, cupping her hand over her cunt. My cock pulsed in my grip.

Enough of this watching shit. Totally overrated. I kicked off my pants and practically stumbled in my desire to reach her. She'd fallen on her bum and closed her legs, her tits heaving with every shuddering breath she took.

I hovered over her, brushing her hair off her face. Leaning forward, she wrapped her lips around my cock. The sensation made my head explode but if she sucked me off, I'd be done in under a minute. I pulled out of her warm, wet mouth.

I cinched my hands around her waist and slid her body up the window. Then with one hand, I pinned her wrists over her head against the glass and kissed her parted lips as my cock skimmed her belly. With her four-inch heels, she was closer to my height, and she pressed her body against mine, skin to skin. I could still feel the heat pulsing from her cunt, and I slipped my finger inside her. She gasped and lurched against me.

I nibbled on her shoulder, peering at the lights on the river. I whispered in her ear. "Maybe someone's watching us right now."

Her body shivered. "Then we'd better give them a show." She sucked my bottom lip between her teeth and murmured, "Fuck me."

Sinking my fingers in the soft flesh of her ass, I hoisted her up, and she wrapped her legs around my hips. I took her hard nipple into my mouth at the same time I dipped the head of my cock into her pussy. When I pulled out, she dug her fingernails into my scalp. "Stop. Teasing. Me."

I slid into her, and she arched, bumping her head against the glass again. Her hands dropped to my shoulders, slick with sweat, and she tongued my earlobe. I moved harder and deeper, each of my strokes drawing a breathy squeak from her.

While I'd been teasing her, I'd been teasing myself, and my release coiled inside me like a feral beast. My heart thundered beneath the ivy tattoo, animating it into a living thing that burned against my chest. As I pounded her, the same feeling overcame me as it did every time I fucked her. Deeper. More. Closer. I wanted to possess her, but at the same time, I knew she'd taken control of my entire being. It didn't matter where it started with her—playful, a base need just to fuck her and shoot my wad, or tender loving—it always ended here. With my need.

I came hard, driving her against the window as she clung to me, her teeth bared against my throat. My body heaved one last time, and I shuddered, my hunger spent and satiated.

She kissed the side of my neck, and my eyelids flew open. I said, "Your turn, baby. Do you want me to go down on you? Or I could keep going."

"Honestly, my legs are tired. If you weren't impaling me with your dick, I'd fall over."

"Poor thing." I brushed the pad of my thumb across her soft lips. "I can carry you to the bed."

"Weak *and* starving." She dropped one leg. "You interrupted me when I was making myself a snack."

"Oh, I'm so sorry. Were you thinking about food the entire time I was fucking you?"

"Only half the time." She reached around and smacked my ass. "And now I need to take a shower."

"You take a shower, and I'll go into the kitchen and get you something to eat."

Fifteen minutes later, Ivy returned wearing the same clothes she'd shed in the bedroom in her sexy striptease. I handed her a plate with some bread and cheese and as she wolfed it down, my phone rang. "It's Jack."

I answered, "Alright?"

"Hey, mate. How'd the session go today?"

"Went great." I sat on the arm of the sofa, while Ivy returned from the kitchen and lifted the lid from the box. She gasped, her eyes widening as she pulled the coat free from the crinkling tissue paper.

"Brilliant, and I've got some good news for you. The suits have agreed to releasing that second recorded version of 'Lost and Found' as the lead single from the album."

Ivy had been twirling around the room in the coat, but when she heard Jack's news, she danced over to me and kissed me. God, I loved her.

I spoke into the phone. "That is good news. Thanks for pushing it."

"Wasn't much of a push. They were thrilled with it. We're going to release it in a few weeks, get it out before Christmas, so get ready for a big promo blitz. Then we'll go with 'Muse' and probably 'Van at Greek' before we release the album. Starting to schedule concert dates based on the buzz alone. We'll look at how the singles perform and ticket sales for the shows in the UK before expanding. We're back, baby."

A sudden spasm of anxiety clutched my heart. What if the singles didn't do well? What if nobody bought tickets to the concerts? What if the critics savaged the record? I ran my tongue around my dry mouth. I'd almost forgotten what I'd called about, but remembering amped up my apprehension even more.

Ivy sat beside me on the sofa, still wrapped in the wool cashmere coat, the sleeve soft against my arm and her lips on my neck even softer. She tickled my ear with a whisper. "Whatever happens. It's going to be okay."

She always knew what to say to me—no false bluster about how every single would be a great hit or how much the critics would love the album or how all the concerts would sell out in minutes. Just the calm reassurance that any outcome would be fine. That she'd be by my side whatever the result. It's all I ever wanted.

I squared my shoulders. "We're not back yet, Jack, but this is a good start, and I appreciate the confidence. But we still have a problem."

"What do you mean? Did Jessica contact you?" Jack's voice went up several octaves.

"Thankfully, no, but it looks like she's back at it. That fishy site you mentioned to me before is the celeb dating app BlueFin, right? Ivy's friend was on there and saw my fake profile and read the fake messages. Ivy thinks Chloe can help like she did before with the Duke Hammer pictures. We need to handle this before the single drops. Seriously."

"Yeah, I got wind of the BlueFin messages a few weeks ago, but it's gotten worse than that, mate."

"Worse? How could it get any worse?" I shot a worried look at Ivy, and she squeezed my hand.

"Jessica has a sex tape—of you—and she's threatening to release it to the highest bidder."

Chapter 25

IVY

I held onto Ian's hand to steady him, as his body vibrated next to mine like a tuning fork, even though a bolt of anger had me sizzling. This threat was a vile attack on his privacy, and I felt like doing physical harm to the perpetrator.

After a long pause, Ian said in a tight voice. "Not possible."

Jack coughed. "Not possible that she's offering it, that someone would be willing to pay for it, or not possible she has it to peddle?"

"Not possible it exists." I loosened my hand from Ian's vise-like grip, and I flexed my fingers to restore circulation. "There is no sex tape, Jack, not of me and her, not of me and anyone."

I knew *we* didn't have one. Any time I'd even playfully asked for a racy picture of us, Ian shot it down.

Jack released a long sigh. "You're sure?"

"That's at least one bit of solid advice I got at the beginning of my career, and I stuck to it. I've never participated in a sex tape and never will." He kissed the side of my head as if in apology. Hell, I didn't need a tape; I had the living, breathing original.

"What do you think she has? Could be something blurry. Could be faked. She seems pretty confident."

"It could be something like that. Videos can be altered, created with AI. If she's looking for a big payday, I wouldn't put that past her, although the whole setup stuns and saddens me at the same time."

"We'll have to handle it one way or another. She must have something convincing."

Ian slumped back, kicking his feet onto the coffee table. "What are you suggesting? That we pay her off, so she don't sell it to some sleazy publication?"

"The record company might even do it. Just end this, Ian. Give the woman what she wants and get out from under it. You can't afford that tape making the rounds...even if it looks like a fake. If she times it to coincide with the release of the lead single, we're fucked."

I nodded. "I agree with Jack. Just be done with it."

Ian jerked his head up, and his jaw dropped. "You're taking the piss, right? Both of you." He pushed up from the sofa and stalked to the window. "It's not me. Even if it were me, I'm not paying someone blackmail. You think it would end there? It wouldn't."

He had a point. I chewed on my fingernail. Did I really believe Matt's blackmail of me would ever stop?

Jack's panicked voice pulsed over the line. "We can't let her do this, mate. She'll ruin you. How long would it take for you to prove it's fake? By that time, your single and the whole album could be buried under this story."

Dragging a hand through his hair, Ian said, "The record company has deep pockets. They also have solicitors. I never consented to be filmed during a sex act, so her release of that tape is a crime. Also, if you have text messages from her threatening to shop the tape around unless we pay her off, save them. Blackmail is also a crime."

"Ian..."

Ian cut him off. "Just do it, Jack. I'm done. Whatever happens, happens."

Stuffing the phone in his pocket, Ian turned to face me. "You really thought it was a good idea to pay her off?"

Of course, I did. I was paying off my own brother.

"I just want you protected. I don't want anything to mess up your comeback. You've worked too hard for it." I shrugged out of the beautiful wool cashmere coat that I could not accept and folded it over in the box. "Why is Jessica doing this to you? Why does she hate you so much?"

He ran a hand across his mouth. "I don't even know if she does. This latest stunt proves she's after money, and she's grown desperate to get it. She has a lot of model-influencer friends, and a few of them are doing alright. Jessica's engagement fell off when we split, but honestly, she doesn't have the work ethic to make a go of it. She's too much of a party girl."

"Did she do drugs and drink when she was with you?"

"No drugs and she didn't drink as much as I did, but she always wanted to go out—parties, clubs, red carpets, openings. I eventually found it exhausting and decided to get sober. Even if she had agreed to change her lifestyle, I knew it wasn't going to work out between us. Different interests, different personalities. When I broke it off to enter rehab, I think she believed we'd get back together when I came out. I made it clear that wasn't going to happen and took off on some travels with a few mates. Then I met you."

"She seems to have found a will to work when it comes to messing up your life. Why are you so confident you can keep this scandal at bay?"

"I'm not." He came up behind me and wrapped his arms around my waist. "But I am confident that it doesn't matter one way or the other... and you showed me that."

"Me?" I rotated in his arms, placing my hands on his chest. "Why are you listening to me? I take it all back—whatever I told you."

"What you said..." he cupped my face with his hand "...was that everything would be okay no matter what happened with the record. When Jack was going on and on, predicting success for the single and the album and the tour dates, you sensed my panic about all the pressure.

Then you told me whatever happens is going to be okay, and I feel that now. If I'm the subject of lewd gossip or I get attacked online—none of it matters to me as long as you're by my side. Are you?"

I buried my nose in his chest and said in a muffled voice, "Always. I love you so much, it hurts."

And if I inspired him, he inspired me even more. I knew what I had to do to get my life back.

* * *

The following day, we returned home. We'd spent one more night in the London flat, holding each other and whispering through the night. As usual, Ian opened up more than I did, and it further convinced me that I needed to take care of business in LA so that I could be a worthy partner for him.

When we got home, Scruffy danced around my feet until I picked him up and kissed him on the nose. "Did Sharon take good care of you?" I carried him into the kitchen and checked his water dish. "I'll play with you outside, later."

Ian followed me into the house with the coat boxes and placed them in the foyer. "You didn't even try them all on. Please don't tell me all my effort lugging them around London was for nothing."

My gaze darted to the boxes as I set Scruffy on the floor. The last thing I needed right now was for Ian to spend money on me. "The coat I tried on was beautiful, but I recognized those labels, and they're too expensive. I can't accept that from you."

Ian rolled his eyes. "You don't accept anything from me."

I spread my arms out and turned around in the middle of the sitting room. "All this and you flew me out here—first class."

"You're living with me. Did you expect me to charge you rent?" His phone buzzed, and he scrolled through it. Without looking up, he said, "Besides, I'm sure I owe you loads of money from LA. You wouldn't let me pay for anything out there."

I aimed a toe at the boxes. "One of those coats probably costs about six grand. A trip to the La Brea Tar Pits and fish on the pier don't even come close."

Grabbing my hand, he tugged me toward him and threaded his fingers through my hair as he cupped the back of my head and kissed me. "Please pick out a coat. As we get into winter, it's only going to get colder here." He held up his phone. "I hate to abandon you, but I have a lot of work to do to prepare for the release of the lead single and the music video, not to mention taking a few meetings with my label's solicitors to handle this sex tape."

"So, you're going to call her bluff and go on the attack."

"It's the only sensible thing to do." He gave me a little nudge toward the kitchen. "Go get some lunch and stop worrying about my problems."

"Do you want me to bring you something to eat?" I patted his flat stomach.

"No. I'll take a break and get some food later."

Once Ian disappeared into his studio, I unpacked our bags and took Scruffy out back for a run-around. This would be the perfect time to head back to LA for a week, as Ian would be busy planning for the release of "Lost and Found." If everything went to plan, I could wrap up in a week.

Our relationship seemed to be rushing toward some sort of climax. Sasha and her husband, Jasper, would be back in England soon, bringing Thea with them, and Ian had hinted that he wanted us to meet. So far, I'd put off meeting his family for Sunday dinner, but with the holidays approaching I'd have to make some kind of appearance, although the thought of family terrified me. He kept assuring me they weren't the Corleones or even the Kardashians, but I'd probably feel more at home with either of those than a normal, unproblematic family like his.

Scruffy finally collapsed at my feet, exhausted, so I tucked him under my arm and brought him inside while I made lunch. Ian hadn't popped out of his studio once since we got home, and I knew he'd probably emerge, blurry eyed, in time for dinner...or later.

He had a lot to manage and decide, and it made my heart sing to see how much he'd taken charge of his own career. I had a suspicion it hadn't always been like this for him.

I made sandwiches for us and sliced some apples and pears into a bowl. I carried his food, along with a bottle of sparkling water, to his studio and stood at the door for a second, listening to his low voice rumble on the other side, one of the songs from the album playing in the background.

When he stopped talking, I tapped the bottle against the door before entering. "I figured you'd forget to eat, so I made you some lunch. You can eat it if you like or have it later."

He'd been reclining on a leather sofa and sat up when I walked in. "I don't know what I did to deserve you." He placed his laptop onto the table in front of him. "Come here."

I had balanced the plate with the sandwiches on top of the bowl of fruit, and I walked carefully toward him and dipped down like a cocktail waitress and set everything on the table next to his computer.

He pulled me into his lap, just as his phone rang again. He tapped the display to answer. "Just one minute, Ronnie."

His hands encircled my waist, and I held his face and planted a kiss on his mouth. As I tried to break away, he deepened our connection. I savored the kiss for another several seconds until Ronnie's voice interrupted us. "Ian, you still there?"

I put a finger to his soft lips and scooted off his lap. He mouthed *sorry* to me as I backed out of the room and blew him a kiss.

I checked the time on my phone and ensconced myself in the room Ian had turned into an office for me. His studio and workspace had no windows and featured dark, heavy furniture along with a collection of microphones and stands, headphones, cables, instruments, and several computers.

In contrast, my light, airy space looked onto the garden, and bookshelves lined the walls. My laptop rested on a gleaming cocobolo desk with wavy lines through the grain. It shouldn't matter where I wrote—I'd written books in coffee houses sitting next to homeless guys and at the beach blowing sand out of my keyboard—but this office seemed to open creative space for me.

I required something other than creativity now, though. I checked the time again and decided I could give Chloe a few more minutes of sleep. I'd already left my lunch here before delivering Ian's, so I bit into a slice of apple while I opened my laptop.

Then I did something I'd put off for months. I went on my social media sites and searched for Ian's ex—Jessica Finch. She'd called one of her accounts *Messica*.

Girl, you have no idea what messy is.

After I scrolled through some of the posts, I figured she was promoting herself as some messy bestie persona with a chaotic, but fun lifestyle, but her content fell flat.

Enlarging one of her photos, I studied the image—tall, a lot taller than I, skinny, busty, shoulder-length light brown hair, lots of makeup or filters, or whatever. I couldn't tell how people manipulated their appearances anymore. I kept studying her face looking for signs of derangement or evil or sadism, but all I saw was a pretty girl, who looked like every other influencer. Maybe I should set her up with Matt.

I shut down everything and grabbed my phone. Chloe answered after three rings. Uh-oh.

"What the fuck, Ivy. Why do you keep calling me at the crack of dawn? Do you need a lesson in time zones?"

"It's seven o'clock there. Cryptobro isn't over for another night, is he?"

"God, no." She made a big commotion with her yawning. "Did you confront Ian about BlueFin?"

"It's not his profile, and the panties belonged to a buddy who was partying at his place—without him."

"His buddy's a cross-dresser?"

"Belongs his buddy's fuckbuddy."

"You're sure."

"Positive. This person who's harassing him has graduated to blackmail, so she's not even trying to conceal her intentions now."

"Gee, that sounds familiar." She blew her nose. "Having a bunch of money isn't that great after all, is it? You'd always have people trying to separate you from it. That's why, if I ever won the lottery, I wouldn't tell a soul. Not even my own mother."

"You wouldn't tell Kelly? After all she's done for you?"

"Honestly, I think my mom likes you better than me, anyway, so hell no."

I took a deep breath. "Can you help Ian mitigate the fall-out from BlueFin? Work your magic? He insists on paying you this time."

"I suppose there are a few things I could do, and why shouldn't I charge him? Everyone else seems to be tapping him for cash."

Toying with a pear chunk, I said, "There's something else. I'm ready to go scorched earth on Matt."

She sucked in a sharp breath. "What does that mean, exactly?"

"I'm prepared to do whatever it takes to get that flash drive from him."

PopWiz Instagram Post

Blind Item #9

The now solo boybander has a new release and
music video on tap, but there's another video
that has nothing to do with music that might
steal the thunder and reveal his renowned
package down under.

Part III

Across the Pond

Chapter 26

IVY

After we made love, I kissed a clearly exhausted Ian good night and scooted out of bed. Without opening his eyes, he reached for me and squeezed my thigh. "Where you goin'?"

"I have a few phone calls to make back home. Go to sleep, baby. I'll be back soon." Before I even finished talking, his hand slipped from my leg and his breathing deepened. He'd gotten so much done today, including getting assurances from the record label's attorneys that they could put a stop to the sex tape with no money exchanging hands.

I hoped for the same outcome regarding my video—which was all too real—but I had other methods in mind for squelching it. And those methods didn't involve attorneys...or anything else legal.

I wrapped up in a robe and shushed a suddenly animated Scruffy, who clearly thought this midnight rendezvous involved him. He trotted after me to my office, and I shut us both inside. I sat at my desk with the phone and opened the French doors onto the garden. The white petals of the fragrant honeysuckle gleamed in the dark, and I inhaled their sweet scent, but I needed something to smack me awake and put me on edge. Lacking a shot of tequila, I pushed up from my chair and stepped outside onto the brick walkway for a few seconds reveling in the chilly air. Scruffy hovered behind me, his head cocked.

"Don't worry. I'm not going to make you go outside." I left the doors ajar and plopped back into my chair. I called Matt. He didn't answer, so I texted him a message of urgency. I knew I wouldn't have to wait too long for him to call me back. When money was at stake, Matt didn't waste time.

"Hey, sis. How's jolly, old England? Livin' large over there?"

"I think we have a problem."

The easy-going surfer dude disappeared, and Matt's tone sharpened. "What kind of problem? You not keeping your man happy? Don't fuck this up, Ivy."

Rage kindled in my gut. Matt sounded so much like Dad I got a bad case of déjà vu, but I needed fear, not anger. "I-it's not that. Everything's good between me and Ian, but I'm afraid someone may have seen that footage from the warehouse. Did you show anyone else?"

"What?" He wasn't expecting that. "I've never shown that to anyone except Dad and then you, years later. Nobody even knows I have the flash drive, certainly not the Brownes. What are you saying?"

"No copies?"

"I have the only copy." His lighter flicked as he lit up a cigarette. "Where's this coming from?"

"I've gotten a few anonymous texts, like warnings, about a video out there. I don't like it."

"Whoa, whoa. Wait." He took a long pull from his cig. "I think I saw something about this online, one of those gossip sites."

"You did?" I practically shrieked, and Scruffy twitched in his sleep. Now, I didn't have to feign the fear. Had someone already seen the fake sex tape of Ian? I licked my dry lips. "When did you start following celebrity gossip sites?"

"The day I found out my sister was dating a popstar."

"What did you read?" I drew my bottom lip between my teeth and clamped down.

"I can't remember exactly, something about a former boybander releasing a song and some sketchy video."

Knots tightened in my stomach, and I pressed my hand against it. This next part was crucial. "Could someone have stolen the flash drive?"

"No way. It's..." he took a drag "...I have it hidden in my place."

"Have you checked on it lately?" *Please don't say yes. Please don't say yes. Please don't say yes.*

He paused. "No."

"Could you? Please. This is serious, Matt. I just need to know that video is safe. I'm paying you fat stacks to make sure it is."

"Alright. Alright. I'm not going to do it with you on the phone."

"But you need to do it as soon as we hang up, and you need to text me back to let me know. I'm not sending you another dime until I know someone else doesn't have the flash drive." Squeezing my eyes closed, I crossed my fingers, and my legs, and my toes.

He grumbled something, and then said, "Okay. I'll check on it. Give me ten minutes."

As soon as I ended the call, I texted Chloe, who was on standby. `He's checking it`.

She gave my text a thumbs up, and I cupped my phone in my hand, staring at the display until my eyes watered. I refused to blink—too scared I'd miss something.

I jerked forward when I saw bubbles in response to my previous message to Matt. The text finally came through. `It's still there someone is fucking with you.`

I gave his message a heart, and with a shaky finger I tapped my phone to answer Chloe's call. "Well?"

"Bingo, bitch. The fuckwad has the flash drive hidden behind his Bob Marley poster in the living room. It must be taped to the back of it or to the wall 'cuz he lifted one corner of the poster and peeked behind it."

I doubled over with a sigh as my head throbbed with the tension of the past several minutes.

Chloe's voice chirped over the line. "Now, I'll put the next part of the plan in action. I'll go over there and steal it."

"No, you won't. You're going to wait for me, so you don't do anything stupid or get into trouble. I have to be the one to get that flash drive. I have a better reason to be at his place than you do. It'll be suspicious if you show up at his place again."

"You're coming home?" Chloe squealed. "I can't wait to see you but hurry up. Matt has the drive behind the poster now, but he could change the hiding place. Maybe he'll finally decide he's too old to tape posters on his living room walls and buy a safe."

"I'll be there as soon as I can arrange it. I'm going to put a stop to this deceit once and for all."

"Are you going to tell Ian everything? I mean *everything*?"

"Yeah, I think it's time."

* * *

I twirled in front of the mirror, grabbing handfuls of the silky material comprising the short, green dress. "I like this one. What do you think, baby?"

Ian looked up from adjusting the cuffs of his fitted black jacket. "You look beautiful in everything, but you look smokin' hot in that one. I'm sorry you have to do this. I know you hate it, but I really want you by my side."

"It's fine. I'm excited to be there for you." Once I had my business settled with Matt, I'd be more than happy to attend public events with Ian. His record company was throwing a bash in a few weeks, complete with red carpet, for several of its artists releasing new music, although Ian would be the biggest star there. This would be our first public appearance together after months of speculation about my identity. Nervous didn't come close to describing how I'd be feeling, but Ian needed me.

"My mate Charlie should be there. He'll be in England because his mum is unwell. I told him he didn't have to show up and to head home to his family, but he said one night wouldn't make a difference."

"I'm sorry to hear about his mom. Is it serious?"

"Cancer."

"That's rough. If he does make it to the release party, I'll be excited to meet him. I hope he'll let me take a selfie with him. Chloe would melt." I winked at Ian in the mirror. "Sorry, Charlie was always Chloe's favorite."

Ian's stylist, Sarah, bustled into the room with another jacket for Ian. "I think this one would be a better fit—ooh." She stopped in the middle of the room. "That dress looks stunning on you, Ivy. Sexy but classy, and we'll pinch it in at the waist a bit."

"Don't she look beautiful?" Ian came up behind me as I faced the mirror.

I turned in his arms. "If you're wearing that suit with the black shirt unbuttoned down to there, all eyes will be on you. Absolute fire."

He took me in his arms, running his hand down my bare back, where the dress cut-away. "My eyes will be on you...always."

As we kissed, Sarah clicked her tongue. "Stop snogging, you two. You're going to wrinkle everything before I have a chance to have it tailored. You might affect the fit."

Ian and I grinned at each other like a couple of naughty children. Then he squeezed my bum and walked back to Sarah, shrugging out of his jacket. "What's wrong with this one?"

"This one's a better fit for an athletic build. You've been working out so much and gaining so much muscle, that other one is too tight across your back and shoulders."

"I might bust the seams like The Hulk." He struck a pose worthy of Arnold and growled.

Sarah rolled her eyes. "Next time we do this, I'm demanding separate fittings for the two of you. There's way too much teasing and touching and messing around, and then there's Scruffy prancing in and out getting dog hair on my *haute couture*."

Ian gave his crinkly-eyed smile *and* wrinkled his nose—peak happiness. The lawyers had shut down the blackmail attempt by Messica, Thea was returning home from Italy shortly, and the hype around his single and album had reached a fevered frenzy.

Leave it to me to deliver the buzzkill.

Sarah finished her notes for the adjustments and started packing up her offerings. As Ian and I helped her with the clothing racks, I said, in a very offhand manner, "I need to go to LA for about a week."

Ian dropped a dress he'd been handling. "What? Now? You'll be back for the release of the single."

"Of course. I wouldn't miss that for the world. It's...Chloe. She's having a hard time right now, and I want to be there for her." As Chloe was always having a hard time, this statement hadn't been too far off the mark.

"Of course, you need to be there for Chloe. She's helped me so much, I guess I can be without my girl for a week." He picked up the dress and put it back on the hanger. "When are you leaving?"

"A few days. I just need to book my ticket."

Holding up his hand, he said, "Call Penny and don't give me any shit about paying for your own ticket. A last-minute reservation like this is going to cost you, and I want to do this for Chloe, too. She needs you. I'm going to make sure you get there."

"Thank you. You'll be okay?"

"Better than okay. I've got so much to do. I need to head into the city for a few days." He tickled my side. "Don't worry. Denny's not invited."

"I'm not worried about Denny, but if I ever see him again..." I balled up my fist and punched the air.

"I'm sure he'd be terrified, Tinkerbell."

I landed one of my punches on his bare shoulder. "What are you doing in London?"

"Several meetings, one with my accountant. I try to meet with him twice a year, and with the new release and tour dates coming up, he wanted to see me to go over some figures."

"So, you'll be busy, and don't worry I'll be back for the release date."

And when I come back, I'll be free to love you even more than I already do.

Chapter 27

IAN

It was almost a relief when I put Ivy on the plane to LA. Her nerves the past few days had the air crackling between us, and I'd been so busy I didn't have the time to settle her down or even discover the source of her tension. Not that she'd tell me, anyway. Helping Chloe would probably give her some peace.

I experienced a vague sense of unease that Ivy had to have a purpose—someone to help. If she didn't think I needed a savior anymore, would she stop loving me? Would she move onto another project? Maybe that's why the vibe between us had shifted before she'd left.

She'd been distracted. My jokes hadn't made her laugh. My touch hadn't soothed her. I'd made it past the two-month boyfriend cutoff, but I could be an outlier. Why didn't she want to meet my family? Why'd it take her forever to accept a fucking coat from me? Would she even come back from LA?

I'd dropped her off at Heathrow at eleven thirty for her two o'clock flight, which was the precise time for my meeting with Julian Abbott, my finance guy. In the interim, I attended a meeting with the PR team and grabbed some lunch.

By the time I got to Julian's office building, Ivy had texted me that she'd boarded and sent me pictures of herself settling in. According to FlightAware on my phone, her plane was still on the tarmac, so before I entered the building, I called her.

"I got your pictures. Are you comfortable?"

"Yes, perfect. I'm hoping to sleep, but I have a few books on my Kindle just in case, and I have your whole album on my phone so I can listen to your voice across the miles."

Didn't sound like she was ready to dump me. I wedged a shoulder against the corner of the building to get out of the wind. "Shh, top secret."

"Don't worry. I'm very good at keeping secrets. Oh, we're pulling away from the gate. I love you."

"I love you, too. Say hello to Chloe for me and be careful."

I muted my phone and dropped it into my pocket. The lift took me up to Julian's office on the tenth floor, and I waited in his reception area for about a minute while he finished a phone call.

I tapped on the open door. "Hello, Julian."

Julian glanced up, the light above his desk gleaming on his bald head and reflecting off his glasses. "Nice to see you, Ian and about time. Jack has been keeping me busy with all these expenses, but it's good to see you releasing new music again."

"Feels good. How are the investments doing?" I sank into a deep leather chair facing his desk, inhaling the sweet scent of tobacco from a recently smoked pipe.

"Excellent. I'll do a top-level review with you. Let me know if you want to dig deeper into anything, and we'll discuss the distribution of all the money you'll be earning this year." Julian unplugged his laptop and carried it around to my side of the desk. He was a hands-on accountant, who wanted to make sure everything was clear for his clients. That's what I liked about him. I'd learned loads about business from Julian.

He took the seat beside mine and put the laptop on the desk in front of us. For the next hour, he took me through my investments, and we discussed selling a few properties.

"You plan to stay in your current house in Woodsbury?"

"Yes, hanging onto that. It's close to my daughter. Was thinking of purchasing something in Los Angeles."

Julian drew his glasses to the end of his nose. "Again? Same area as before?"

"Not sure. I'll have to consult my…friend about a location." I wanted to buy a house for Ivy, for both of us. If I admitted it was for her, she'd raise all kinds of objections. I'd have to pretend that I needed a residence there for business. My lips turned up thinking about what a fuss she'd make.

"Let me know when you're ready to look at properties." Julian tapped his screen. "Just want to review Jack's expenditures that he submitted over the past six months, and then we're done. I'll send you an email with an attachment of your financial summary."

My eyes glazed over a little as Julian went through Jack's expenses for Sarah and Penny, clothes and travel, studio time, payments for the musicians. The voice of Julian's partner from the other room jolted me out of my revery.

Julian took off his glasses and pushed back his chair. "Excuse me one minute while I see what Robert needs. You can look over the rest, if you like."

When Julian left the room, I pulled the laptop closer to me and scanned the spreadsheet. My gaze skimmed down the rows until an entry caught my attention. I tapped my finger on the cell and read aloud. "Chase Arts."

"All done?" Julian entered his office and hovered over my shoulder.

"What's this expense? Chase Arts." I drove two fingers into my temple to massage the sharp pain that had penetrated my skull.

Julian shoved his glasses on his face and leaned in. "Not sure, really. It's a newer expense. By the color-coding I use, I can tell it's a charitable expense but not tax-deductible. Here, let me bring up the spreadsheet detail."

He reached over me and highlighted a tab at the bottom of the spreadsheet that brought up an itemized account. He studied the data for a second. "Right. It's a donation to the arts, private, so it doesn't come under the tax-deductible category. Looks like Jack started monthly payments in October for $25,000 US dollars. Just made a payment for December. Do you have a problem with this? Not authorized?"

Yeah, I had a problem with it. What was it? Why was Ivy's last name on it, and why did it start in October, the month she moved to England?

I cleared my throat, which seemed to have closed up on me. "Can you tell what the payments are for?"

"Not really. I'm assuming it's supporting some kind of community art project. I know you like to help struggling artists by paying for supplies and classes and such, and as they're not a 501c, the donations aren't tax deductible. So, this isn't a tax issue."

"I-it's just that I've never heard of this Chase Arts." Coincidentally, I knew a Chase. I just didn't realize I was paying her for her art...or anything else. Something else caught my eye on the spreadsheet, and I stayed Julian's hand before he closed it. "Wait. What's that name?"

Julian read it aloud. "Matt Russo. Ring a bell?"

"Not one. What's his name doing on this Chase Arts organization?"

"He's the coordinator for the fund, I suppose. I'd suggest you talk to Jack about it. He's usually good with his accounting. I haven't had any suspicions about him at all."

Oh, I planned to talk to Jack, alright, and I had plenty of suspicions of my own.

＊＊＊

As I stood outside the building waiting for my car, I turned up my collar and pulled my coat around me to stave off the chilly, damp air that rose from the river. My teeth started to chatter, as I checked Ivy's flight. She'd been in the air for over an hour and was just leaving the UK. She had another ten hours to go.

She'd also sent me a text message letting me know the flight was taking off, telling me she loved me, and including a bunch of silly emojis. Even the eggplant emoji couldn't raise a smile from me. What the hell was Chase Arts, and who the fuck was Matt Russo?

I bobbled my phone and dropped it on the ground. *Matt.* I knew that name. When I'd been in LA with her, she'd gotten a few texts from a Matt. Was I giving my money to Matt? Was this all some kind of huge scam?

I ducked down to retrieve the phone just as my Uber pulled to the curb. When I got into the car, I stabbed Jack's number on my display. He didn't answer, so I texted him to let him know I was coming to his place, and I'd wait for him. I didn't want to give him a heads-up about Chase Arts or Matt Russo. Didn't want to give him time to formulate a lie. Jack didn't do well thinking on his feet.

Numbness seemed to take over my brain on the way to Jack's place. My thoughts moved like sludge. Could this be some coincidence? Wasn't Chase a common name in the US? I knew Matt was a common name. Had someone conned Jack into thinking this organization was connected to Ivy? If this was for Ivy, why didn't she just ask me for a donation?

Took a good forty minutes to get to Jack's place, battling traffic all the way. He'd texted me back that he be home in thirty. I could wait in the lobby of his building.

Didn't take me long to convince the doorman of my identity and that I was Jack Davies' client. While waiting, I did a search for Matt Russo in LA. I got about a million hits. I tried Matt Chase and got about two million. I pocketed my phone and clasped my hands in front of me, my mind still roiling with questions.

Jack came through the lobby door, his ruddy cheeks more flushed than usual. He pulled his blue scarf off his mouth. "Hope you weren't waiting long, mate. Did Ivy get off okay?"

"She's probably somewhere over the Atlantic about now."

"Good, good." Jack twitched his head, birdlike. "Was there a problem with the PR notes? I thought the meeting went well."

"Meeting was good." I stood up from the chair in the lobby and unbuttoned my coat. "Speaking of meetings, I just came from my meeting with Julian."

"Julian." Jack's Adam's apple bobbed in his throat, and his fair English complexion grew mottled. "Oh, right, your semi-annual financial review. I-is there a problem?"

"Are we gonna stand down here and talk, or are you going to invite me up to your place?"

"Yeah, yeah." Jack loped to the elevators with his long stride, and I followed him, knowing in my gut I'd caught him out. I just couldn't suss out his crime.

He babbled all the way to his floor about the PR meeting, stroking my ego about the music. He dropped his keys at his door and scooped them up hurriedly.

Ushering me inside, he asked, "Something to drink? A fizzy drink? Water?"

"I just want the truth." I kept my coat on and shoved my hands into my pockets.

"The truth about what, Ian?" He left his coat on too and even secured the scarf around his neck.

"I saw the item in the spreadsheet you sent Julian, the item for Chase Arts. What is it, Jack?"

"It's uh..." He wiped a hand across his mouth "...some funding for an art project in LA."

"Bollocks. Why does it have Ivy's last name? Why did the payments start the month she came out here to live with me? Why *did* she come out here to live with me suddenly, after dumping me in LA?"

"Mate..."

I drilled him with a hard stare. "Don't mate me...mate. Just give it to me. Am I paying Ivy a monthly salary to be with me?"

"It's not like that, ma...Ian." Jack mopped his face with his scarf, even though I could almost see my breath in the cold apartment. "We're paying her, but it wasn't her suggestion."

There it was. Jack's words, although expected, hit me like a bowling ball to the chest. I think I even swayed on my feet for a second. "It was your idea."

Jack paced to the window, twirling the ends of his scarf, almost strangling himself. *Would save me the trouble.* "You know how it was, Ian. You missed that woman so much I was afraid it would derail the new music—and it almost did. I figured you'd relapsed, and I was nervous it would happen again. You don't know what it's like. The record company breathing down my back"

I gave a sharp laugh that almost choked me. "*I* don't know what it's like. You're really trying to tell me I don't know what it's like to have the record company on my ass."

"I mean, I know you do as an artist, but it's a whole different level as a manager. They threatened to drop you, Ian. It would've ruined your career. I did it for you, mate."

"And your own job."

"I'm not denying that, but you were so close to a comeback, and it was because of Ivy. I knew if she was back in your life, it would put you on track—and it worked. You finally chose the right person, Ian, someone who's mad about ya."

"So mad about me she has to be paid to be with me." I balled my hands into fists and kept them in my pockets so I wouldn't put one through Jack's wall.

"Look, I'm not gonna pretend that I know why she split with you. I thought it might be a money thing, but when I first called her with the plan, she turned it right down. Then she changed her mind and called me a few days later and accepted the deal. What does it matter? You love her, and she loves you."

"Does she, though. If you love someone, you want to be with that person freely. Love isn't a transaction, but I guess it is with me." I didn't know what I wanted to do—smash something, take off for Lapland, go home to my mum, but I knew what I didn't want to do—drink. The idea of boozing in response to this latest failure actually made me sick.

"One other thing..." Jack held up a finger as if making an argument in High Court "...she doesn't know it's your money."

"What does that mean?"

"She believes the record company is footing the bill. I didn't think she'd agree if she knew the money was coming directly from you."

"How fucking...noble." I grabbed the back of my neck and took a turn around the room. "One more question, Jack before I fire you."

Jack's blue eyes bulged from his sockets. "Wh-what?"

"Who the fuck is Matt Russo? He's on the Chase Arts invoice, like he's a fucking CEO or something. Maybe he's Ivy's lover, and I've been cucked twice over."

"Matt Russo." Jack's face scrunched up. "Can't be her boyfriend."

The throbbing in my head had receded to a dull ache. "How can you be so sure?"

"Must be a relation or something."

"A relation?"

"Yeah, 'cuz that's *her* name."

My head finally exploded. "What the fuck are you talking about? Whose name?"

"Ivy's. Her real name is Maddie Russo."

Chapter 28

IVY

As soon as I could, I took my phone off airplane mode and tapped my text messages. My bottom lip jutted out. Ian hadn't responded to my last I love you and my silly emojis. I missed him already.

I sent him another text to let him know I'd landed at LAX and watched my phone anxiously for a reply while I grabbed my carry-on. Nothing. It *was* one o'clock in the morning there, but I guess I expected him to be waiting for me to land. Thought he'd be tracking my flight on his phone. He'd probably fallen asleep. He'd been so busy the past week, taking charge of the lead single's release and promo. Couldn't be prouder of him.

It didn't take me long to get off the plane and through customs. I'd taken just a carry-on. I didn't have big plans here in LA—just a burglary. I'd already texted Chloe from the plane, and I headed out front to wait for her.

On the curb, I zipped up my jacket. I'd finally relented and picked out one of the gorgeous coats Sarah had chosen for me, but I didn't need it here. I wouldn't call it a particularly warm evening by LA standards, but it felt like a sauna compared to the UK.

I pulled my phone from my purse and scrolled through my messages. Still, nothing from Ian. I probably wouldn't hear from him until tomorrow morning, his time. I'd stay up late tonight if I could, to catch his text, and then I'd call him. I needed to hear his voice. Even though he didn't know what I was really doing here, talking to him would give me confidence to deal with Matt.

Chloe and I hadn't formulated our plan yet, but at least we knew where Matt was hiding the flash drive, and I believed the dumbass when he said he had no copies of it—not that he expected anyone else to be interested in it, and I'd never fought back against my father or my brother before. Until now. I had something to fight for now.

Thirty minutes later, Chloe pulled up in her BMW and popped the trunk. I tossed my carry-on inside and climbed into the passenger seat. Chloe gave me a one-armed hug as she immediately maneuvered away from the curb. The faster you got out of LAX, the better.

"You look great, babe. England agrees with you, or maybe it's just love." Chloe put her hand beneath her chin and batted her eyelashes.

"It's everything. You know, his house is near John Milton's cottage, and we went to Oxford one day so I could visit the college I attended for that summer program. We went to Stonehenge, of course, and spent a few days in Bath and went to that fabulous costume museum there. We even went to Stratford and saw 'As You Like It.' It was so funny." I glanced at my phone cupped in my hand for the tenth time since getting into the car.

Chloe whistled. "Are you trying to seduce the man or bore him to tears?"

"I don't have to try to seduce him. He's thoroughly seduced. The sex is..." I fanned myself with my hand "...*muy caliente*."

"So, he feigns interest in your tedious pursuits to get into your pants. Okay."

I stuck my tongue out at Chloe. "He doesn't pretend. He enjoys all my little excursions...well, most of them. He does have an irrational hatred of Milton, though. I think he was forced to read 'Paradise Lost' in school."

"Hatred of Milton is *not* irrational. Not to change the subject from the love of your life, but did we nail it getting to Matt's hiding place, or what?" She held out her fist for a bump, and I complied.

"Nailed it. Now we just need to figure out how to get our hands on it."

"Planning sesh right now, if you're not too tired."

My gaze strayed to the phone in my lap. "I'm more wired than tired."

"Perfect. Diego is waiting for us at Paco's. I figured you could use some proper Mexican food after subsisting on bangers and mash and spotted dick."

* * *

When we got to Paco's, which sat on the 18th floor of a hotel in Santa Monica with a view of the bay, Diego waved at us from a prime window seat.

As we approached the table, he jumped from his seat and threw his arms around me. "So good to have you home, Ivy. Missed you."

I kissed his cheek. "Missed you, too."

"How's the fabulous popstar?"

"He's fabulous. Wait until you hear his new album. You're gonna love it."

Diego waved a hand over the table. "Already ordered three of those little pitchers of margaritas for us, and you can pick out the appetizers." He rubbed his hands together. "I'm just thrilled you're letting me in on one of your little escapades—even though you won't tell me specifically why you're breaking into your brother's place."

"The less you know, the better." Chloe dropped into a chair and picked up a plastic happy hour menu.

I snapped a chip in half. "Are we going to break in or just pretend we're there for a perfectly normal reason? I vote for the latter. We don't need to commit a crime to get into his place. I'm his sister."

"A sister who never visits him and avoids him like the bubonic plague." Chloe ran her finger down the menu. "Nachos, taquitos, and quesadillas."

"Sounds good to me, but that's going to ruin my diet." Diego patted his mid-section, and Chloe snorted.

"Diego, you drink like a fish. A few taquitos aren't going to send you over the edge."

After the drinks came and Chloe ordered the food, we got back to business. "True, I don't visit Matt often, but we're kinda in this thing together now. I have a good excuse to visit him."

Chloe swirled her drink. "And I'm coming with you. You're not doing this alone. One of us can be a distraction while the other..." she glanced at Diego happily making his way around the salted rim of his glass "—gets the thing."

"Okay, so I make up some excuse to drop in on him, or maybe we just surprise him, and you come along. He's always thrilled to see you, anyway."

"He is." Chloe did a little shimmy, which caught Diego's attention.

"Eww, you still think he's hot?"

"He may be a douche, but he is a snack."

I held up my hands. "There will be no snacking involved. We both go into his place, and then you get him outside somehow. While you're out of the apartment, I'll retrieve the...um...item, and then we'll dip out of there. He won't even realize what we've done until I break it to him—once I'm out of the country again."

"Okay, how am I going to get him outside if I'm not going to use my feminine wiles." Chloe cupped her breasts and hoisted them up.

Diego tapped his glass with his painted fingernail. "Girl, put those things away. Ain't nobody at this table interested."

We all giggled, and I felt a warm glow suffuse me, which had nothing to do with the single sip of margarita I'd taken. Chloe had been my friend since high school, and we'd seen each other through many ups and downs. Diego had joined our clique about four years ago when Chloe had been working for his then-boyfriend. When they broke up, we got custody of Diego.

I coughed. "You could show him your car. He likes cars, and he hasn't seen your Beamer yet."

"Okay, that's our plan." Chloe smacked the table, rattling our glasses. "You think of some reason why you need to drop in on him, I ask him if he wants to see my new car, you grab the thing, Matt and I return for some more BS conversation, and then we leave with the...thing."

"I think that'll work." I pointed at her empty mini pitcher and said, "I'm driving home."

"Oh, go ahead and enjoy yourself. I can leave my car here and we can Uber back tomorrow morning."

"Eh, I don't even like drinking anymore to be honest."

"Ugh, Ian's turned you into an abolitionist."

I exchanged a smirk with Diego. "I think you mean prohibitionist, and that's another reason why you're not driving us home."

We finished catching up with each other, and then Chloe and I waited with Diego for his Uber. Once he sped off, I took Chloe's keys and drove us home. We stayed up talking for a few more hours, which allowed me to kill more time until Ian woke up. By the time Chloe fell asleep on the sofa, and I retreated to my bedroom, it was still only six AM in England.

I'd left my Ian Pope pillow in LA—'cuz I had the real thing—and now I hugged it to my chest as I lay on my bed. I couldn't wait to be free of the sword hanging over my head. Once I had that flash drive and destroyed it, I could tell Jack to take his twenty-five grand and shove it and could tell Matt to take his blackmail and shove that, too.

I must've drifted off. My phone, which had slipped out of my hand, buzzed against my hip. I squinted at the glowing green numbers on my digital clock, and I jerked awake. It would be ten o'clock in the morning for Ian.

I felt for my phone, which had stopped vibrating, among the bedcovers. I untangled it from the sheets and brought it to my face. Jack, not Ian. I tapped on his text message and froze as I read his words: **Ian knows**

Chapter 29

IAN

I chucked Scruffy under the chin. He'd been looking for Ivy all over the house and finally decided to slump at my feet. "I feel ya, Scruffy, unironically."

I scrolled through the text messages from Ivy since she'd left. I knew she landed safely and that she missed me. She didn't text me again until this morning. **I'm sorry. I love you**. Short, to the point...and bollocks.

Jack must've clued her in that I'd discovered her scam. My thumb hovered over the option to block her number from my phone, but Scruffy whined, and I couldn't go through with it...yet.

Instead, I rang up Jack. Hadn't blocked him yet, either. When he picked up with a tentative hello, I said, "I ain't forgiving you or hiring you back, but I already paid your salary for this month, and I want you to do something for me."

"Anything, Ian, but don't cut off Ivy. She doesn't deserve it."

I swallowed the lump in my throat. "You still have contacts with a private investigator, right? You must have. I'm sure Ivy herself never told you her real name."

"Th-that's right. I have a guy."

"Tell your bloke to get on this Matt Russo. Find out who he is to Ivy and anything else about him. I deserve to know who's been working with Ivy to con me."

"I'll get on it." Before I could end the call, Jack spoke very quickly. "Still good for the first interview in four days, right?"

Then I ended the call.

I had no intention of backing out on or missing any of my promo engagements for the release, but I'd let Jack sweat it out. My mind had been in total confusion since I found out Ivy had been taking money from me...and that her name wasn't even Ivy. Who was she? Had she targeted me somehow? Was this a setup from the beginning?

How could it be? How could she have known I'd be at that book festival? I did know she was a real author. She had an author page on Amazon and everything, and she had real books listed there. That part wasn't a lie. Ivy Chase was probably her penname, but Chloe and her neighbors all called her Ivy. Why would she change her name in real life?

What else had she faked? I knew now that she was just having me on when she pretended not to want me to pay for anything. I huffed out a breath as I sank my head in my hands, bracing my palms against my forehead. She couldn't have faked loving me, could she? I'd never felt so seen, so understood, so cared for by someone.

My fingers curled into my scalp. "Mate, that's probably her job."

She was a fiction writer. She made up stories for a living and apparently had a side hustle of scamming people.

I did a good job of distracting myself for the rest of the afternoon. Had a silly facetime with Thea where she tried to teach me some Italian. Her bond with Jasper didn't hit as hard this time. I was glad Thea's mum had found her happiness, and I couldn't complain about Jasper. Thea adored Jasper's older daughter. Ivy had been right—about that.

She'd been right about so much. That's why her betrayal hit so hard. Why kind of game had she been playing with me?

I dumped Scruffy off my lap and ran up to our room, taking the stairs two at a time. When I burst into our bedroom, I stood in the center of it, my gaze darting to every corner and surface as if I could find the answer to the mystery of Ivy in the stuff she'd left behind.

But the essence of her that lingered—her flowery scent, the echo of her laughter, the lipstick print of her kiss on the mirror she'd left me before she departed on her trip—brought me to my knees, leaving me more confused than ever.

When I recovered some sense of will, I staggered to my feet and rummaged through her drawers, checking for secret hiding places. I barreled into her closet, searching in pockets and snatching boxes from the shelves. I had no idea what I was looking for—maybe some sign of Maddie Russo.

Had she created Ivy Chase from her imagination, just like one of her characters? Did Ivy Chase even exist?

I tore down the stairs with Scruffy barking at my heels and made a beeline for Ivy's office. She'd taken her laptop with her, but I sat at her desk and yanked open the drawers. Journals full of handwritten notes, printed charts with character traits filling the boxes, and sticky notes with names crowded the drawers. I grabbed one of the notebooks, hoping for insight into Ivy or Maddie, but she'd filled it with story ideas and phrases and half-written scenes and even single words. All make believe, all fiction—just like her.

My phone rang on the corner of the desk, and I didn't even look up. I was done with business today, but Scruffy wanted me to answer it.

"Stop yer yapping." I pulled my phone toward me and froze when I saw **Tinkerbell** on the screen. She was ringing me? My thumb hovered over the display. If I talked to her now in this state, she could tell me anything, and I'd be begging her to come back and giving her even more money to do it. I had to get a grip.

The phone rang four times and stopped. I checked my text messages, but she hadn't sent one since the apology text earlier. As I put the phone back on the desk, it dinged. I snatched it up again. Voicemail. She'd left me a voicemail. Nobody left voicemails anymore expect my mum.

My finger trembled as I held it over the play arrow. Then I stabbed it and put it on Speaker. I didn't trust myself to hold the phone steady.

"Hi, baby." Her whispered voice gave me chills.

"I-I guess I can't call you that, anymore." She cleared her throat. "Ian, I'm leaving you this voicemail because I didn't want to write a book in text message. I don't even know if you'll hear this or listen to it. I'm thinking you haven't blocked me yet, or my call would've gone straight to voicemail, and it didn't.

Scruffy cocked his head and barked. I scratched behind his ears. "I know, boy."

"I'm not calling you to make excuses. I don't have any. What I did was wrong, and I did it for selfish reasons. I deceived you to protect myself and maybe to protect you just a little—but mostly I did it for myself. I got into some trouble and accepting Jack's offer seemed the easiest way out."

Trouble? My heart pounded in my chest as she paused.

"And don't blame Jack. He cares about you and just wanted to make sure you stayed on the right path, and okay, maybe he had selfish reasons, too. We both made a mistake, but it didn't come from a bad place or with the idea of hurting you or taking advantage of you." She sobbed, and the sound reached out and squeezed my heart.

"I just want you to know that nobody would ever have to pay me to be with you or love you. I always wanted to be with you from the minute we met, but...certain things got in the way of that. Jack's offer seemed to solve all my problems at once, but it created one, big, huge one—and that was lying to you."

Ivy blew her nose, and I pressed a thumb against the corner of my twitching eye.

"But I'm here in LA, and I'm gonna fix everything tomorrow night. I don't expect you to want me even after I make this right, but now I'm doing this for myself, and you did that. You inspired me. When you defied your blackmailer, even though that video could've derailed your comeback, you gave me the confidence to stand up for myself. I knew what I had to do."

I ran my hand through my hair. What was she on about?

"I know you always say you needed me and that I saved you, and I like to think I helped you a little bit, but you were already prepared to save yourself. I know you'll be fine because you're strong, and I know you're strong because you saved me. So, we helped each other."

Listening to her sweet, husky voice, I closed my eyes imagining her next to me. She could fill my head with lies, and I'd be happy to listen to her forever.

"You know maybe that's why we met that afternoon. Maybe the power of Fabio brought us together for one magical moment in time when we each needed a little support. Maybe we just weren't meant to last forever, just long enough to make a difference in each other's lives. And you did. You showed me I could be lovable and even more than that, you showed me I could love. You're so special, and I lo..."

Her message ended, cut off by the impatient system. I scooped up the phone and brought it to my face as if I could bring her back.

"What do you think, Scruffy?" I tickled his furry back with my toes. "Do you think she's spewing a load of shit? She knew an easy mark when she saw one and used me for money. All the rest of it, being in trouble, needing help...all convenient lies."

Scruffy gave me a side-eye. He was right. Even I could hear the uncertainty in my voice. Nobody could fake being in love like that, could they? Her body couldn't fake anything, but then that was sex, not love. That wasn't even true. When we made love...that *was* love. I didn't just want to fuck her because it felt good and got me off. I wanted to meld with her, body and soul.

What the hell did she have to take care of tomorrow night? That could all be rubbish. The woman straight-up lied to me about her identity and about taking money off me, all the while acting like she didn't want me to pay for a thing. I checked the time on my phone—two PM in LA right now.

I jumped when the phone in my hand rang, my heart racing. Seeing Jack's name on the display caused a mixture of disappointment and relief to course through my body. I wasn't ready to talk to Ivy, yet. Maybe I never would be.

I tapped the phone. "Alright?"

"Ian, the PI got back to me already. He can do a deeper dive on Matt Russo, if you want, but I got some info right off the top."

"Give it to me." I leaned back in Ivy's chair and stared at the ceiling. I wasn't ready for this so soon after Ivy's voicemail.

"Matt Russo is thirty-two years old, a few years older than Ivy."

"Three years older."

"So, he's probably her brother or cousin. Definitely not her father, and not her boyfriend with the same last name."

"Husband?" I felt sick to my stomach at the thought.

"No, Matt Russo is single. He does live in LA though, apartment in West Hollywood...and he has a record."

I jolted forward, sending Scruffy scrambling for the corner. "What kind of record?"

"An arrest record, mate. The bloke's served time for loads of crimes."

"He's a criminal? Ivy's...brother is an ex-con? What kinds of charges?"

"Hmm, burglary, carjacking, auto theft, a few drug and weapons charges, fraud, nothing too serious."

"Nothing too serious?" I was shouting, and Scruffy whimpered. "Weapons? That's not serious?"

"He's a Yank." Jack took a gulp of something. "They all have weapons."

I wiped a hand across my mouth. "You said fraud."

"Yeah, my guy didn't get into any details."

"Blackmail."

Jack clicked his tongue. "I didn't say blackmail."

"I know you didn't. Ivy did."

"Ivy? You talked to Ivy? That's great, mate. How's she doing?"

"You seem more worried about her than me. I didn't talk to her. She left me a voicemail."

"Who leaves voicemails? Me mum leaves voicemails, that's who."

"Yeah, mine too." I shook my head. "That's beside the point. In her voicemail, Ivy mentioned Jessica's blackmail attempt. Said the way I handled it gave her courage to take care of something in her own life."

"You think Matt's blackmailing her? Over what?"

"I have no idea, but the fact that she's out there in LA by herself planning to deal with this...ex-con gives me a bad feeling. How likely do you think it is this guy's gonna give up twenty-five thousand quid without a fight?"

"I thought she was visiting her friend, Chloe."

"She lied. What a surprise. Besides, that doesn't make me feel any better. Chloe's good at her job, but she's daft."

"Are you going to call Ivy back?"

"No. I may not know Maddie Russo, but I know Ivy Chase, and she's determined to see this through. She wouldn't listen to me, and if she thought I was coming out there to stop her, she'd move her plans up."

"Move them up?"

"She told me she was gonna take care of business tomorrow night."

"Wait, wait a minute. Go out to LA? Who said anything about going out to LA?"

"I did. Just now. I'm not going to let her put herself in danger because she thinks she needs to prove something to me."

"You're going out to LA to stop her?"

"Fuck, yeah."

Chapter 30

IVY

It had been almost twenty-four hours since I left that cringe voicemail for Ian. Who left voicemails anymore? Chole's mom, that's who. I wished I could reach through my phone and take it back. With any luck, he wouldn't even notice it or listen to it. Thank God I'd been cut off before I could utter any more embarrassing confessions. I'd claimed I wasn't calling to offer excuses but then went right on to serve up the lamest excuse ever. I'd pulled the pity card. Poor me. If he had listened to the message, he'd probably seen right through it.

Always the optimist, I'd kept my hand curled around my phone in a death grip ever since—just in case. I hadn't left the message to get him back, and I didn't expect him to want me back, but a little ray of hope kept me checking my phone every five minutes.

"Can you just stop looking at your phone? It's not gonna make time go any faster." Chloe misinterpreted my agitation.

I hadn't told my bestie about Ian's discovery. How had he found out, anyway? I didn't contact Jack after that single, devastating text, and he never explained further. We both knew what those two little words meant.

Chloe didn't need to know what was happening with Ian. She'd probably call him and launch into my defense. He'd think I put her up to it, and everything would be worse than it already was, although I don't know how it could be any worse. I'd lost my man, and he thought I was a piece of shit scammer.

I put down my phone, wiped my hand on the seat of my jeans and grabbed a Diet Coke from the fridge. "I just hope Matt doesn't call and cancel or get suspicious. It was hard enough to get him to agree to a meeting at his apartment tonight."

When I called Matt to let him know I was in LA and needed to see him, he'd suggested meeting at a bar. I convinced him that I didn't want to discuss this subject in public. Then he said he'd come to my place, and I had to assure him that Chloe and I were going to be in his neighborhood, anyway, and we'd drop by. Mentioning Chloe's name had been the golden ticket.

Chloe pointed to my can. "You need chamomile tea to calm down, not caffeine."

"I need to be alert and on my game. This is no time for serenity."

"You wanna go through it one more time?" She wrapped her black hair around one hand and tossed it over her shoulder, as I nodded my head.

She launched into the plan for the hundredth time. "We'll take my car. I probably won't be able to find a parking place in front of his building anyway, since this is West Hollywood we're talking about, but even if I do, I'll park down the street a bit. He won't question that."

I picked up the narrative. "We'll go to his place, shoot some shit, and then you'll mention to him that you bought a new car and ask him if he wants to see it."

"Right. He'll want to go, of course, because it'll give him a chance to ogle my tits." She shimmied her shoulders.

"Ugh." I covered my ears. "Don't wanna know."

"While I'm showing him my...beamers, you'll be visiting Bob Marley. Grab the flash drive, shove it in your pocket, and then when I bring Matt back, you can make up some BS about your plan. What are you going to say? You can't drop the ball at that point because he might get suspicious."

"I'll tell him that I can get more money out of Ian. He'll be so pumped at the thought of more cash, he won't be thinking about anything else. Believe me."

Chloe dusted her hands together. "We bounce out of there with the flash drive, you can destroy it and go back to the popstar with a clear conscience."

I chewed my bottom lip. I'd have to explain to Chloe at some point that I wasn't going back to the popstar. I could just say we broke up over the pressure of the new release. Ian would be touring soon, anyway. He'd forget all about me.

"Matt's going to realize I took the flash drive."

"So what?" Chloe shrugged.

"I don't want him to come around here, hassling you wh-when I go back to England.

"Don't worry about me, babe. I can handle Matt, and if you don't tell him he won't have any proof we took it. I can pretend to be shocked." She crossed her hands over her chest and widened her baby blues. "You mean the flash drive is gone? Your little blackmail vehicle is no more? Guess the party's over. The key tonight is to get him out of the apartment and leave you there. Have you thought of an excuse for staying?"

"I could come in limping, but I don't want to add more lies to the story in case I forget to limp in front of him. I can just say, I don't need to see your car, or I can get on the phone or use the bathroom at an opportune time." I couldn't stand it anymore and picked up my phone. *Nothing*. "I'll play it by ear."

"Okay, I'm going to do some work before show time." She paused at the entrance to the hallway. "Have you heard from Ian lately?"

I almost dropped my phone. "Uh, no, why?"

"I texted him yesterday about Project BlueFin, and he didn't get back to me. I think I squelched all that nonsense. I just wanted to give him an update." Chloe smacked the wall with her hand. "He did pay me already, though. I should switch my clientele from Fortune 500 companies to celebrities. The celebs pay a lot better."

"I'm glad it worked out. He's really busy with the release, but I can pass on the update."

Once Chloe disappeared into her bedroom to work, I collapsed on the sofa. Ian had paid off Chloe to get us both out of his life. His actions couldn't be any clearer. I expected it, but the knowledge only twisted the knife even more.

After staring at my phone, almost comatose, for thirty minutes, I shook myself into action and vacuumed the house, cleaned my bathroom, and went out to pick up groceries for dinner. I didn't feel like eating anything, but Chloe could eat through an alien invasion.

She didn't emerge from her room until I was well into cooking the pasta. She strolled into the kitchen, stretching. "I thought I smelled garlic cooking out here. You didn't have to make anything. We could've gone out to eat in West Hollywood, made it worth our while to trek out there."

"Getting that flash drive is going to make it worthwhile." I stirred the linguine in the pan with the tomatoes, basil, onion, and garlic. "It's not a big deal. Nothing I cook is a big deal."

She poked me in the back. "You'd better expand your repertoire. Englishmen do not live by spotted dick alone." She couldn't get enough of that joke, but I didn't feel like smiling.

"Oh relax." She massaged my shoulders. "This is going to work."

It had to work. Once Matt knew Ian and I were no more, nothing would stop him from exposing me with that video.

* * *

A few hours later, with my stomach in knots and my hands clenched in my lap, Chloe circled Matt's neighborhood. "Damn, I can't even find a place to park on his block."

I hit her arm. "There, there. That guy's pulling out."

She made an illegal U-turn in the middle of the street and put on her signal. "I'm nervous about parallel parking my baby. Can you guide me into the spot?"

Grabbing my purse, I exited the car and stood on the sidewalk, waving my hands in the air. Chloe had every electronic parking feature known to mankind on her car; she shouldn't have needed my efforts. If she was as nervous as I was, we were fucked.

With her Beamer snug against the curb, Chloe jumped out of the car. "Let's roll."

My legs felt like the pasta I just cooked as we walked down the block to Matt's old-style apartment building. We veered onto the property that sat flush with the sidewalk. Each unit of the complex opened onto a cement quad with planter boxes filled with dead foliage and a few towering palm trees in the corners. The quad smelled like weed and damp clothing.

We planted ourselves in front of unit number five, and I knocked on the screen door, rattling it and causing a cat to jump from a basket chair nearby and flick its orange tail.

Matt swung open the door, and the smell of cigarettes wafted through the mesh of the screen. "Hey, you. Welcome to my humble abode." He winked at Chloe, who was all smiles. "I plan to upgrade real soon, though. What's the emergency?"

Damn. Too fast. I put my hand to my throat as if dying of thirst. "Can I get something to drink? And I never said emergency, did I?"

He narrowed his eyes so like my own. "You're here, aren't you? Across the pond."

"I had to come home, anyway. Just thought I'd check in with you." I pounded my throat with my fist. "Can I please have something to drink? Water." As if we'd just crossed the Sahara Desert instead of the urban landscape of LA.

"Sure." He eyed Chloe up and down like a starving man checking out the buffet. "Something for you, Chloe?"

"You have some wine?" She ran her tongue around her glossy lips. "Red, white, pink, doesn't matter."

My fingers dug into my thighs. She didn't need to be drinking at this crucial moment. Flirting, yes. Drinking, no.

"I think I might have some white in the fridge. You're lookin' good. Still with that dickwad boyfriend of yours?"

"Nope. All broken up. White's good."

When Matt turned his back to walk into the kitchen, I sliced my finger across my throat. She lifted her shoulders and tipped her head toward the Bob Marley poster over a bookshelf crammed with old albums, CDs, DVDs, Xbox games, and a few books. Looked harder to reach than I had imagined.

When Matt returned with our drinks, I shifted my gaze from the poster and picked up a pamphlet from the sofa. My eyes bugged out when I saw the sleek Tesla on the front. "Don't tell me..." I thrust the pamphlet at him.

"Yep, all mine. Bought her last week." He handed me the glass of water with a smirk, and I had to grind my back teeth together to keep from smacking it off his face.

"How'd you manage that? You've gotten just 75 grand from me. That model costs more than 75K." Chloe sidled up next to me and drilled her knuckle in my back as she took her wine from Matt.

Matt cocked his head. "From you? It's not your money, sis, and duh. You ever hear of car payments? I put a down payment on it."

"You qualified for a car loan?" I snorted, and Chloe drilled harder. "Did they actually do a credit check on you?"

"It's not the best interest rate, but I gave them a hefty down...thanks to Ian Pope."

The blood in my veins simmered, and I was two seconds from throwing my water in his face and throttling him.

Chloe took a big gulp of wine. "I got a new car, too, a BMW. Wanna see it?"

Shoving his hands in his pockets, Matt got a big grin on his face. "You show me yours, and I'll show you mine. Kinda like that?"

"Sure." Chloe set her glass on the cluttered end table. "Let's go."

Was that my cue? I dragged my phone from my purse and studied the picture of Scruffy on my home screen, my mouth twisted to the side. I tapped the screen as if entering a text message.

Matt brushed past me and opened the front door. Holding it ajar, he made a half turn. "You coming, Ivy?"

"Maybe in a minute. I have to answer this text from my editor. You guys go."

Matt's step faltered over the threshold of the door, and I held my breath, my eyes glued to Scruffy's picture. Matt finally moved. "Alright. Hurry up, and don't touch any of my shit."

As he and Chloe stepped outside, they bumped into someone. Matt said, "Hey, Buzz. Whaddya need?"

"Nothing, man. Just dropped by to see if you wanted to have a beer." Buzz poked his head inside the apartment, his long hair swinging over his shoulders, and I lifted my hand in a wave.

Go away. Go away.

Matt gave Buzz a fist bump. "Hit me up in about a half hour. My sister and her friend are here, and we're gonna look at my car."

"Sweet ride." Buzz tucked his hair behind his ear. "I'll come by later."

Matt and Chloe turned to leave, but Buzz hovered in the doorway. I stretched my lips into a tight smile. "Yeah, nice to meet you."

"You wanna have a beer with me while we wait for Matt and your friend?"

"No, thanks." I clutched the Tesla pamphlet to my chest as if it were an important document. "Actually, my brother and I have a little business to discuss. Like he said, we'll be done in about thirty."

"I gotcha, I gotcha." He held up his hands and backed away from the door.

As soon as the screen door slammed, I rushed to the poster. Reaching over the bookshelf, I felt along the bottom of the glossy paper with my fingertips. I lifted one corner, peeling the sticky putty away from the wall. I slid my hand behind the poster, running it along the plaster. No luck.

Standing on my tiptoes, I smoothed both of my hands across the slick paper from Bob's elbows down to the bottom of the poster. I didn't feel any lumps or bumps, and I couldn't reach above his elbows.

I twisted around and spotted a kitchen chair pulled up to a round table. I tripped across the room and grabbed the chair by the back and dragged it to the bookshelf. I stood on top of it, and leaning forward, I reached for the poster again. I started at Bob's elbows and ran my hands upward. My fingers tripped over a lump just under Bob's chin—dead center in the middle of the poster.

I'd have to peel it back from the very top. My fingers crawled up the paper to the top edge, and I loosened one corner. If I could just get a little higher. I glanced down at the bookshelf. I put one foot on the top shelf, bracing my hand against Bob's crotch.

The screen door banged open, and Matt yelled. "I knew it! I knew you were up to something."

I jerked to the side, my hand grabbing at the flash drive beneath Bob's throat through the paper. I curled my fingers around it and ripped. With the flash drive and a bunch of poster paper in my hand, I teetered backward.

Matt charged toward me and finished the job. He tackled my legs and took me down from the chair, falling on top of me. I formed a fist around the drive. He'd have to pry it from my cold, dead hand 'cuz there was no way I was giving this up.

As he grabbed my wrist, the screen door bashed open again, and I screamed. "Come and get the flash drive, Chloe. I have it in my hand."

Instead of Chloe's voice, I heard the sweetest sound in the world and figured Matt must be choking the breath out of me, causing me to hallucinate.

That low voice with the English accent shouted, "Get off my girl."

Chapter 31

IAN

The man sitting on top of Ivy cranked his head around. "Who the fuck are you? Oh, hold on, you're the popstar. This was all a setup."

"Ivy, are you alright?" My adrenaline was pumping hard and fast through my system, and every one of my senses was on fire.

Ivy's round eyes took up half her face, but she didn't look like she was in any pain. The guy on top of her was pinning her down, but he didn't have his hands on her, except his fingers circled around her small wrist. "I'm fine, sort of. What are you doing here?"

I lunged forward, fists at the ready. "Get off her, mate, or I will fuck you up."

Matt, I'm assuming it was Matt, laughed. "Come at me, pretty boy. I'll fuck up your face so bad, you'll never sing again—not that you can sing now. Total shit."

I advanced and loomed over him and Ivy on the floor. Matt didn't have any weapons, so I closed my hand around the back of his neck to pull him away from Ivy. "You don't wanna try me, bro. I trained with Marky Mark."

Ivy's head shot up. "Who? Get off me, Matt."

"When was that, at bandboy bootcamp? That's supposed to scare me?" Matt shifted a little, and I saw my chance, although he looked so much like Ivy, this would hurt me more than him. I landed a punch on his jaw with a satisfying smack, and his head snapped back, a surprised look on his face.

Ivy took advantage of her brother's incapacity and wriggled from beneath him, dancing to her feet. The screen door crashed behind me, and I swung around, my fists still clenched, one hand throbbing from the punch.

Chloe, her hair a wild nest, her makeup smeared, tripped to a stop. "Ian?"

Ivy held up her fist. "I got it. What did he do to you?"

"He shoved me into the back seat of the Tesla and locked me in. Took me a minute to find the fucking door handle." She reached into her purse. "Make a run for it. I've got my pepper spray."

These Yanks and their weapons.

Ivy spun around and rushed toward the loo, and I took off hot on her heels as Matt began to lumber to his feet, squarely in the bullseye of Chloe's pepper spray.

I squeezed in after Ivy just before she slammed the door and locked it. I took her by the shoulders. "Are you okay? What's going on?"

She fell against my chest and wrapped her arms around my waist. "I can't believe you're here. How'd you find me?"

"Find my phone. Will you tell me what's happening?"

"I will later. I need to do something first." She opened her fist, revealing a green flash drive. Pinching it between two fingers, she held it over the toilet.

"You're going to flush that?"

She nodded. Her hand trembled as she chewed on her bottom lip. Then she jerked her hand back and stuffed the drive into my front pocket.

"I can't do it."

* * *

The following afternoon, I sat behind the wheel of my rental car in the parking lot of the Federal Building in Westwood—not too far from where I first met Ivy.

We stayed up all night talking, and she told me everything—about how her father had used both her and Matt in some of his cons, how he involved her in a scam against a crime family in LA, how she and Matt suspected the hit and run that claimed her father's life was no accident, and how Matt had video of her participating in that con. He'd then used it to blackmail her for my money.

My heart broke for her when she explained that she'd done what her father asked because her mum had already left her, and she didn't want to lose her father too, no matter how flawed he was. How could she think I'd ever blame her for that?

Finally, she emerged from the building. Her clothing hadn't been replaced by an orange jumpsuit, and she wasn't sporting handcuffs, so I figured things had gone well with the FBI.

I got out of the car and when she spotted me, she started running towards me. I met her halfway and picked her up in my arms. "Is everything going to be alright? They're not going to charge you. Even if they do, I'm here for you."

Cupping my face with one hand, she said, "Agent Reynolds told me that while the statute of limitations for bank fraud is ten years and my father did, in fact, commit bank fraud, I wasn't a party to that. The statute of limitations is five years for fraud, so I'm past that, and he told me they would've certainly taken my situation under consideration, and the fact that I'd been coerced into participating, and wouldn't have charged me, anyway. I'm free."

I kissed her and led her back to the car. When we were seated inside with the engine running, I turned to her. "I can't believe you've been living with that all these years. I just wish you would've explained everything to me from the beginning."

"I told you, baby. Matt would've made your life...and mine, a living hell."

"I wouldn't have allowed that to happen." I smoothed her hair back from her beautiful face. Her eyes had lost their mystery, but the light that shone from them now made them even more addictive.

"I know that now. You were always stronger than I thought, stronger than you thought." She glanced down at her hands in her lap. "I-if you want to go home now, that's fine. I understand."

"You mean without you?" I gripped the top of the steering wheel and stared at the cars rushing down Wilshire Boulevard. She'd lied to me. Tricked me. Hid her identity from me. Had run cons with her father. Had a dirtbag for a brother. My brain was screaming at me to run in the opposite direction. But my heart knew her smile, her touch, the way she believed in me like no other. The way she saved me.

"I don't think I could ever do anything without you by my side, Ivy Chase." I covered her hands with one of mine, and a little sob escaped her lips. "I have my issues, and I can't guarantee I won't fuck up. I've just been allowed to see my own daughter unsupervised in over a year. What does that tell you?"

She sniffed. "It tells me you worked hard to overcome your demons and beat them into submission." Skimming her fingers across my forearm, she said, "You inspired me to beat mine back, too. That's why I couldn't destroy that flash drive. It was time to come clean. Even if I never saw you again, your example gave me the courage to face my mistakes."

"But you *are* going to see me again." I slung my arm around her shoulders and pulled her close. "Over and over and over. You're going to see me so much, you'll plead for a break. You're coming on tour with me—for as long as you can. And you're coming with me for the holidays to meet my family. And you're going to meet Thea. And you're going to be in my bed every night because I can't even go to sleep without you next to me."

"I think I can handle that, but you're going to have to walk me through the whole family stuff. It's foreign territory for me." She pinched my chin. "I just have one question for you."

"What's that? How'd I find out about my...not my record company's... payments to Chase Arts?"

"Oh, yeah, that too. How *did* you find out? I know Jack didn't tell you."

"You know that meeting I had with my accountant the day you left. I saw the payments then and confronted Jack. He never could lie."

"You're not holding it against him, are you? I know he wanted to protect his job, but he really cares about you."

"I already hired him back. He's been texting me every five minutes to return to England for my first interview on the Brit Morning show in a few days."

"And you'll be there."

"Only if you're coming with me."

"I wouldn't miss it for anything, but that wasn't my question."

I teased her earlobe with my thumb. "What's your question?"

"Did you really train with Marky Mark Wahlberg?"

Laughter bubbled from my lips, and I rested my forehead on the steering wheel. "I can't believe I said that. It's the first thing that came to my head. Are you going to be able to put up with all that rubbish from me?"

"You have a lot more to put up with from me, including my annoying brother." She patted my arm. "No more crimes, though."

"Yeah, about your brother."

"I know. He's the worst, but we don't have to deal with him. I mean once he knows we're back together, he'll probably hit you up for money, but we can ignore him."

"I paid off his Tesla today."

She snapped her head around. "You did *what*? Why would you do that for him."

"I don't know." I stroked her hair. "While we were talking last night and you were telling me all about your childhood, I felt sorry for Matt. Your mum left him, too. Your dad used him, too. Yeah, you were able to turn out okay, more than okay." I kissed the side of her head. "But experiences affect everyone differently, look at me and my brothers in the band, and Matt probably would've been a different bloke with a different background."

"You have to be the sea lion." She shook her head. "It's a good thing I'm coming back to England with you. You're a babe in the woods." She rubbed my thigh. "Emphasis on *babe*. I can spot a con a mile away, and I'll make it my mission to protect you from the vultures."

I grabbed her hand and pressed a kiss against her wrist. "And I'll make it mine to protect you from yourself."

Epilogue

Two weeks later, Ian released "Lost and Found" to critical and popular praise and a week after that, it hit number one on the UK charts and was climbing the top ten charts in the US. When he released the second single, it looked as if it was ready to follow the same arc.

We spent the holidays with his family, who weren't scary at all. His mom took me right under her wing, and his dad didn't even ask me to commit any crimes with him. I met his adorable daughter, who had me re-thinking my entire stance on having children. Thea's mom and her husband were gracious and allowed Thea to spend a lot of time with us ahead of Ian's tour.

Even Jessica had conceded defeat and moved on with a bad boy from some reality show.

Ian's tour started in two days, and I was coming along for the ride. He had several dates in the UK. The US leg of the tour was up next, and I'd definitely be there for that. Not sure what my days and nights would look like, but I knew I wanted to be with him. He'd made it clear to his musicians and the rest of the crew, that this was going to be a sober tour—no alcohol or drugs allowed on or backstage.

As he opened the car door for me, he said, "I feel like I'm back in the Five2Go days when I had to be the responsible one. It kind of sucks."

When he slid into the driver's seat, I said, "I know at least one of the musicians will be happy, as she's two months clean and sober."

"She?" He raised his eyebrows. "You don't have to tell me who that is."

"Oops." I covered my mouth. "I just gave that one away. She'll probably end up telling you herself. She's very grateful."

As he started the powerful engine of the car with a roar, I put my hand on his arm. "Where are we going?"

"You'll see. It's a surprise." He put the car in gear, and we zoomed off, startling every living creature in the English countryside. He gripped the steering wheel. "Charlie reached out to me this morning with the date of his mum's funeral. The tour will still be in the UK at that time, so I'll be going, and he'd like you to be there, too."

"I was so sorry to hear about his mom's death. I'd be honored to go with you."

We rode in silence for several minutes until I recognized our direction. "We're going to John Milton's cottage."

"I thought something very calming and very English for you before we start on this whirlwind. I don't think you know what you're in for, but I'm not going to tell you because I don't want you backing out."

"I'm not going to back out." I tapped on the window as we blew past the sign for the cottage on the road. "Is it still closed?"

"It is."

"And you used your popstar status to get us in again?"

"My popstar status is even greater now." He primped his shirt collar. "Just ask Marky Mark."

I flicked his earlobe. "You...wanker."

Ian wrinkled his nose and shook his head.

"Too much? How about tosser?"

"A little better." He wheeled into the small dirt lot next to the cottage where a single white Ford Fiesta stood sentry. "And before you say anything, Vera was working today, anyway."

"Vera, is it? I think we're going to make a Milton fan of you, after all."

Vera met us at the door and ushered us inside. "If you have any questions, just let me know." As she turned, she winked at us. Did she think we were going to make out among the manuscripts or something?

We wandered through the rooms with Ian practically hopping from one foot to the other with impatience. I finally wedged a hand on my hip and said, "You could've waited in the car."

"Can we go out to the garden? Loads of pansies, camellias, crocus, even in winter."

"You're a flower guy now?" He opened the door for me, and I strolled into the garden, which boasted surprising splashes of color for this time of year. I shuffled down a path littered with pink petals toward the fountain formed from a bust of Milton.

"It's so nice here, tranquil, but I don't know why all these rose petals are on the ground. Where'd they come from?"

Ian didn't answer. Had he fallen asleep? I turned and put my hand to my mouth when I saw him down on one knee. "Wh-what are you doing?"

"Come over here, so I don't have to hobble over there on my knees."

I took two steps closer on wobbly legs and put my hand in the one he held out to me. He kissed my fingers with his soft lips sending a river of chills down my spine. "Before we go on tour, I want to make this official. Will you marry me, Ivy Chase? Or, whoever you are today. Doesn't matter—I want them all. I love you. Can't live without you. Don't wanna live without you. I want to keep you safe and protect you and put a smile on your beautiful face every day."

I dropped to my knees in front of him and traced his jawline with my fingertip. "There's nothing more in this world I'd rather do. No one I'd rather be with."

I glanced at the huge sparkler as he slipped it on my ring finger and then turned my gaze to the brighter shine in my love's clear eyes.

Paradise Lost. Paradise Found.

PopWiz Instagram Post

Blind Item #8

This former boybander has gone through a lot of
loss recently, including the loss of his voice
in a very public way. Is his career done, or
will he be back another day?

*Carol Ericson's Five2Go Boyband series continues
with Charlie's story, Sweet on Charlie Beck*

About the Author

Best-selling, award-winning romance author, Carol Ericson, has written over 65 books, mostly romantic suspense for Harlequin Intrigue. Also indie pubbed, Carol is working on a spicy popstar romcom series about five members of a boyband. A California girl and graduate of UCLA, Carol lives near the beach with her husband and their giant dog. For more information about Carol's books, please visit her website at www.authorcarolericson and follow her on Instagram @author.carol.ericson